"I am sure in your profession you must have some days in less than your petticoats, Miss Kensington."

"Miss...Kensington?" Her voice sounded rusty, the fright evident in every single syllable, for she trembled as she took in breath. "I think...you are indeed...mistaken."

"Acacia Kensington?" He heard the horror in his tone. "You are Miss Acacia Kensington, the paramour of my cousin Thomas, are you not?"

She shook her head hard, the long blond hair falling loose now in a swathe across her shoulders and down over her chest.

"I am not, sir. I am...Lady F-Florentia Hale-Burton... youngest daughter...of the Earl of Albany." Each breath was raw with the effort of talking.

"Hell." He could not believe it. "Hell," he repeated and all the clues fell into place. The servant running down the road before the park screaming. The ring. The priggish dress. Her voice.

He'd kidnapped the wrong woman, rendered her unconscious and subjected her to the sort of danger and terror she'd probably never ever manage to recover from.

For the first time in his life he was almost speechless.

Author Note

I love characters with secrets from the past, and if that past is intertwined with danger then it is all the better.

James Waverley, Viscount Winterton, is again back in England after ruining Lady Florentia Hale-Burton's chances of marriage.

But the spark that ignited between them six years ago is about to burst into flames, and this time Florentia has devised an ingenious plan to discover just who Winter really is.

SOPHIA JAMES

Ruined by the
Reckless Viscount

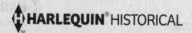

HARLEQUIN® HISTORICAL

Recycling programs
for this product may
not exist in your area.

ISBN-13: 978-0-373-29936-2

Ruined by the Reckless Viscount

Copyright © 2017 by Sophia James

This edition published by arrangement with Harlequin Books S.A.

For questions and comments about the quality of this book, please contact us at CustomerService@Harlequin.com.

® and TM are trademarks of Harlequin Enterprises Limited or its corporate affiliates. Trademarks indicated with ® are registered in the United States Patent and Trademark Office, the Canadian Intellectual Property Office and in other countries.

Printed in U.S.A.

Sophia James lives in Chelsea Bay, on the North Shore of Auckland, New Zealand, with her husband, who is an artist. She has a degree in English and history from Auckland University and believes her love of writing was formed by reading Georgette Heyer on vacations at her grandmother's house. Sophia enjoys getting feedback at sophiajames.net.

Books by Sophia James

Harlequin Historical Romance

The Penniless Lords

Marriage Made in Money
Marriage Made in Shame
Marriage Made in Rebellion
Marriage Made in Hope

Men of Danger

Mistletoe Magic
Mistress at Midnight
Scars of Betrayal

The Wellingham Brothers

High Seas to High Society
One Unashamed Night
One Illicit Night
The Dissolute Duke

Stand-Alone Novels

The Border Lord
Lady with the Devil's Scar
Gift-Wrapped Governess
"Christmas at Blackhaven Castle"
Ruined by the Reckless Viscount

Visit the Author Profile page
at Harlequin.com for more titles.

Chapter One

⁅⸻⁆

London—1810

The door of the approaching carriage opened as it stopped beside her in a sudden and unexpected haste.

'Get in now.'

'I beg your pardon.' Lady Florentia Hale-Burton could not quite believe what she had heard even as the stranger standing above her on the top step of the un-liveried coach repeated it again more loudly.

'I said get in now.'

The man frowned when she did not move and leaned forward so that his face was not far from her own. A beautiful face, like an angel, she thought, though his voice held no notes of the celestial at all.

'Look, unlike your long-suffering paramour, I am not up to playing this silly game of yours, madam. If you don't get in this minute I will drag you inside and be done with it. Do you understand?'

'I will do no such thing, sir. Of course I will not.' Finding her voice, Florentia looked about wildly for some help from her maid, Milly, but the girl had dropped back, her mouth wide open in alarm as she turned to run. It was like some dream, Flora thought, the horror of it appalling, like a nightmare where no matter how much you wanted to escape you could not. Fright held her simply rigid. The sky was grey and the day was windy. She could smell cut grass and hear birds calling from the park across the road. An ordinary Wednesday on a walk she had done a hundred times before and now this…

As the stranger stepped down from the carriage and took her arm she finally found resistance, swinging her heavy reticule at his face and connecting with a thump. The two books inside the bag were weighty tomes on the history of art, leather bound and substantial. The edge of one cut into the skin above his right eye and blood gushed down his cheek, though instead of looking furious, which might have been expected, he only began to laugh.

'Hell,' he said, 'Thomas damned well owes me for this though he did warn me you might not come easily if he was not present. But enough now. We are beginning to attract some attention and if I am going to be of any help to you we have to leave immediately.'

Grabbing at her, he pulled her hard against his body and she bit into his hand. Swearing, he brought one arm down across her breast when she screamed as loud as she could manage. Then he simply clamped his fingers on the top of her right shoulder and all she knew was darkness.

James Waverley, Viscount Winterton, couldn't believe he was doing this, kidnapping his cousin's whore before Hyde Park and rendering her unconscious. But

Tom had insisted, pleaded, cajoled and finally called in any favour James had ever promised. So he had.

'She's a feisty one, you will find,' his second cousin had insisted, 'and if I was in any position at all to go and get her myself I would, but…' He'd looked down at his leg cast from the ankle to the thigh. 'She needs to be out of London, Winter, needs to be safe from those who might hurt her.' And because one of his own unruly horses was responsible for his cousin's broken leg, James had consented.

'What does she look like?'

'Blonde and sensual. She will be wearing red, no doubt, as she always does and will be waiting on the corner of Mount Street opposite Hyde Park at five o'clock precisely.'

Lord help me, James thought. Tom hadn't mentioned that she would be the type to scream her head off in fury or whack him with a heavy bag full of books.

She didn't have the appearance of a whore either, with her demurely cut pink and red day dress and old-fashioned hat, but then what was the look of one? He'd never required the services of a lady of the night before, though he had seen them around Covent Garden and the Haymarket and many of them had appeared… quite ordinary. Perhaps Acacia Kensington was one of those girls, thrown into the game by dire circumstance and the need to survive.

She certainly had good teeth. The bite mark on his hand stung badly having cut the skin to leave it swollen and throbbing.

Laying her down on the seat opposite, he took off his jacket and placed it under her head as a pillow. She'd wake up soon and there would be all hell to pay, the journey north taking a good few hours to complete. With a frown he looked away.

Is this who he was now? A man who would hurt a woman? A man who might take the path of least resistance when quite plainly it was the wrong thing to do?

Swearing, he sat back and glanced out the window. A young maid was running along the pathway and shouting at the top of her lungs, another couple joining her. When the man raised his hand in a fist the first shudder of things not being quite as they ought to be went through him and he was glad when the carriage turned into the main road north, its speed increasing.

The blood from the cut above his right eye had begun to blur his vision and he swiped at it with the sleeve of his jacket, blotting the redness against dark linen.

Thomas could do his own courting next time, broken leg or not, he thought, and if the girl came to as angry as she had been he didn't quite know what he would do next. Put her out, he imagined, and let her make her own way from London, or not. In truth he didn't care any longer.

She had a damn expensive ring on the third finger of her right hand, the diamonds winking in the light. No false gold or cut glass either, the patina and shape of the piece telling him this was the real thing. Perhaps a paramour had gifted it to her. Tommy had the funds to procure such a bauble, should he have wished it, so maybe this was his doing. He was a man inclined to the grand gesture.

The anger that had been his constant companion threatened to choke him and he pushed back the familiar fury. Once he would have told his cousin exactly where to go with his hare-brained schemes of procuring women, but now…

The war had knocked the stuffing out of him and he had returned from Europe and the first Peninsular Campaign unsettled. He did not fit in here any more, having neither property nor much in the way of family, save a father who had taken more and more to the drink. He wanted to be away from the London set and its expectations, but most of all he needed to be away from the brutality of war. It had settled into him the aftermath of violence, making him jumpy and uncertain, the ghosts of memory entwined even in the ordinariness of his life here.

He swore again twenty moments later as sky-blue eyes opened and simply looked at him, the paleness of her cheeks alarming.

'I think… I am going…to be…sick.'

And she was, all over his boots and on her dress, heaving into the space between them time after time and shaking dreadfully. Her eyes watered, her nose ran and the stench of a tossed-up lunch hung in the air as she simply began to cry. Not quietly either.

Banging his cane against the roof, James was glad as the conveyance drew to a halt, the countryside all around wide and green, the road empty before them and behind. He didn't stop her hurried exit as he threw water he carried for the journey on to the carriage floor, drying what he could with great bunches of wild grasses pulled from the side of the road.

She was gone when he had finished, disappeared into a tract of bushes behind a stone fence. He caught the hue of her red gown at some distance dashing between the trees of a small grove.

Part of him wanted to simply leave her there and go on, but it was getting late and dusk would soon be upon the land. If she fell into a ditch or in with the company of someone who might really hurt her…

Cursing again, he bade Thomas's driver to wait for him and went in after her.

Florentia ran from tree to tree, her breath ragged as the asthma she had had since childhood came upon her with this unexpected exertion.

She was crying and running and trying to draw in breath, sharp branches tearing at her gown and at the exposed skin on her arms and legs.

Would her kidnapper follow? Would he kill her? Would he chase her and trap her here in the woods and the oncoming darkness and so very far from London?

She tripped and went down hard, then got herself up again, the pathway more difficult to discover now, the sound of a stream further on and dogs.

Dogs? Her heart leapt in her throat. Big dogs? The horror of it kept her still, the sound of crashing feet drawing nearer as two enormous black and brown hounds padded out from a break in the undergrowth and came towards her, lips bared and teeth showing.

'Keep very still.' His voice. The man from the carriage. Raw. Brutal. Furious. He sounded as though he would like to kill her along with the canines though the hackles of each dog were raised along bony spines, ready to spring.

He'd stooped to pick up a few of the bigger stones around his feet and threw one hard and fast. A direct hit to the flanks had the lead dog crouching down and slinking backwards. Two long scars at the back of her abductor's head were easily visible in the fading light. She wondered how anyone could have survived such wounds as that.

'Get back, damn it.' His words seemed to be having some effect as the second dog followed the other.

'Walk slowly towards me.' This was directed at her now. 'Don't run. They are hunting dogs trained to protect and defend. Any quick movement will have them upon you and my pistols are still in the carriage.'

'You…would…shoot them?'

He laughed at that, a harsh and savage sound. 'In an instant, were I armed and they were attacking. Now do as I say.'

She did because just at that moment the slobbering teeth of the hunting pair were infinitely more worrying than the possibility of this stranger hurting her. Again. She was pleased when he stood before her shielding her from the threat. 'Now, walk backwards, keeping my body in a direct line with the dogs. Don't make eye contact with them. Don't trip. Look as if you are in charge until you get through the green shelter at the edge of the clearing and then turn and run for the carriage as fast as you can go and get straight in. Do you understand me?'

'And…what…of…you?'

'I will be fine.'

He picked up another of the big rocks with one hand and a dead branch from the ground as a weapon and planted it before him. One of the dogs growled loudly in response and the noise had her moving back past the shelter of the bushes and away. As she scampered through the scrub at the edge of the clearing she simply turned and ran for the carriage, screaming at the driver about the dogs and the danger and slamming the door shut behind her.

It was wet inside and smelt like hay, though the dress she wore bore the stronger stench of vomit. Taking a flask of water from a shelf at the back of the conveyance, she poured it across the skirts of her gown, the cold seeping through the red-sprigged muslin and making her shiver.

Her breathing was worse. She could barely take in air now and the panic that she knew would not aid her was building. Placing her head back against the seat, she closed her eyes. This sometimes helped, but she needed the expectorant and the anti-spasmodics that her mother procured from Dr Bracewell in Harley Street. She needed calm and peace and serenity.

Would she die here on the side of a country road and alone? Would her family even know what had happened to her? Would her body be left to the dogs to devour after strangers had stolen her jewellery and books and her dress?

Not to mention her virginity.

The dreadful terror of it all had her sweaty and clammy and she began to feel strange and distant from things. It was the air…she couldn't get enough of it.

Finally, and with only the slightest whimper, she fell again into the gentler folds of darkness.

Hell, this whole journey was turning into a fiasco, James thought as he rejoined Thomas's mistress in the carriage. She was on the floor now in a puddle of water, the cold liquid seeping into the red dress and darkening the fabric to scarlet. She was breathing strangely, too, the skin at her throat taut and hollow and a blue tinge around her lips.

Finding his blade, he leaned forward and slit the tight fabric of her gown from bodice to hem, peeling it away from her. Without hesitation he threw the stinking wet dress straight out of the window and tucked his jacket about her before lifting her to sit up on the seat opposite. An erect position would make breathing easier, he thought, for he'd seen a soldier once with the same ailment on the icy roads between Lugos and Betanzos, and the man had insisted his head should be above his lungs or otherwise he would perish.

Reaching over to a net shelf at the back of the carriage, he searched for the tin of peppermint grease he'd bought at an inn from a medicine man on the way down to London. His cousin was prone to a weakness of chest and the vendor had been so insistent on the healing properties of the treatment James had found coin and purchased it.

Now he fingered a large translucent blob into his palm and rubbed at the skin around the girl's throat, though the fumes of the ointment were strong and his eyes began to water. Surely such potency must have some effect on allowing breath. He wished she would speak to him so that he could see how she fared, but she simply sat there, a tight and angry presence. He knew she was now conscious—years of hard soldiering had taught him that difference—but he did not wish to harry her with the malady of her condition and the skimpiness of her clothing so he left her to herself and willed the miles gone.

Her legs were badly scratched beneath the skirts,

he'd seen that as he had lifted her and the shoes she wore were nothing more than thin leather and silk. A woman used to the boudoir and an inside life. Her hair in the fading light was the colour of honey and gold. He had imagined whores to be cheap and brassy somehow, an artificial enhancement on show for the customers they would be trying to attract. Acacia Kensington's locks looked natural and unfussy.

Forty minutes later as the carriage slowed to rest the horses at an inn, her eyes opened. When she moved his jacket pulled away from her neck and her cheeks paled again as she registered her extreme lack of outer wear.

Such false theatrics irked him. 'I am sure in your profession you must have some days in less than your petticoats, Miss Kensington.'

'Miss…Kensington?' Her voice sounded rusty, the fright evident in every single syllable for she trembled as she took in breath. 'I think…you are indeed… mistaken.'

'Acacia Kensington?' He heard the horror in his tone. 'You are Miss Acacia Kensington, the paramour of my cousin Thomas, are you not?'

She shook her head hard, the long blonde hair falling loose now in a swathe across her shoulders and down over her chest.

'I am not, sir. I am… Lady Florentia Hale-B-Burton…youngest daughter…of the Earl of Albany.' Each breath was raw with the effort of talking.

'Hell.' He could not believe it. 'Hell,' he repeated and like the tumblers in a safe all the clues fell into place. The servant running down the road before the park screaming. The ring. The priggish dress. Her voice.

He'd kidnapped the wrong woman, rendered her unconscious, stripped her almost naked and subjected her to the sort of danger and terror she'd probably never ever manage to recover from.

For the first time in his life he was almost speechless.

'How old are you?'

'Eighteen. This…was my…first…Season.'

Young. Unprotected. Defenceless.

'Are you married?'

His eyes searched the fingers on her left hand and saw them bare.

'I am…not, sir…but I soon…may be. I…have a… suitor…who…likes me and I am…sure that we… will….'

She didn't finish for shouts filled the courtyard of the inn as another conveyance reeled wildly into view. Several men alighted and came towards them and as the door was snatched open all James felt was pain as a firearm exploded into his face, the smell of gunpowder one of his last and abiding memories.

He was dead.

Her father had killed him, the blood oozing from his neck and his mouth in a slow dribble of frothed red.

The sound of the shot had deafened her so that all she could see were people with open lips and corded throats and wildly gesticulating hands.

She felt him fall and she went with him, the green-eyed stranger who had taken her. She saw the spurt of his blood and the quick steps of the horses as they danced against the movement. She saw the rough broken face of her father above her, too.

Crying.

That single thing shocked her more than anything else had, his tears against her face as he tried to pull her up.

Everything smelt wrong.

The blood. The gunpowder. The fear of the horses. Her sweat. The last tinge of vomit in the air.

It smelt like the end. For him and for her. A quick and final punishment for something so terrible she could hardly contemplate just what might happen next.

He lay on the ground beneath her, her abductor, young and vulnerable, one arm twisted under himself, a bone sticking out through the linen shirt and blood blooming. She wanted to hold on to him, to feel the lack of pulse, to understand his death, to allow him absolution, but her father was dragging her away, away from the people who had gathered, away the driver who was shouting and screaming, away from the light of a rising moon.

The smell of peppermint followed her, ingrained and absolute, the heat of it sitting atop her heart which was beating so very fast.

He had rubbed the ointment there. She remembered that. He had lifted her on to the seat and placed his jacket around her shoulders to cover her lack of clothing, to keep her hidden. He had removed her dress so that she might breathe, protecting her as he done against the threat of the dogs.

The wrong person.

He had said so himself.

The wrong punishment, too. She began to shake violently as her father discarded the jacket she'd clung to before calling to his driver and footman. Then the horses jolted forward as they left the country inn and raced for the safety of Mayfair and London.

A warm woollen blanket was tucked carefully about her and she heard the soft sound of her father praying. Outside it had begun to rain.

'Is she ruined, John?' Her mother's voice. Tear filled and hesitant.

'I don't know, Esther. I swear I don't.'

'Did he…?' Her mama's voice came to a stop, the words too hard to say out loud.

'I do not think so, but her petticoats were dishevelled and her dress was disposed of altogether.'

'And the cuts all over her legs and arms?'

'She fought him, I think. She fought him until the breathing sickness came and perhaps it saved her. Even a monster must have his limits of depravity.'

'But he's dead?'

'Yes.'

'Who was he?'

'God knows. Florentia could hardly draw breath and so we left. I don't want to send anyone back either to the inn to make enquiries in case…'

'In case our name is recognised?'

'Milly said the Urquharts saw Florentia in the park a moment before the abduction and that she had spoken to them. They are not people who would keep a secret easily. I doubt Milly is a girl of much discretion, either. But they did not see our daughter as I did.

They did not see her so underdressed in the company of a stranger, her gown gone and her hair down. There might be some hope in that.'

Her mother's sob was muffled and then there were whispered words of worry, the rustle of silk, the blown-out candle, the door shutting behind them and then silence.

She was in her room in Mayfair, back in her bed, the same bunch of tightly budded pink roses bought yesterday from the markets on the small table beside her. It was dark and late and a fire had been set in the hearth. For heat, she supposed, because all she could feel was a deathly cold. She wiggled her toes and her hands came beneath the sheets to run along the lines of her body. Everything was in place though she could feel the scratches incurred during her flight through the woods.

She breathed in, glad she could now gather more air than she had been able to in the carriage. Her neck throbbed and she swallowed. There was a thick bandage wrapped across her right thumb and tied off at her wrist.

He was dead. All that beauty dead and gone. She remembered the blood on the cobblestones and on her petticoats and in the lighter shades of his hair.

The beat of her heart sounded loud in a room with the quiet slice of moonlight on the bedcovers. A falling moon now, faded and low.

Was she ruined because of him? Ruined for ever?

She could not believe that she wouldn't be. Her sister had not come to seek her out and extract the story. She imagined Maria had been told to stay away. Her maid, Milly, had gone too, on an extended holiday back to her family in Kent. To recover from the dreadful shock, her father had explained when he first saw her awake, but she could see so very much more in his eyes.

The howls of the dogs came to mind. Her abductor's voice, too, raw but certain. She remembered his laughter as she'd hit him hard with her books. There was a dimple in his chin.

Where would he be buried? She'd looked back and seen the servant lift him from the ground, carefully, gently, none of the violence of her father, only protection and concern.

She was glad for it. She was. She was also glad that she was here safe and that there was nothing left between them save memory. His pale clear green eyes. The shaved shortness of his hair. The two parallel scars evident on his scalp. The smell of wool and unscented soap in his jacket. She shook away such thoughts. He had ruined her. He had taken her life and changed it into something different. He had taken her from the light and discharged her into shadow.

The deep lacerations on her arms from the trees in the glade stung and she could still smell the peppermint even after her long soak in a hot bath scented with oil of lavender.

The scent clung to her and she recalled his fingers upon her as he had rubbed it in. Gently. Without any threat whatsoever.

He was dead because of his own foolishness. He was gone to face the judgements of the Lord. A deserved punishment. A fitting end. And yet all she could feel was the dreadful waste.

A tap on the door had her turning and her sister was there in her nightgown, face pale.

'Can I come in, Flora? Papa said you were sleeping and that you were not to be disturbed till the morning. But Milly has been sent home and she was so full of the horror of your abduction it began to seem as if you might never be back again. What a fright you have given us.'

Florentia found her sister's deluge of words comforting.

'Mama says that there is the chance we might have to leave London for a while and retire to Albany. Did he hurt you, the one who took you from Mount Street, I mean? It is being whispered that Papa shot him dead somewhere to the north?'

Flora's stomach turned and she sat up quickly, thinking she might be sick, glad when the nausea settled back into a more far off place.

Warm fingers curled in close as Maria positioned herself next to her and took her hand, tracing the scratches upon each finger and being careful not to bump her thumb. 'You are safe now and that man will never be able to hurt you again, Papa promised it would be so. At least we can leave London and go home for it's exhausting here and difficult to fit in.'

The out-of-step sisters, Flora suddenly thought. She had overheard that remark at their first soirée. One of a group of the *ton*'s beautiful girls had said it and the others had laughed.

They were an oddness perhaps here in London, the two daughters of an impoverished earl who held no true knowledge of society and its expectations.

Heartbreak had honed them and sharpened the

edges of trust. But she would not think about that now because she was perilously close to tears.

'I heard Mama crying and Papa talking with her and she asked if we were cursed?'

'What did Father say?' Flora stilled at Maria's words.

'He said that only the weak-willed can be so stricken and that the true curse would have been to never find you. He also said while there is life there is hope.'

Life. Breath. Warmth. No hope for him though, the stranger with his blood running across the cobbles.

'Papa also said that perhaps we should not have come to London in the first place, but Mama asked how are we to be married off otherwise. Father replied there was an unkindness here that he found disappointing and I think he's right for people laugh at us sometimes. Perhaps we are not as fashionable as we should be or as interesting as the others are? Papa's title is something that holds sway here, but I suppose they also realise there is not much more than that behind our name.'

Flora pulled herself together and spoke up. 'We are who we are, Maria. We are enough.'

'Enough,' her sister repeated and brought her fingers up into a fist.

This was an old tradition between them, joining hands and making a chain. Pulling them together. Keeping them strong. Maria was only a year above her in age and they had always been close. But even as she tried to gather strength Florentia felt that something had been irrevocably broken inside her, wrenched apart and plundered. She wondered truly if she would ever recover from a sadness she could not quite understand.

* * *

Her father called her to his library the next morning and he looked as tired as she was, the night past having been a long and fitful one to get through.

'I thought we should try to remember something of yesterday between us, my dear. To keep it in memory so to speak, in case we have to think about it again in the future.'

'In the future?'

'If he has left you with child—?'

She didn't let him finish. 'It was not like that, Papa. He did not...' She stopped. 'I think he thought I was someone else entirely. Some woman who needed to be escorted north because she was in trouble. He did not touch me in that way.'

Relief lay in the lines of his face and in the lift of his eyes. 'But your dress and the scratches?'

'I had been sick and used water to try to make my gown clean again and he took it off me because it was wet and I was shaking and breathless. I also ran through a forest to try to get away and the branches snagged at my skin.'

'He is a monster to do what he did.'

'Is? I thought the man was dead. Are you saying he could still be alive?'

Her father's hands came up. 'I am certain he is not, but we shan't stay in London to find out. I have ordered the town house to be closed and have put in motion the means to remove us once again back to Kent. We shall leave on Friday.'

Albany Manor. Two days away. The bloom of thankfulness made Flora dizzy.

'There is something else that I think you should know.'

The tone of his words was gentle.

'The story of your abduction is all over London this morning. There were people near Mount Street who spoke when they should not have and Milly was not… careful with her own words either.'

'I see.'

'Well, perhaps you do not see it all. There will not be a gentleman here in London who would now offer his hand in marriage. Quiet ruination is a completely different thing from this utterly public condemnation and I doubt that we can recover from such a spectacle. If I had more capital behind me or the title was not an entailed one…' He stopped and took another tack. 'For the moment I think withdrawal might be our best defence. Your mother has the same thought. The Honourable Timothy Calderwood has sent a message to say he shall not be able to call upon you again, but he is sorry for your trials.'

Sadness welled. She had enjoyed Timothy's company with his laughter and his conversation. When she had danced with him a few days ago at the Rushton ball he'd intimated that he would like to know her much better and she had smiled back at him as if all her world was right. A kind man. A man of integrity. The first man who had made her feel special.

Her father's eyebrows raised up.

'Did your abductor say anything at all about who he was?'

'He didn't.' Florentia wondered if she should mention the name of Acacia Kensington and a man called Thomas. She decided against it, though, reasoning if her kidnapper was identified and still alive he'd be badly hurt and unable to fight off any further recriminations against him. 'I am sure he imagined I was another and had just realised his mistake when you came and shot him.'

'And mark my words I would do exactly the same again for I am not sure how you might recover from this travesty.'

'With fortitude, Papa.'

Her reply made him laugh though there was no humour in it. 'I wish Bryson was here…' he said and stopped, realising what he had just uttered.

Her brother stood in the empty space between them. Beautiful funny Bryson with his golden hair and blue eyes and his cleverness. The glue in a family that had come unstuck ever since his passing.

The son. The heir to an entailed property. Florentia's twin.

She sat down on the nearest seat, trying to find breath. It had been so long since his name had been mentioned out loud even though he was silently present in every moment of every day.

'I no longer think the fault lay with you, Flora, and am sorry that I once implied it such.' These were words she had heard before and foolish apologies that she had long since ceased to refute. 'We will get through this. All of it. There will be an ending to the pain, I promise.'

But there wasn't. There hadn't been. There never would be.

The nausea she had felt in the carriage returned and she forced it down. She hadn't been able to eat anything and although she felt hungry she just could not swallow even the smallest morsel of food. A new symptom that.

Perhaps she was going mad in truth. The completion of a process that had started as she had sat there with her brother dying in her arms and both their clothes splashed in red.

Her fault. Her dare. Her imprudence. She began to shake in earnest.

'Shall I fetch Mama, Flora?'

'No.' She shook her head hard and the memory shattered.

The ache was lessened now, the burn and throbbing of it where his neck met the collar bone. Tommy was beside him.

'Here, take this. It will help.'

Bitter like almonds. James screwed his face up at the taste, but after a few moments he started to feel as if he was floating, as if the land was somehow below him and he was flying through the clouds on a murmur.

He liked the sensation. He liked the freedom though his head still throbbed with each beat of his heart, leaving him squinting his eyes against the light.

'What happened?'

'You were shot.' His cousin lent closer, eyes shadowed. 'It was the wrong woman, Winter. You got the wrong damn woman.'

The red dress. The dogs. The breathlessness. It all came back in a fractured whirl.

'Is she safe? The girl I took?'

A curse and the shifting of light was his response, quiet between them until his cousin spoke again. 'She's fine. It's you we are worried about.'

'I…won't…die.' He managed to get the words out one by one.

'Why the hell do you think you won't, when you've lost so much blood?'

'Because…need…to say…sorry.'

'Her father shot you by all accounts, for God's sake. Point blank and without dialogue.'

'Deserved…it.'

Then the dark came and he slipped away from the hurting light.

Chapter Two

Albany Manor, Kent—April 1816

'Come to London with me, Flora. I am tired of you never being there and that ridiculous scandal from years ago is old news now. No one will remember it, I promise. There are far worse wrongdoings in society catching people's imaginations. Your downfall is barely recalled.'

Her sister, Maria, had always been difficult to say no to, Florentia thought, as she finished the final touches of a painting depicting the faces of three men caught in dark light at a dinner table.

'Roy will be there, too, and his mother. We will have a number of people all about us at every important social occasion. It won't be like the last time at all, I promise.'

The last time.

Three years ago when Florentia had finally decided to step again into society the whole thing had been a disaster. No one had wanted to talk to her, though Timothy Calderwood to his credit had made an effort to try and converse before his new wife had pulled him away. The memory of it stung. She had felt like an outcast and even Maria's marriage to one of the *ton*'s favourite sons, Lord Warrenden, had not softened her dislike of social occasions.

Shaking away the memories, Flora stood and took off her smock before hanging it across the back of her easel.

'If I did decide to come, I'd need your promise that I can leave as soon as I want and return to Albany without argument.'

Maria smiled. 'I'd just like the chance for you to see the worries you harbour are totally unfounded. You cannot possibly let the unlawful actions of one unhinged individual ruin your life for ever. A stranger. A man who has never been apprehended for the heinous deed and one who in all probability is long dead. It's finished and over. You need to live again and find someone like I have. Roy has been a blessing and a joy to me. He has made me happy again.'

That certain look came across Maria's face as she spoke about her husband of eighteen months with the true contentment of a woman in love and knowing it.

Placing the paint back in their glass containers, Flora wiped her easel with turpentine. She could not work in a mess and she hated waste. The yellow ochre had dribbled into the cobalt blue to make a dirty brown-green, the swirl of the mix blobbing on the cloth.

For over a year now she had been sending a new portrait every second week to London and to an agent she had acquired through word of mouth from Roy. Mr Albert Ward had been hounding her to come and visit him in the city to meet some of his private clients, many who had expressly asked for her by name to draw their portrait.

By name…? Well, not precisely, she thought, frowning at the mistake.

Mr Frederick Rutherford was making a splash in the realms of the art world with his dark and moody portraits, and his reputation was growing as fast as his list of prospective clients. A young man with a great future before him, if only he would show up at the events planned around his unique style of painting.

A sensation. A mystery. A talent that had burst on to the London scene unexpectedly and with a vivid impression of genius and worth.

The letters from Mr Ward were getting more and more insistent on a meeting face-to-face. The agent needed to understand what sort of a man he was, what had fashioned his sense of design, what had shaped him into a muse who could seemingly interpret the feelings of those he chose as his subject in each painting so brilliantly. Hopelessness. Loss. Grief. Love. Passion. Deceit. All the shades of human emotion scrawled across a canvas and living in the application of pigment.

Ward's letter had been full of exaggerated prose and superlatives. The agent had seen in her paintings many of the themes that she herself had no knowledge of and yet her silence had seemed to propel him into a fiercer and more loyal promise.

It was worrying this temperament of his and Florentia often doubted if the ruse was even worth going on with, but as a woman bound by her past to never marry she had been somewhat forced into finding a vocation that did not include family and children. And she loved painting. If her life was not to follow the direction she once had thought it might have, she did not wish to be derailed into another that she hated.

It could be worse, for the money she garnered was supplementing her father's lack of it and as Albany Manor was entailed the promise of a longevity of tenure was gone without a male heir. After her father's death the Manor and title would pass to her deceased uncle's oldest son, a fact that Christopher, the heir, reminded them of every time he came to visit.

She'd thought to send her youngest cousin Steven in her place to see Mr Ward in person, instructing him on his conduct and in what to say, but she knew for all his good points he was a tattlemouth. The fact that she had duped one of the prominent art critics in London in her role as Mr Frederick Rutherford would be gossip too salubrious to simply keep quiet about was another consideration altogether and she did not think her parents would be up to a further scandal.

So she was essentially bound to the charade she had thought up. Besides, a new idea had begun to form at the back of her head. She could go herself to London. A young artist who was slight and effeminate would not be much remarked upon and if she gifted him with a cough and a propensity for bad headaches and poor health she might not have to stay around anywhere for very long.

A quick visit might suffice to keep her hand in the game, so to speak, and with her father's bouts of despondency that took him to bed often and her mother's insistence in looking after him, she would have much freedom to move around.

Her sister could help her, too, for she had been in on the deception from the very start.

'If I agreed to come to London, I would not wish to attend any major social events, Maria. If I went anywhere it would have to be something small and select.'

'An afternoon tea then would be the thing to begin with. A quiet cultural affair at Lady Tessa Goodridge's, perhaps, and afterwards a play in the Haymarket.'

Flora unbundled her hair and shook it free. She always placed it up when she painted in a messy and oversized bun fastened with two ceramic clips that she had been given by her sister.

Her good-luck charms, she called them, because after receiving them things had improved and she had survived. She smiled to herself. Perhaps that was putting too good an interpretation on it, she ruminated, for in truth she had become the sort of woman who was decidedly eccentric and superstitious. She'd been enclosed in the Hale-Burton country seat of Albany Manor for the last six years and had seldom ventured out, apart from her one sojourn to London, the small world she called her own allowing her much time completely alone.

She used to like people. Once. Now they simply frightened her. She could not understand them or interpret their true meaning. The inspiration for every portrait she had completed and sent to Mr Ward by mail had come from the pages of books of drawings in the extensive library at Albany. Fictional, altered or copied.

Save one, she amended, but then she did not think about that.

So many topics now that were out of bounds to her sense of peace. She wished she were different, but she did not know where to begin to become so.

'We will go to the dressmaker in Bromley, Flora.

She will fashion you some clothes and she is as talented as the expensive modistes in Paris. One of her patrons is a friend of mine and every person who ever orders a gown from her is more than delighted with it.'

Listening to Maria's plans for their sojourn made the enormity of what she had agreed on to become real. Appearance was so important in the city and the old feelings of being not quite good enough resurfaced with a dread.

'I don't want anything fancy, Maria, and I shan't be wearing bright colours at all.' Last time their mother had insisted on gowns that were so dreadfully noticeable and so very wrong for their colouring. Since her abduction she'd never worn that shade of red again.

'Roy prefers me in pastel,' her sister was saying and even that sent a chill of horror down Florentia's neck. Women in society had so little say in anything. They were mute beautiful things, needy and powerless. Well, the paintings had given her back her power and she knew that she would never willingly relinquish it.

'I also need to visit Mr Ward in South London.'

Maria was silent, her brows knitted together. 'He thinks you are a man, Florentia. How can you see him at all?'

'It will just be quickly and I shall be dressed as Frederick Rutherford.'

'I hardly think you could do that for it would be… scandalous.'

Flora laughed. 'Well, I am an expert in that field by all accounts, so I should manage it effortlessly. I'll wear Bryson's clothes and his boots. They would fit me well.'

'What of your hair? Mr Ward would not think that to belong to a boy.'

'A wig and a hat would be an easy disguise. I can procure a moustache, too, and stuff paper in my cheeks to change the shape of my face. That should make me speak differently.'

'My God, Florentia.' Maria simply stared at her. 'You have been thinking of this for a while? This dupe?'

'The art of pretence lies in painting just as truly as it ever would in the world of acting. It just requires sure-mindedness, I think.'

'And you truly imagine you could pull off such a character?'

'I do.' She smiled because her sister's face was stiff with disbelief. 'I've been practising, Maria. The walking. The talking. The sitting. I am sure I could be more than convincing.'

'And what of the serving staff at the London town house of the Warrendens? I am certain they should notice if one moment you are a girl and the next a boy and goodness knows who they might tell. Your true identity would be all over London before we ever got to our next appointment if the stories of the gossip-mongering between the big houses is to be believed.'

'Then perhaps I should simply go as Mr Frederick Rutherford right from the beginning. The Warrendens' staff in London does not know me and it would completely do away with the need for new gowns and shoes. I shan't have to even take a maid with me. I shall simply arrive as Mr Frederick Rutherford and leave as him with no questions asked.'

'I don't believe I am having this conversation with you, Florentia. You cannot possibly be serious.'

'Oh, but I am, Maria. I have no wish to be out and

about in society again, but I do have a need to continue selling my paintings. I could, of course, simply go up to the city alone and in disguise, but…'

'No. If you are going to do this ridiculous thing I want to be there to help you, to make certain that you are safe.'

'Thank you.'

'You have forced my hand, dreadfully, but I do want to state quite forcefully that this is a terrible and dangerous idea.'

'I know I can do it, Maria. Remember the plays we used to put on as children. You always said I was marvellous at acting my parts.'

'That was make believe.'

'As this is, too. It's exactly the same.'

'If you get caught—'

Florentia cut her off. 'But I won't. I promise.'

'My God, I can't believe I should even be considering this. I can't believe you might talk me into it.'

'Try, Maria. Try for my sake.'

'All right. I'll visit the wigmakers if you fashion a drawing of your wants and I can simply say it is for a play we are putting on at Albany for Christmas. Did you have a preference for a colour?'

'Black.' Flora was astonished to hear such certainty coming from her mouth. She could mimic Bryson because she had known him so very well, his habits, his stance, the way he walked and watched. His hair had been golden just like hers, so she needed something distinctly different.

'And I would require some height inbuilt in the boots. I have seen that done so it should not be difficult.'

Maria groaned. 'I cannot believe that we could even be contemplating this farce, Florentia. God, if we are discovered.'

'It will never happen.'

'Well, Roy needs to know at least. I will not lie to him.'

Flora walked to the stream late that afternoon through the small bushes and the flowering shrubs, through the birdsong and the rustle of the wind, through air filled with the smell of spring on its edge and the promise of renewed warmth.

She had always come here to think ever since the time she had returned in disgrace from London.

The glade reminded her slightly of the woods she had run through besides the North Road as she had tried to escape the carriage of the man who had abducted her.

Her kidnapper.

That was how she named him now and here she allowed him to come into her thoughts just as surely as she had banished him from everywhere else.

His smile was what she remembered most, slightly lopsided and very real. He had a dimple in his chin, too, a detail that she had forgotten about until, when painting from memory, she had rediscovered the small truths of him.

Beautiful. She had thought him such then and she still did now, his short hair marked in browns of all shades from russet to chestnut and threaded in lighter gold and wheat.

She wondered why she still recalled him with such a preciseness, but she knew the answer of course. He

had died for a mistake, his own admittedly, but still…
He was like a martyr perishing for a cause that was
unknown, his blood running on the forecourt of the
inn in runnels of red, the dust blending indistinctly at
the sides so that it was darker. She had used that colour when she had drawn him, that particular red on
the outlines when first she had formed his face and
body on canvas and now even when the painting was
finished the colour was a part of who he was, both his
strength and his weakness.

She'd bundled up the portrait with its power of grace
and covered it with a sheet before placing it at the very
back of her large wardrobe. Often, though, she looked
at him even as she meant not to. Often she lifted the
fabric and ran her finger across his cheek, along his
nose and around the line of his dimpled chin.

It made her feel better, this care of him, this gentle
caress, this attention that she had not allowed him in
life even after he saved her from the dogs and wrapped
his jacket around her shoulders to deter the chill of
spring.

Contrasts. That was the worst of it. The disparity
of caring or not.

Her kidnapper had made her into a woman of detail and fear. He had changed her from believing in the
hope of life to one who dreaded it. At times like this
sitting in her private grove she wondered if perhaps
this introspection was exactly the thing that made her
take up the brush, for she had never lifted one until
she had returned in shame to Albany Manor after her
fateful London ruin.

Seeing yellow paint on her nail, she scraped it off
with her thumb, the small flakes falling into drops of

water caught on a green waxy leaf and turning the colour yellow. With care she tipped it over and the hue ran into the mud and the soil, swallowed up until it ceased to exist at all.

Like him. Perhaps?

Sometimes she imagined he still lived, scarred and angry, as closeted away as she was, afraid to be seen and exposed. Did a wife live with him now? Had he found a woman who might listen with her whole heart to the story of his narrow escape and then stroke his cheek in comfort, just as she tended to the image in the painting? A mistake to forget about, or to laugh over.

Crossroads for them both.

Him in death and her in life. Everyone seemed to have moved on since for good or for bad. Her father to his penchant for sickness, her mother in her willingness to play his nursemaid, Maria in her love of a husband who suited her entirely.

Everybody but her, stuck as she was in this constant state of inertia.

That was the trouble, of course, the puzzling hopelessness of everything that had happened. The scandal she could have coped with easily. It was the grief of it all that had flattened her. Everything for nothing.

Picking up a stick, she began to draw lines in the earth. Six lines for the years. She wanted to add a seventh because this next one would be no different. Then she embellished the lines with twelve circles each representing the months. Seventy-two of them. A quarter of her lifetime.

She wanted to live again. She wanted to smile and laugh and dance. She wanted to wear pretty clothes and jewellery and have long dinners under candlelight. But she couldn't, couldn't make herself take that first little step out and about.

It had got worse, her lack of air. In winter now she gasped and wheezed when she walked further than she ought to.

Sometimes she wondered if she were indeed addled by it all. Pushing that thought away, she concentrated on another.

Mr Frederick Rutherford.

With care she raised herself up on to her heels and walked across the clearing with a swagger, her head held high, her shoulders stiff. Then she ambled back, this time with a stick in hand shaped from a branch that she had stripped from a tree.

The accoutrements of a gentleman. Better. It felt more…right. So many parts made up a man, though. Stride. Voice. Arrogance. Certainty. Disdain.

She walked faster as though she was important, as though in the wasting of even the tiniest of seconds there lay a travesty. Men about town knew where they were going. They did not falter. They acted as though everybody might wish to know of them and their opinions. There was a certain freedom in being such a one as that.

Lengthening her stride, she tried again and again, all the while adjusting things slightly so that it felt more real, this person whom she was becoming.

She could do it. With spectacles to hide her eyes and a moustache to disguise her lips. A neckcloth tied in the high manner would see to the rest. The cane her grandfather had owned sat unused in the attic, just another prop to draw the eye away from her with its silver dimpled ball and dark walnut wood.

Everything was beginning to fall into bands of colour. Her wig. The clothes she would sport. The heightened leather Hessians that would easily come to her knees.

Like a painting established layer by layer, of substance and structure. Drawing the eyes. Finding the essence. Creating the illusion.

Chapter Three

'I think you are a veritable tease, Lord Winterton, and if half the things that are said of you are true I should imagine you find us very dull.'

James glanced down at Miss Julia Heron, soft blonde ringlets falling around her face and smiling brown eyes. One of the beauties of the Season, it was said, though there was a wide ring of other young ladies around her who looked every bit as charming. He wished they would not look at him as if he was the answer to all their heartfelt dreams. He wished he could have simply crossed the floor and left, to feel the rain on his face and puddles beneath his feet, and smell the green of London in the spring.

How he had missed it.

His neck ached as it always did at about this time of the night and he breathed through the pain with a measured practice.

Lady Florentia Hale-Burton was not here, he was sure of it, and from what he had managed to find out about the family in the last few weeks he could well imagine why. His actions on the road across from Hyde

Park had ruined the youngest daughter of the Earl of Albany. For marriage. For the hope of a family. For life. For ever.

Her sister was present, though. He had met Lady Maria Warrenden, once Hale-Burton, on the arm of one of his oldest friends as he had alighted from his coach. Roy Warrenden had introduced his wife with pride, giving him her unmarried name to place her in a context and James prayed his surprise and shock had not been noticeable.

She'd showed no recognition of him or his name at all which was a comforting thing leaving him with a decided uncertainty as to what he wanted to do about the whole sordid affair. An apology to the Hale-Burtons would be a good start, but by all accounts the father had taken to bed with a broken spirit and he could well see that his very presence would be a nightmare for the entire family; a memory of a time they would have no want to recall or relive.

Lady Florentia Hale-Burton would be twenty-three now or twenty-four, he thought, and gossip had it she resided in Kent and only occasionally visited town.

James looked around, wishing he could simply leave and figure out his choices in peace, but as it had been only an hour since his arrival he thought any withdrawal would incite comment. Better to have not come at all, he thought, as he swallowed his drink.

Miss Heron before him was weaving her fan this way and that, a dance of wonder he found himself mesmerised with and repelled by, the female tool of flirtation and provocation holding no interest for him.

He had come home to England half the man who had left it, but with twenty times the fortune. There was a certain irony to be found in all he had lost when weighed against that which he had gained, here in a place where money mattered most.

'You promised me this dance, my lord.' There was a note of supplication in Julia Heron's eyes. He could not remember making such a promise and frowned slightly.

It was the way of the London set, he supposed, a world of chimera and delusion underpinned by a steely determination to marry well.

'I've written it in, Lord Winterton,' Miss Heron insisted, showing him the name placed in small and precise letters upon her dance card.

With a nod, he acquiesced. He'd never particularly liked dancing, but as the orchestra began into a quadrille he was at least grateful that it was not a waltz.

Moving on to the dance floor, James saw that many patrons watched them, smiling in that particular way of those who imagined an oncoming union. The jaded anger inside him rose with the thought and he pressed it down. A crowded ballroom was not the place for excessive introspection or regret.

As he fished about for a subject that might interest the young woman beside him came up with a topic of her own.

'Papa is having us all drawn by Mr Frederick Rutherford, the artist, my lord. He hopes the portraits will be begun as soon as possible.'

The words were filled with a delight tinged in trepidation.

'Have you seen anything at all of his work, Lord Winterton?'

James shook his head, the heady world of art a long

way from anything he'd ever been interested in. 'But I am sure he will capture your likeness with alacrity.'

The girl's face fell. 'Well, in truth he tends to embellish things with his own interpretation, though Papa says he cannot imagine the man wanting to do so with us.'

'Because perfection cannot be improved upon?' He heard the tone of irony quite plainly in his voice, but Julia Heron simply trilled and blushed, her hand tightening around his as her glance came fully upon him.

His heart sank further. He would need to be careful if he were to escape the gossip so often associated with these soirées and emanating from even the simplest of familiarities.

His fortune had singled him out now as highly sought after husband material and if beneath his clothes there lay deeper shades of tragedy no one else here knew of it.

The older Herons were watching them closely, another younger daughter of the same ilk beside them glowering at her sister. When the dance brought them together again Julia had a further question waiting.

'Are you here in London long, my lord?'

'Just for the next few weeks, I think, Miss Heron. I am hoping to move west.'

'To Atherton Abbey?'

'I see you have heard the rumour.'

'Who has not, Lord Winterton, for the Abbey is said to be one of the loveliest homes in all of Herefordshire as well as one of the most expensive.'

James gritted his teeth and smiled, glad as the complexity of the quadrille pushed them apart again, though the other woman on one point of the square was unexpected and he tensed as he saw her visage.

Lady Maria Hale-Burton, now the new Lady Warrenden, smiled at him politely. She was taller than her sister and much more rounded. Her hair was darker, too. He waited to see if in private she might mention the plight of her sibling in connection with him, but she did not, chancing instead on a mundane and social propriety.

'I hope you are enjoying your return to London after so long away, my lord.' Her voice was soft and carried a slight lisp.

'I am, thank you. It was good to see your husband again. We were at school together.'

She was about to answer, but the change in the figure took him back to Julia Heron who claimed his arm in the final flurry of the dance, her colour high and her smile wide with enjoyment.

Accompanying the girl back to her parents he gave her his thanks and went to find Roy Warrenden, grateful to see the Baron sitting at a table with a bottle of wine before him and a number of empty glasses, though he was in full conversation with another James had no knowledge of. Maria Warrenden now joined them, brought back to her husband on the arm of an older man whom she promptly thanked. As her dancing partner left she sat down and made her own observations.

'Roy said you led him astray more than once, Lord Winterton, but your presence here has made his night. He is usually desperate to get home early.' She laughed heartily, a joyous natural sound that was nothing at all like Julia Heron's practised society giggle.

'Are your parents here tonight, Lady Warrenden?' He'd looked around the room before just in case the visage of Florentia Hale-Burton's father should be peering back at him, his face full of violent memory, and had been relieved to see no sign of the man.

'No, I am afraid they seldom venture far from Albany Manor in Kent any more. Papa suffers from bad health, you see, and Mama feels it her duty to be there to wipe his brow.'

'A woman of responsibility, then?'

'Or one who enjoys playing the martyr?' Close up the resemblance between Maria Warrenden and her sister was more noticeable and he found himself observing her with interest even as Roy Warrenden stood and clapped him on the back.

'It's good to have you in England, Winter. I saw that my wife managed to find you in the quadrille. She said she was going to try.' His glance went further afield. 'I should probably warn you that the Misses Heron are fairly overwhelming and are not ones to take no for an answer lightly either.'

Glancing over, James was concerned to see them all looking his way, eyes full of the hope of more than he had offered them.

Maria laughed at their interest. 'The Heron girls are handsome, granted, but if I was a man I should not wish to wake up to only beauty each morning.'

Her husband concurred. 'No, indeed not, my love. Beauty and brains is what you are after, Winter, and the ability to be entertained for every moment of your life. Miss Heron looked particularly chatty in your company?'

'She was telling me of a portrait she is having done

by Mr Frederick Rutherford. Seems the artist holds a reputation here that is more than salutary and he has been commissioned to paint the three sisters.'

Lady Warrenden choked on the drink she had just taken a sip of, but it was the look of consternation in her eyes that was the most arresting.

'The man is indeed talented.' Roy had now taken up the conversation and James had the idea it was to give his wife time to recover her equilibrium. 'But I doubt the Herons will entice the fellow to London, for from my knowledge Rutherford does not do sittings in person.'

'No, he certainly does not.' Maria Warrenden was shaking. James could see the tremble of her hands as she placed the glass down on the table, though she immediately dropped them into the thick fabric of her skirt and out of sight. 'He would be appalled at such an idea, believe me, Viscount Winterton, and I cannot understand how they could think such a thing might happen.'

'You sound as though you know him well?'

The woman shook her head. 'Only a little,' she returned and changed the subject entirely. 'We will be walking in Hyde Park tomorrow, my lord. Perhaps you might wish to accompany us for the foliage of the trees there this spring is particularly beautiful.'

The past seemed to collide with the present and James shook his head. 'I am out of town tomorrow, I am afraid.'

'Of course.' Maria Warrenden looked uncertain. He would have liked to have asked her of the health of her sister, but could find no way to broach the subject. Perhaps if he met Roy alone one day he could bring her up in a roundabout sort of way. He had no mandate to be truly interested and besides Florentia Hale-Burton could have no wish ever to meet up with him again if the scale of the scandal that had ensued at their last meeting was anything to go by.

He wondered if the youngest Hale-Burton daughter was married and had a family now. He wondered if she was happy…

Her sister came to her room late that evening, having returned from the Allans' ball full of a bustling gossip.

'Lord Winterton graced the ball this evening, Florentia, and the Heron girls were all over him, though in truth I did not see him complaining. I think he had danced with each of them by the end of the evening.'

'Winterton is the Viscount newly home from the Americas?' Flora had heard of the man, of course. He was the newest and most interesting addition to the *ton*, a soldier who had made his fortune in the acquisition of timbers from the east coast and transported them back to London.

'That's the one and he is every bit as beautiful as they all say him to be. It's his eyes, I think, a true clear and pale green. You would love to paint him, Flora, but that's not my only news. No, indeed, my greatest morsel is that the oldest Heron girl, Miss Julia, apparently told Winterton that Mr Frederick Rutherford would be painting all three daughters at their town house in Portland Square across the next few weeks.'

Florentia put down her book. *A true clear and pale green and every bit as beautiful as they say he is.* The world tilted slightly and went out of focus, so much so that one of her hands twisted around the base of the chair on which she sat in an attempt to keep herself anchored.

'Are you all right, Flora? You suddenly look awfully pale.' Her sister moved closer as Flora made an attempt to smile.

'I am tired, I suppose, for London is a busy and frantic place when you have been away from it as long as I have.' Her heart was racing, the clammy sheen of sweat sliding between her breasts. Could it be him? Could her kidnapper have survived? Was he here now in London, living somewhere only a handful of miles from the Warrenden town house? She made an effort to focus.

'Mr Alfred Ward did ask me to consider the Heron commission in a letter he sent after we met him on Monday, but I declined.'

'Well, it seems he has not relayed your answer to the prospective clients.' Maria removed her hat and shook out her hair. 'I knew something would go wrong with this scheme of yours, Flora. I knew that we could not trust Mr Ward with one meeting. He is a schemer and he wants more and more of you for I could tell from his demeanour and by all the words he did not say. Goodness, if he keeps this up you will be unmasked summarily and then what?'

'He is a greedy man, Maria, but also an astute one. I told him if I am pressured too much I am inclined to bouts of severe melancholy. I inferred I was…brittle, I suppose, a highly sensitive artist who is not of this world so to speak. The cough helped, I think, though it has left me with a sore throat and a hoarse voice from having to do it so much.'

Maria looked aghast. 'We should leave London then and just go home.'

Florentia frowned for suddenly she did not want to desert the city with such haste.

A true clear and pale green.

The words kept repeating over and over.

'Is Lord Winterton married?'

Her sister's mouth simply dropped open. 'No. At least I do not think so. He is an old friend of Roy's, so I could ask him of it. Why would you possibly be interested?'

Ignoring that query, she asked another of her own. 'But he will be staying here? In London, I mean.'

'He's rumoured to be acquiring a substantial home somewhere to the west. He is also rumoured to be dangerous.'

'In what ways?'

'In every possible way, I should imagine. He is neither for the faint hearted nor for the timid. He looks as though he could eat the whole world up should he want to and everyone there at the Allans' ball was a little afraid of him. It's his wealth, I suppose, and the fact that he is said to have a scar upon his neck that makes it appear as though his head was almost torn completely off from his shoulders at some point long ago. He wears his neckcloth high to hide it.'

'I see.' Florentia stood and turned towards the mirror on one wall of her room.

For she did see. Everything. Too much. All of it.

It was him. She knew it. Knew it from the bottom of her racing heart.

She could ruin him in an instant as surely as he had ruined her. She could give her truth out loud and watch him suffer as she had, this lord of the *ton* with all his wealth and his connections and his beautifulness.

She felt sick and scared and elated and horrified. Every emotion melded into shock and then shattered again into coldness and fear.

But she could not just go home and leave it. To fester and burn and hurt her. Not again. She could not weather another six years like the last ones. The drawing she'd done in the dust of her grove came into recall. Seventy-two months. So very many lines.

'Did you speak to him, Maria? To Lord Winterton?'

'Yes.'

'And he knew your name? Your unmarried one, I mean?'

'I suppose so. Yes, I remember Roy introduced me by using it. Why? Why should that matter, Florentia? What is it that you are not telling me?'

But Florentia had ceased to listen altogether, lost as she was in her own desperate worry. Did Lord Winterton remember her? Had he recognised the Hale-Burton name? Had the world already tilted in a way that could not be stopped or altered?

The smallness of the room here in the Warrenden town house on Grosvenor Square suddenly felt like a trap and she longed to be out of it, walking and thinking.

She wanted her grove of trees and the soil of Albany Manor, but she wanted the truth even more.

Six years of hiding. It was enough. She just could not do it any more. Not for a day or a moment or a second. She needed to see Winterton, to look upon his face and understand what it was that lay between them, what it was she needed to do.

She could confront him personally or amongst a selected company and yet even that thought made her blanch. Her protections were no longer in place. Her father was ill and Maria's husband was an old friend. If she told her sister Winterton was the one who had kidnapped her, Roy would imagine it his duty to issue him a challenge and gain a penance.

Winterton was a soldier and from all she had heard he was not timid. Roy wouldn't stand a chance against him and if he died Maria would be miserable for all the rest of her life. Her parents would suffer, too, and the news would kill her papa. Had not the doctor said he needed to be kept in a calm and safe state of mind if he was to ever have a hope of recovery? Lately he had seemed happier, more himself, and she did not want to compromise that. Everything for nothing, but how could she meet him without being completely exposed in the company of society?

The higgledy-piggledy of it all whirled in her brain around and around until finally one perfect solution presented itself. She turned to her sister and her voice was certain.

'I should like to draw him, this Lord Winterton. If he is as beautiful as they all say he would be the ideal subject for a sitting. It also sounds as though he could afford to pay. Well.'

Maria's mouth dropped wide open.

'You would draw him while you are dressed as a youth? Winterton is no milksop lord who would be easily duped, Florentia.'

'If he is so very beautiful, I am sure that he would be flattered by the chance to sit for the first and only portrait I am ever likely to do in person. There is also the added advantage that if I complete this commission Mr Ward may leave me alone for a while. Perhaps this portrait is the answer we have been looking for.'

'You sound strange, Flora, unlike yourself. You have never drawn anyone before in this way, right in front of you—'

Florentia interrupted her. 'Then perhaps it is well past time that I did, Maria. A new direction, so to speak, a different turning.'

'And the Herons?'

'I shall leave London for good after completing the portrait of Viscount Winterton. After that it will all be finished. I can do other paintings to augment our income, but the requirements of Mr Ward will no longer concern me. I will be free of it and you won't need to worry about anything at all going wrong.'

When her sister had left Flora stood at the window and looked out. There had been so many times in the past six years when she had thought to try to find out about her kidnapper's family, the cousin Thomas and the woman Acacia Kensington that he had mentioned. But where did she even start to look without attracting attention? Quietly she had trawled through the books of the peerage at Lackington's because the man she had met was obviously from the aristocracy, but she had never managed to identify anybody, the small information she had more frustrating than none at all. Besides, if she had managed to find out his name what could she have truly gained from it?

Catching her eye in the glass she saw her lips move in the reflection.

'Please God, just let me understand him.'

* * *

James upended the brandy Roy Warrenden had handed him at Whites and called to the waiter to bring them another.

The night was warm for this time of the year and the windows along the whole east side were open. It had been three days since the Allans' ball and the most surprising of correspondences had come to his home in St James's Square yesterday morning.

'The artist Mr Frederick Rutherford has sent word that he wants to draw me. His agent, a Mr Ward, came to see me late yesterday afternoon.'

For a moment James saw complicity on Roy's face but dismissed the idea as ludicrous. Maria Warrenden had said they barely knew the fellow and Winter could not see what an ailing reclusive country artist might have in common with a wealthy baron and his wife.

'The agent intimated this commission would be the first and the last painting done in this manner, the fellow being a very private soul.'

'I see.' Roy watched him carefully. 'And you are agreeable, Winter?'

'I am not altogether certain, though the fact that he has sought me out personally does interest me.'

'Perhaps he is intrigued by the way society flocks to your side in admiration, particularly the women?'

James shook his head. 'I think there is more to it than the fleeting consideration of appearance. Your wife said she knew him slightly. How slightly is that?'

'Mr Frederick Rutherford made our acquaintance most recently so I should not like to give you any advice as to his sincerity or otherwise based on my knowing his character well.'

'Your wife has a sister, does she not, a Lady Florentia Hale-Burton if I am not mistaken?'

Horror crossed Roy's face as he asked it, giving
James the impression of something being awfully
wrong with the girl. His heartbeat quickened because
he did not want to be told her shortcomings were his
fault or that her abduction on Mount Street had led to
some sort of a mind disorder that had never been resolved.

'Why do you mention her in conjunction with Frederick Rutherford, Winter?'

'Pardon?' The conversation had seemed to have got
away from him and he waited for the other to explain
the query.

'Florentia, my sister-in-law, is somewhat timid. She
does not enjoy London at all but prefers the quiet of
her parents' home of Albany Manor in Kent. But as to
the other matter of the portrait—perhaps it is not to me
that you should be addressing your queries. The agent
you spoke of would hold a far better understanding of
these things.'

With care James swallowed his brandy, liking the
way it brought warmth into the coldness.

Secrets and lies. His own and Roy Warrenden's.
There was a sense of wrongness here that he could not
quite put his finger on, something held back and concealed and the mystery had to do with the artist Frederick Rutherford, he thought.

'I think I shall agree to the commission of the portrait, though the price is extremely high.'

'Well, look at it as a painting for posterity, Winter.
A foothold into history.'

'But I won't take up the offer of using the agent's gallery in South London as the place of sitting. I want it done at my place in St James's.'

'The lad may find it difficult to get there with all the accoutrements needed for such a task. I doubt any artist is all that flush.'

'Then I shall send a carriage to pick him up. Where does he reside in London? No one I ask seems to know.'

'Here, there and everywhere, I expect. Rutherford is like a gypsy in his constant changing of addresses. My wife accompanied him on the first visit to see Alfred Ward, actually, so he spent the night at our town house.'

'Yes, I had heard of that.'

Warrenden smiled. 'I thought perhaps that you might have. Rutherford is a chameleon, Winter. You might be wise to get the sittings completed as quickly as you are able and without asking the fellow too many questions.'

'You think he might abscond otherwise.'

'I sincerely hope not for I'd like to see him settle,' Roy replied, 'and you could be just the one to do it.'

'You think it might be the beginning of a more lucrative career for him? Already he is a painter with many admirers. Does he wish for more?'

Roy's laugh was harsh as he stood. 'I leave you to make your own assessment of his ambition, Winter, when you meet him, but for now I'm off home. I am, however, more than interested in seeing exactly how this romp of yours turns out.' He stopped for a second as if debating if he should say more. 'Frank Reading intimated you had returned to England to try and understand something of your father's untimely demise.'

'He's right. I never believed William committed suicide and am looking for the truth of it.' The words came out with a strained anger that he could no longer bother hiding. He liked Roy Warrenden as he was not a man inclined to gossip.

'Reading also said he had word you were asking around in the more unsavoury parts of town. Sometimes there are consequences in uncovering secrets, Winter.'

'And I should welcome them if they allow me to understand more about the nature of my father's death.'

Roy nodded. 'Well then, I hope you find some answers that might make more sense to you. If you need any help…?'

James was quick to shake his head. 'I am better alone, but thank you.'

He watched as Warrenden threaded his way through the last of the patrons of White's and lifted the bottle of brandy up to pour himself another glass when he could no longer see him.

Roy was not quite telling him the truth about Rutherford, that much was certain. There was some faulty connection, but he couldn't put his finger on it.

He knew the Warrendens were better acquainted with the artist than they let on. The lad had returned to their town house on Grosvenor Square for all the nights he'd been in London and once passing by late on an afternoon in his carriage James had noted Maria Warrenden holding the fellow's hand with more than a little delight.

God, was the sister cuckolding her husband right under his nose? And where the hell did the reclusive Lady Florentia Hale-Burton fit into any of this picture?

* * *

The blow came from behind as he was walking to the corner to hail a hackney cab, a sharp blinding pain that had him on his knees and clambering for consciousness, and all James could think of was that the danger Roy had spoken of had suddenly come to pass.

A boot came next to his face, the edge of the tread connecting with his lip, but the shock was kicking in now and with it came the strength.

Grabbing his assailant by the leg, James brought him down and within a moment he was on top of him, a punch to the side of the head having the effect of keeping the other still.

'Who the hell are you and what do you want of me?'

'Perkins sent me, from the Red Fox Inn at the docks. You have been prying around and he don't like it. It's him who sends us on to see who is asking too many questions.'

James realised this man was only a messenger boy, all brawn and muscle and no idea at all as to what this was all about. Letting him go, he stood back, watching the fellow collect his hat and move away.

'Can I speak with Mr Perkins? I'd pay well for a few moments of his time.'

The other nodded. 'If he wants to talk, you will hear from us.'

With that the stranger turned and disappeared into the night, leaving James to wipe the blood from his lip and find his own hat spilled into the gutter by the unexpected retribution.

His father's death had rocked him and he had been trying to track down some of William's gambling partners to get some answers. Suicide was a shameful thing and he could not believe that his father had killed himself. Two parents lost to suicide painted a worrying family weakness, though in his mother the failing was almost to be expected.

He swore again and looked up into the sky. A small rising moon tonight. It had been much the same sort of moon when he had kidnapped Florentia Hale-Burton. Clenching his fists, he lent back against a stone wall and felt in his pocket for both light and a cigar in order to steady himself. He wanted to see her again, to tell her that it had all been a mistake and that he was sorry for it. He wanted to take her hand in his own and let her know that he had not thought her abduction a small thing and that it had changed his life as much as it had ruined her own.

Like a pack of cards, one fell and then the next and the next until finally in the remains of what was left was the realisation that there was nothing at all of value or of honour.

His neck ached and he drew on the cigar, liking the way the red end of it flared in the night and his heartbeat slowed.

Florentia Hale-Burton had had asthma. He wondered if she still had it. She'd had a suitor, too, and a bag full of books. He'd heard her name mentioned in the card room at some ball. It was said that she had always been odd, but that if the Earl of Albany's girls had made a bit of effort with their appearances they would probably have outshone every other woman in the room.

Perhaps it might be true, though the girl in the carriage had been either unconscious, furious or sick so he had no honest picture by which to measure this.

He did remember her face after her father's gun had gone off, though, for she had reached out for him, her hands around his neck, trying to contain the damage, his blood between her fingers and her blue eyes sharp with pain.

They had both fallen then, out of the door on to the road, her body wound about his own, like a blanket or a cushion. He had felt the softness of her and the honesty, her hair falling around them in shelter until she had been torn away.

'God.' He spoke that out loud. 'God, help me,' he added as if in that second and under the darkness of a spring London night he had understood exactly what he should have always known.

Florentia Hale-Burton had tried to help him even after everything he had done to her. After all the hurt and the dogs and the chill and the fear. She had reached out and tried to stem the damage of the shot, placing her own body between him and his assailants and the promise of another assault.

The realisation was staggering.

Roy Warrenden had said she was timid and seldom left Kent so how could he meet her? To thank her. To make certain that she was…recovered?

His life seemed to be going into a vortex swirling around truth. The artist. Roy's wariness. His wife's fear. The sister banished to Kent after he had ruined her by his own stupidity.

But first he had to deal with Perkins from the inn at St Katharine Dock, for the ghost of his dead father demanded at least some attention.

Spitting out the pooling blood in his mouth, he stood, waiting for a moment as the dizziness lessened. He was on the right track at least if he was being threatened.

It was a start.

Chapter Four

Winterton had agreed to everything Florentia had stipulated save the place to meet.

His note was in her hand, the letter stamped in wax and delivered that very afternoon.

His writing looked as beautiful as he himself was purported to be—a long slanted hand with an air of arrogance in the words alongside a tinge of question.

Dear Mr Rutherford,

I was pleased to receive your letter and would be most interested in your offer. I hope that my visage will indeed do your style a justice.

I would, however, prefer to have the painting completed here at the town house I am renting for the Season in St James's Square. The light is good and I should enjoy it more than sitting for hours in the gallery of a stranger.

If you could give me by return post the time and day you would like to commence I shall have my carriage sent for you. Warrenden intimated

you have been staying with his family on and off.
Is this the location you would want to be met?
   I look forward to our association on this matter.
Yours sincerely,
James Waverley

He had used neither his title nor his crest. The wax was of a plain sort one could buy for a smaller coin than the scented kind in any of the market places of London.

Not a man inclined to waste, then? Not a man who might lay his cards on the table either, for all to admire.

You should be careful of Winterton, Florentia. Her sister's words came back. *He is not a milksop lord who would be easily duped.*

She swallowed. Well, she was not a milksop lady either. The shrieking sharpness inside her had been honed in anger for years and years and her kidnapper was a great part of that. To be thrown off into a netherworld and away from society made one more independent, more resourceful.

The commission of a portrait was a medium to understand Winterton, to weigh up her options, to evaluate which way her dice would roll and what pathway her vengeance might take.

Vengeance?

She had never imagined herself as a vengeful person, even the word made her slightly horrified, but if Lord Winterton was indeed her kidnapper then he had to understand the ramifications of what he had done to her, to her family, to her father in particular who had withdrawn to Albany Manor much changed after his flight north to save her.

Ruination came in a series of degrees, it came in sickness and sleeplessness and in fright. It came in the nights when she would wake in a sweat and wonder what else she could have done to make it different. It came in the mornings when she looked in the mirror to see the fear there lurking in her eyes and the dark sleep-deprived circles beneath them.

Maria had married and was talking of having children, but she herself had faltered, trapped in the horror of her history and hiding from all that it had exposed. She needed to see Winterton privately in order to understand what she might do from now on, what pathway to a better life she would follow.

Forgiveness might bring around absolution. She only hoped she could find such mercy within herself.

She'd dressed this morning carefully, in Frederick Rutherford's clothes. She had jammed cloth down into the edges of her cheeks and practised breathing through her mouth so that her voice was more hollow and stuffed up. When she looked at her reflection she could barely remember the frightened woman she had been when she had first donned her disguise before coming to London. She seemed to have grown into the role in every way that mattered and was heartened by such a fact.

Lord Winterton had not seen her for six years and even then in the brevity and tenseness of the whole situation he probably had not observed her closely. These clothes would maintain her anonymity, she was sure of it.

As an added insurance she had placed a small paper

knife in her left pocket wrapped in leather and within easy reach.

She knew she would not use it on him, but it was a protection to keep him at bay if all else failed. She would avoid confrontation if she could, but if it was impossible she at least wanted to have a weapon in order to escape.

Her sister knocked on the door and came in, her face set in an expression that told Florentia she was not pleased.

'I think you should reconsider this whole mad scheme of yours, Flora. This may be the last chance for you to do so for once you are in that carriage—'

Florentia interrupted her. 'I shall be fine. Winterton is hardly going to jump on a young and sickly artist. He is from society, for goodness sake, and a product of years of manners and propriety.'

This observation did not seem to alleviate her sister's worries whatsoever, nor her own, in fact, given what had already transpired between them.

'Manners and propriety are not words that come easily to my mind when I think of Winterton, Flora. I could come with you?'

'No.' They had had this conversation a number of times. 'I do not need you there and from what I have read of the workings of a private commission it would be very odd to take an onlooker.'

'But the whole thing is odd and you should not be risking the chance of discovery. There might be others there.'

'He has said there would not be.'

'He might be able to see through your disguise.'

'Can you?'

'Well, no. If I did not know any of this, I would barely recognise you myself.'

'The painting shall take at the most four mornings. Twelve hours. After that I'll have a good amount of money for Papa and Mama and me to live on. My reputation with Mr Ward will stay wholly intact as well and so hopefully more sales of work will follow.'

And I will know exactly what I am facing, for better or for worse.

'I have already said to Papa that I can help, but he won't accept it.'

'Because it would be Roy's money, Maria, and Papa is too proud a man to take it.'

'Proud and foolish and if any of this leads to a problem for you I shall berate him for ever. I do hope you are not late back and if you need me at any time…'

'I won't.'

'Roy said if Winterton hurts even one hair on your body he will kill him.'

Privately Flora wondered if her sister truly believed in this absurdity. Roy was slight and short whereas everything she remembered of the Viscount was the exact opposite. 'I will bear that in mind.'

There were tears in her sister's eyes.

'Trust me, Maria. Please.'

The brown curls jolted up and down as she nodded and then the butler was there with Florentia's coat and hat and she simply followed him out.

Winterton's town house on St James's Square was far grander than any she had ever seen before. Certainly the Viscount must be somewhere at the very top of the social tree and climbing higher by the moment if the tales Maria told were anything at all to go by.

Suddenly Flora felt less certain, the clothes she wore that had seemed like a shield at home were now only thin layers over the heart of her deceit. But it was too late to back out and when the man waiting at the bottom of the wide steps leading up to the house asked her to follow him in she did so.

Once at the front door a different and even sterner-looking servant indicated a chair just inside the reception hall and, taking her prepared canvas and the small satchel filled with paint and charcoal, Flora sat down to wait.

Thirty minutes later she was still there and the bravery garnered over years of hurt had dissipated into a much lesser force beneath the heavy ticking of a clock in the corner.

The same servant finally returned, his face as dismissive as before. A mere artist was not to be bothered with or coddled, she supposed. She was surprised she had not been dispatched around to the back door when first she had come, reasoning it would be the carriage, no doubt. Anyone who arrived in his lordship's own conveyance was probably to be treated with some amount of care.

The room she was now taken to was darkened, the curtains pulled and a single candle glowing on the desk behind which a figure sat quite still.

'Thank you for coming, Mr Rutherford.' A hand gestured to the seat in front of him but he did not come to his feet.

Florentia sat as carefully as she could and as her eyes became accustomed to the dimness she saw exactly what she had hoped…and feared.

James Waverley, Lord Winterton, was indeed her kidnapper.

Still undeniably beautiful, but dishevelled somewhat, one pale and clear green eye wholly shot with red and his bottom lip split at the corner.

Her heart began to thump rapidly and she hoped the movement did not show through her clothing. The cloth at her neck felt as if it might rob her of all breath with its tightness. Please God let the asthma stay at bay, she found herself thinking, the catch in her throat worrying.

'I have been indisposed, Mr Rutherford, and I apologise for keeping you waiting.' The Viscount said this quietly and the voice was nothing like the one she remembered. It was hoarse and scratchy and deep.

Tipping her head by way of response, Florentia sniffed without decorum. The lump in her throat was so large she thought suddenly that she might just begin to cry. In deliverance? In shock? In the solace of seeing that he was alive and that her father had not killed him after all.

Years of guilt and anger melded into this one moment of utter relief. She swallowed a number of times to try to find a balance, uncaring as to what the Viscount might think of her and glad for the dimness in the room.

Another clock above the mantel beat out the seconds. This house was full of clocks, she thought, the sound of time passing, life disappearing by the second. Or rediscovered, she mused, the stoppage of life between them now running on again with a different rhythm, another truth?

The hand nearest to her lying on the table held deep bruising, the fight echoed on his face. The violence of such lacerations made the room seem smaller. Last time she had met him there'd been blood, too. And force.

He'd spoken again and she made herself listen.

'I thought to set your easel up here in this room, Mr Rutherford. It's the one I feel the most comfortable in.'

'I would need much better light, my lord.' Lowering her voice, she liked the way her words sounded. She breathed through her mouth as an extra measure and made certain to cough. Four times.

'I promise that the curtains will be pulled back when next you come.'

He smiled as he said this and Florentia's whole world stopped. The memory of him was so strong that she lost her train of thought, fumbling with her glasses as she jammed the spectacles on tighter just because she needed a distraction.

His hair was longer now. Much longer. It touched his shoulders and fell down his back, a heavy swathe of light browns and gold. The scars that had once been visible would now be gone entirely. His skin was darker, too, as though the lands he had travelled had been warm ones, brushed with summer. The hue suited him, suited his pale eyes, suited the shades in his hair. The years had been much kinder to him than they had been to her, she thought, and frowned at such a notion. The dimple in his chin was deeper.

'I wondered if you were a figment of someone's imagination, Mr Rutherford, because so few have ever

seen you. I also wanted to ask you some questions before we started.'

'Yes, of course, my lord.' Subservience was a further disguise, a way to lead Winterton away from her
true identity and as all the pieces of her ruse seemed
to come together Florentia forced herself to relax. His
grim frown heartened her. Please don't smile again,
she thought, and glowered back.

'How is it you know Lady Warrenden?'

A different question from the one she had thought
he might ask. Very different entirely. The chills down
her spine returned in abundance.

'The Warrendens live near me in the country, sir.
In Kent.'

'So you know the family well?'

'They have a penchant for my work, my lord.'

'Who does not, Mr Rutherford? It seems as if you
have many admirers here in society.'

'Not as many as you seem to have garnered, Lord
Winterton.'

He looked at her directly and raised an eyebrow. 'I
haven't seen you at any of the soirées of the Season
across the past few weeks. Do you not enjoy the plea-
sures of society?'

Averting her eyes, Florentia coughed for a good
twenty seconds. 'I am more interested in painting,'
she managed when she had caught her breath. 'I fear
it takes up most of my time.'

'A passion then, this craft of yours?' He lowered his
voice and gave her a quote. '*Of all base passions fear
is the most accursed.*'

'Shakespeare?'

'One of the Henry's, I think. I forget which.'

'*Henry the Sixth*, sir.' Her answer was quiet. She had not expected him to rattle off Shakespeare so easily, a soldier with blood on his hands and danger imprinted into every line of his body. A man who was still fighting for his place in the world by the looks of him. The bruise under one eye would be worse on the morrow.

'You are both a scholar and an artist, then, Mr Rutherford?' He sounded amused.

When she gave no reply he stood and poured her a brandy. At least she thought it was such by the colour.

My goodness, she had not thought of this trap. A man would drink with another man and, as a woman who seldom sipped at anything stronger than a punch with very little alcohol within it, she was more than unsure as to what she should do.

Be the character, she thought, and lifted the glass to her lips. The heat of the brew warmed the blood from her toes to her hairline and after a moment or two she started to feel decidedly light-headed.

This would not do at all. Another lapse in her concentration and he would begin to wonder. Already she could see a frown of puzzlement on his brow as he watched her.

She resorted to the coughing again, taking the large kerchief Maria had procured from her pocket and blowing into it, the sound hideous and fabricated.

The longer this went on the harder it became. She felt like an insect under a microscope, peered at and questioned, everything about her turned on its head. Did he suspect? Could he know? The horror of discovery made the effects of the alcohol seem more heightened than they actually were. How many sips did one need to take to become drunk? It was frightening to feel the control she'd always had loosening.

Mr Rutherford barely looked old enough to be out of the schoolroom with his smooth cheeks and his thinness. He also looked as though he should be in an infirmary somewhere laid out on a bed with camphor and peppermint.

Peppermint. The memory of the debacle in the carriage resurfaced and James swore under his breath. God, his head ached, his knuckles stung and the lucky strike the adversary had landed last evening had broken some blood vessel in his eye so that the whole thing was a violent showy red.

He had not wanted to meet Rutherford this morning for shafts of light hurt his vision, but Mr Ward's last words had prevented him from simply cancelling the appointment.

'The lad is brilliant, Lord Winterton, so brilliant that he does not know it, the brilliance that comes from inside and not from any formal education. This painting could be worth twenty times what you will pay for it within a few short months, you mark my words, but if you frighten him off he will not be back either.'

That warning now irritated him. So far everything he'd learnt about the lad was baffling and contradictory.

'Have you always worn spectacles, Mr Rutherford?' The thickness of the glass made it seem as though the fellow was only one step away from blindness.

He nodded. 'Since I was young, sir.'

James noticed that he had pushed the brandy aside as though it were a danger, knotting his fingers together on the desk before him. Small hands and very smooth. There was a good-sized scar across the top of the thumb. When Rutherford saw his interest he immediately dropped them out of sight.

'A strong tipple does not help you creatively?' he ventured, thinking of those artists he had met in the Americas who swore the contents of a bottle allowed them their best work. The moustache above full lips looked awfully out of place amidst the smooth skin of youth. He wondered if it could be false.

'How old are you?'

'Twenty, sir. Almost twenty-one.'

He'd been caught at that age by the French in the battle for Madeira and when he'd finally got free four days later he thought it would have been better if he had simply died.

'Do you have family?'

'I do, sir, they live in Kent.'

James saw hesitation and tension cross into what little he could see of the blue eyes. Was Rutherford afraid? Was he overwhelmed? Was the drink starting to make inroads?

He raised his own glass.

'To the painting, then.' He lent forward. 'Would you mind if we did not begin today, for I have an appointment in an hour that is unexpected and urgent.'

'Of course, my lord.'

'Perhaps in private you could call me Winter.'

The lad nodded, a vulnerability and uncertainty about him so touching James wanted to protect him. That thought had him sitting back again. Rutherford's black hair was scraggly and dull, but there was a beauty about the lad that was fragile and unexpected, a quiet oddness that made him interested in knowing more, a sort of tragic undertone that shouted his life had not been easy.

He would have liked to have reached out and laid a hand across his bony shoulders, just in reassurance. But of course he did not.

'Is there something special you would require me to wear for the sittings, Mr Rutherford?'

For the first time a true emotion ran across the lad's face.

'Wear anything that makes you feel the most comfortable. It is not a showpiece I shall make for you. It will be only who you are.'

'And you can see that as you paint? Who I truly am, I mean?'

'Would you want me to, Lord Winterton?'

The room stood still suddenly, so still that James felt his hand grasp the desk he sat at, a giddy feeling that told him all was not quite as it seemed. A sort of feeling that was so foreign he could not quite decide if he was sickening for something or if a lack of sleep had finally caught him up.

The darkness inside him spiralled out through the careful face he managed to portray to society. His wealth had protected him here somewhat, but the forces of change were looming, the danger he had always lived in creeping back through the cracks of manners and propriety. He wondered if he might have a sort of delayed concussion from the blow of his assailant last night and had an image of a painting with the scar at his neck emblazoned with broken hearts and betrayal.

Nothing was safe any more.

He should send Mr Frederick Rutherford away from

the house, pay him the money owed and tell him he had changed his mind. But he couldn't. Something held him connected to this lad, bound by a thought he could not quite decipher.

'It is not a showpiece I shall make for you. It will be only who you are.'

But who was he now? The truth of not knowing had him standing and bringing this first meeting to a close.

He obviously expected her to leave, but as Florentia gathered her canvas and leather satchel the door opened and a woman and a man came through, the female throwing herself fully against Lord Winterton to kiss him on the lips and not timidly either. Looking away Florentia waited until he broke away from the caress.

'Mr Rutherford, may I present Mr and Mrs Rafael and Arabella Carmichael.' He turned to the others and smiled. 'Mr Frederick Rutherford, the celebrated artist, is here to paint my portrait. For posterity and prosperity,' he added, 'in the words of his agent.'

'I doubt anyone could do a fine job with a likeness in such semi-darkness?' The woman stated this with humour in her tone. 'It would be a wonder if he can even see you.'

Arabella Carmichael looked her over carefully as she said this. She was simply the most beautiful female Flora had ever seen anywhere, each lady of society paling against her vivid colouring. The red in her hair was that of rust and rubies and dying autumn leaves and with her full lips and her flushed cheeks she was all fire and fertility, the colour of joy and summer and success. The sort of red Flora used only sparingly in her paintings, the hue that made every other colour fade into insignificance. Her husband was just as striking. He wore a ruby pin on the lapel of his frockcoat, a dozen diamonds embedded around the shape of a serpent.

Florentia felt like a dowdy pigeon beside them, swathed in grey and brown and hidden, the patina of her deceit unattractive and ordinary. With the sensuality in the room and an undercurrent of question she wanted to be away and gone quite desperately.

Of course she knew who Mrs Arabella Carmichael was, even sequestered as she had been in the depths of rural Kent. She was a famous courtesan, trained in the profession of serving men with her body and her mind. The man Rafael Carmichael looked as though he had stepped into the room from some old painting as well, all black hair and golden eyes. An engraved silver ring sat in his left ear.

The day felt suddenly flatter, the truth of all she was and wasn't dragging her into worry. Her ruse felt wrong somehow as she had stood and watched the kiss, the hope and grief in her heart changed to only a more honest understanding.

She had built her kidnapper up as both a martyr and a miscreant, as a man of too much principle and one of none at all, and now she was uncertain as to where the truth lay. The middle ground, the grey without the black and white, the place where Winterton had left her all those years before with so many questions and so many memories?

It was his smile, she thought. It confused her now as much as it had done the first time they had ever met. She wished she had not suggested this painting. She wished she could just leave London and go home. She wished Winterton had not been beautiful and that he did not have the look of a battered angel who needed saving.

She mostly wished she did not care at all.

'I shall see you out.' His words as he came over to her. 'Perhaps tomorrow we could begin earlier. Shall we say at ten o'clock?'

As the others gave their goodbyes the same servant as before came to the door, shepherding her down the corridor, past the chair and the grandfather clock and out into the cool London day.

The sumptuous interiors of the house and the people within it stayed with her on the carriage ride home, but another thought also surfaced.

The masculine gender saw a lot more than a woman was ever allowed to, it was a freer world for them and a much more interesting one. Drink. Sex. A lack of rules and the ability to flaunt them.

The worry of a few minutes ago began to subside and she laid her head back against the smooth leather of the seat.

Well, she had done it. She had survived the first foray. Winterton hadn't suspected her and she knew initial impressions always lingered. It would be a protection and the answers she was seeking were beginning to be understood.

She would not confront the Viscount yet because underneath the strangeness she felt a kinship and a vulnerability she had not expected in a man she barely knew. It was surprising and worrying, both vengeance and absolution tumbling into another feeling entirely.

She clenched her fists together until they shook before releasing the tension.

'Enough,' she whispered to herself. 'I am enough.'

* * *

'You look worse for wear, Winter, for your wounds are visible even in this dim room and God knows what fracas you have been in now.'

Moving forward, Arabella turned his cheek into the light and he winced as one finger brushed across the bone beneath the reddened eye. 'The artist is very beautiful. I think he should have been a girl. Do you know him well?' Raising the brandy he had poured for her, she drank a good third of it. Rafe wasn't drinking at all, a fact that surprised James.

'I have just met him, Bella. He has come to do my portrait.'

'A lovely job, then, to look at you for hours. Would you not agree, Rafe?' She laughed, the sound filling the room.

'I'd say you have not told Winter that you are pregnant, Arabella, and you are teasing him in that way you regret later.'

'A baby.' James snatched the brandy from her. 'I read an academic treatise in America that warned against consuming too much alcohol whilst with child. It was most adamant in its conclusion.'

'I've told her about that already.' Rafe spoke now. 'And I have stopped drinking to try to convince her to do the same.'

'He would put me in isolation and keep me there, Winter, and nine months is a long while to worry. Frederick Rutherford was trembling quite markedly. Did you notice?'

He was used to Arabella's penchant for changing the subject when it suited her and he smiled. 'I am the boy's first private commission. Perhaps it's nerves?'

'And you would scare anyone, James, especially with your blood-red eye, let alone an unprepossessing and effeminate artist.' When Bella stated this, the timid uncertainty of Rutherford came back, a young man caught in the expectation of others.

James had felt his tension and desperation. He had also understood that the lad was lying about everything. He had been in the game of deceit for too long to believe otherwise and he'd known many a man trying to hide his identity.

The cough was the first giveaway, of course, a means of diversion that was poorly executed. Rutherford had not coughed even once with Arabella and Rafael in the room. The glasses were also wrong for he doubted anyone so young needed all that magnification, especially one adept at building a detailed and intricate likeness of a stranger in the precise medium of charcoal and paint.

But what could Frederick Rutherford want of him that a hundred others had failed to discover?

'Well, I think that the little artist is intriguing.' Arabella said this as she pulled back the curtains.

'In what way?' He couldn't help taking the bait, as he squinted against the light.

'Frederick Rutherford looks at you as though you are a prize, but then everybody is inclined to admire you, if only you could see it. But you never stop in a place long enough to notice those who would lay down their lives for you and there are so damn many of them. Perhaps this artist, Rutherford, is just another you will not notice because you do not love yourself enough.' She shook her head as he went to speak. 'You are flawed in some way, Winter, that is incomprehensible, you with all your money and beauty and strength. You who can lead men anywhere you want them to go and they will follow.'

He could hear the blood hammering in his ears. 'You are spouting nonsense, Bella.' He looked across at Rafe for support, but Arabella was not yet finished, not by a long shot.

'We are all of us too good friends to lie to each other, James, and you have been my best friend since I was ten. Now it is my turn to help you. You will be thirty before you know it and for the past years, from what you say, you have not let a woman into your life. Not in any way that matters, at least. Oh, granted, you flirt with the possibility and allow your paramours to believe that there is a chance for everything, but you never take it further. A quick romp and then a parting, no true emotion in any of it. In Boston it was said you could have had your pick of any of the women and I have heard accounts of it being exactly the same in London. The Heron daughters, for example, have apparently spoken of nothing at all save of your allure since the Allans' ball. There is also talk of a stately home in Herefordshire.'

'How could you know this? You abhor society, Bella?'

'Rafe hears things in the same way as you do, Winter, because the channels of intelligence are never still and because once you are part of an underworld you never truly escape it. As for me, well, I was not born in such elevated circles as you both were, but in the worlds below that of the *ton* everyday life is most connected. The servants talk. The shopkeepers gossip. The man on the corner who sells herrings for a shilling has a story to tell for the right price and your name at the moment, Winter, is exchanged for the top currency. And I listen well to all of the gossip.'

'God help me.' He began to laugh. Arabella had always been beautiful, but few had understood the cleverness that ran along with it or the iron will that she had had to cultivate to survive.

Rafe finally pushed himself away from the wall and spoke.

'It is rumoured that the Rutherford chit is related to the Warrendens.'

'I'd heard that said. Do you know how?'

'Closely, by all accounts. Mr Rutherford has brought no servants with him from Kent, not even a valet, and those in Warrenden's employ are not allowed anywhere near the locked room that Rutherford uses at his town house. The most worrying thing is that the artist has also been asking questions about you, Winter, about your past. Quietly, I will give him that, but still…'

The shock of Rafael's revelation had James lifting his glass and drinking the last of his brandy.

'My past?'

'Your time in the Americas. Your family. That sort of thing. He will know that you are looking into buying Atherton Abbey and that you have returned to England wealthy. Was the portrait expensive?'

'Very.'

Rafe laughed. 'Well, then, perhaps there is method to his madness after all. Choose one wealthy mark and milk his vanity for all it is worth and then go on to the next. It could indeed work for a while.'

James shook his head. 'From what I have heard the man is prone to alter the appearance of his subjects.

At the Allans' ball the oldest Miss Heron told me she was worried that she might not be drawn with quite the fineness she would hope to be. I do not think an artist like that would pander to the shallow conceits of the very rich.'

'Interesting.' Arabella took hold of Rafe's hand and held it close. 'I'd like him to do my portrait then, for I am sick of all the wooden beautiful ones I seem to engender.'

'I doubt Rutherford will be tempted. I think this is his first and last effort at pleasing his agent. He told me as much.'

'It gets more and more fascinating. But why you, in particular, Winter? Do you know him? Have you met Mr Rutherford before?'

'No.'

'Could your father have?'

That thought had not occurred to James. William Waverley had gone bankrupt after a gambling spree that had lasted for ten years. Could the Rutherford family have been somehow involved in that scandal?

The artist did not look well off for a start with his old-fashioned clothing and scraggly hair. But in the lines of his body there was a fineness that was easily discernible and a watchfulness that hinted of other things.

He'd observe him more carefully tomorrow and try to ask his own questions. He'd make certain that no one was expected to visit either to allow him the hours of uninterrupted time he might need to persuade the lad to trust him.

He wished Rafe and Arabella had arrived when they were supposed to have, for he would have liked to speak with Rutherford longer. He'd seemed frightened and timid. James wondered how he had injured his hand for the scar upon it looked so very out of character.

Flora visited the church she'd found near Grosvenor Square because after her day she felt as if she needed to pray for guidance and help.

Her reactions to Lord Winterton made no sense. She should be loathing and blaming him for all the trouble that he had caused in her life and here she was wishing that he could look beneath the disguise and hurt to understand just exactly who she was. Ridiculous. Foolish. Imprudent.

The anger that had been building all afternoon under bewilderment and question bubbled over as she sat in the pew in the third row from the back of the empty church.

The candles were burning and she tried to concentrate on them, tried to inhale their scent and pull herself free from this fear she was consumed with. A statue of Jesus on the cross in marble looked down at her from the font. She wished the sculptor had made his eyes more believable. The lines of his arms were wrong, too. Foreshortened and thick.

Her sister had wanted to know everything that had happened with Lord Winterton, every nuance and word that had passed between them when she'd arrived home. Maria had been waiting in the front room, worry crossing her brow and darkening the blue in her eyes, but had then immediately taken her hand and shepherded her upstairs where their privacy was assured.

Flora had told her a little of her time at Lord Winterton's, but left out many of the more pertinent facts. She'd said nothing of the Viscount's unexpected visitors or of the offered brandy. She had not told her sister how she'd been made to wait either or of the darkness of the room she was finally ushered into or of the battered beauty of the man within it.

Shallow she knew to base so much of her opinion on simple appearance, but there it was.

By all accounts he was a womaniser. The kiss Arabella Carmichael had given him in front of her husband had been scandalous and it told her that the Earl ran in fast company and did not apologise for any of it.

She wondered what had happened when she left. Had they spoken of her? Had they laughed at her countenance, recalling her cough and her glasses and the dull colour of her wig? Or had she been a person of no consequence and very little thought? Dismissed completely the moment she had left the room.

Mocked or forgotten, both options had her bringing her hands together and praying…for what?

For his redemption. For her forgiveness. For her vengeance. For his atonement. For some resolution. For a hundred different things that could never be. For the life she'd been forced to live and for her papa who had slid into a depression fed by the worry of an entailed property and an unmarried ruined daughter.

She frowned and stood. The Lord above would not want to hear such complaints and whining from a woman who was hardly as desperate as a thousand others. Oh, granted, she had had her trials, but even those paled against the everyday life of many Londoners without enough food to eat or a warm and safe place to sleep.

No, she needed to deal with this effectively by herself. Tomorrow she would go to meet Lord Winterton again and begin the portrait. She knew his face. She could have closed her eyes and drawn him from memory. And she had done so for the painting in her wardrobe at Albany held a likeness she would never better, not even with him there right in front of her.

It was the essence of her subjects she loved the most to draw and his spirit was vivid and strong and clear. She couldn't show him any of it, though, this reality she knew, because he would understand who she was, where they had met, what had passed between them on the road north all those years before. She was not ready for that just yet.

It was a fine line she was treading between lies and the truth, the diverging pathways of exposure, scandal and ruin all a part of it, too.

The quiet of the church was comforting, the solace of a space to breathe and consider. The smell of candles and incense was embedded in the polished wooden benches and ornate hangings, the scent warm across the cool darkness. Light streamed in from all angles above, the smallest sound echoed back from the walls and the roof. As a woman she would never have been able to walk these streets alone or steal into the worshipping place with such an untroubled ease.

A man's life was a different life from the one that she had been brought up to. The boundaries were wider and there was a freedom that was exhilarating.

She wouldn't leave London just yet. She had accepted no money and she had signed no contract, but the strictures of her life were opening again, the dullness of the last years exposed in the running risk of what she was now a part of, an animation of stillness, an exuberance that made her breathe faster and more deeply.

She wanted the liberty and the emancipation that this charade allowed her. She wanted the independence to walk exactly where she desired to, a thought that was increasingly more fascinating and satisfying.

She wanted to draw what she could see here in the hidden parts of the world she had not been allowed to venture into before as a woman. The buildings. The river. The people who hurried across the parks in the wind who looked nothing at all like those who inhabited the *ton*.

Chapter Five

The next morning she was shown into the company of Lord Winterton without delay, past the wicker chair and the clock, down the corridor and into the library that was somewhat changed.

Today the curtains were drawn back and the light of springtime flooded into the room, making it look bigger and much more inviting.

Lord Winterton's appearance was different, too, his clothes this morning a reflection of his elevated station in life. He had shaved and pulled his hair back into a cue tied with leather. A severe style, but it suited him. His left eye did not look so reddened or his lip so broken. The purple bruise on his cheek, however, was much darker. It made him look rakish and dangerous.

'I hope the room and its brightness meets with your expectations, Mr Rutherford.'

'It does, my lord.'

Her glance was drawn to the books in long shelves on each side of the room. Milton. Edmund Burke. Swift. Shakespeare. The Viscount was a well-read man.

'Can I help you with the canvas? It looks heavy.'

He'd come closer now, much closer. It was the first time he'd been so near and she felt herself stiffen.

Don't touch me. Don't touch me for if you do...?

'No, it is fine, my lord, and most easy to handle.'

She thought she should cough, but yesterday's marathon had left her exhausted and her throat sore and so she decided to depend on the fact that he'd have her demeanour of sickness in his mind already.

'I have not sat for a portrait before.' He sounded uncertain now and a little shy and Florentia felt the tension inside her soften.

'It won't hurt, Lord Winterton, as long as you remain very still. Here.' She angled a small armchair in front of a window and invited him to sit, liking the way he crossed his legs in a long line and placed his arms on the chair rests.

No tightness in the gesture. No pretence. An easy subject and so very beautiful. Sliding the thick glasses down her nose so that she could see over the top, she began.

His eyebrows had risen as she watched him, arched in something akin to humour. She saw he almost went to say something, but did not as she raised the charcoal and squinted. Sliding her thumb up and down the length of the shaft, she tried to get down the proportions in a way she was happy with. His legs. His body and his head. The quick freedom of the medium began to fill the empty canvas, as it came alive with the essence of James Waverley, Viscount Winterton.

His hands came next, the line of the fingers and the shapes of each. His nails were square and short. There were many scars across the knuckles of his right hand and her glance inadvertently went to the one at the top of her own thumb. Hurts lingered in both skin and mind. She wondered if he had other marks beneath the linen and superfine apart from that which she knew would be on his neck. Some inner sense told her that there would be. He was a man who wore his history like an armour.

She moved on to his face next for the eyes were the strongest point of any portrait, though when his glance met hers straight on it was she who looked away first. There was laughter in the clear and pale green but also question. His cheekbones were high and angled, the play of light from the window drawing them up into sharpness.

The dimple on his chin she hurried over. She did not wish to remember the portrait she had already finished of him.

The Belvedere Torso sketched in red chalk by Michelangelo came to mind, the vitality and the beauty. But this Adonis was fully clothed and she was glad of it.

For the first time since meeting him Frederick Rutherford looked as if his fleeing was not imminent, his whole attention centred on the canvas and charcoal, his mouth pursed in focus.

'Can I talk? Or would that ruin the composition?'

He asked this carefully, fearing that even the slightest of movements might spoil things.

Rutherford looked up at the question, the surprised frown between his eyes giving the impression that he had just remembered the person he drew was alive after all.

'Drawing is not an exact science, sir. The interpretation of your face does not lie only within what is seen.'

'You try to look inside?'

'You quoted Shakespeare yesterday and I can see that your many books are well loved and used. Those things are a part of who you are and should be reflected in a portrait. But there is danger in you, too, and a contrast if you like. Stillness against energy. It must be hard to be so very noticeable when there is such a lot you want to keep hidden, Lord Winterton?'

He tried to keep his face clear of surprise. 'Are you a soothsayer, Mr Rutherford? A man who might think to read people's minds?'

'Bodies tell stories as succinctly as any words. The skin holds tales as surely as the eyes and face hold history. Even hands have a narrative to impart.'

He watched her straight on. 'Uncomfortable truths. Are you surprised when you are wrong?'

'Are you saying I am, my lord?'

'Age must be fairly definable, heartbreak less so. What if I told you my life has been a comfortable and joyous one thus far, without any trial or tribulation?'

'I might congratulate you out loud on your luck, but I doubt that I would believe you. Tragedy makes each of us stronger and I can see you are that, my lord. Strong, I mean. Perhaps you have had to be?'

He began to laugh because this was one of the most illuminating conversations that he'd had for a great deal of time.

'And what of you?' he asked after a moment. 'Has the loss of some great hope made you who you are? Has it boosted empathy?'

Winter saw the lad's eyes in full focus as he tipped his head, the pupils flaring over the top of heavy glass.

They were the blue of summer skies and gentle seas. But apprehension danced across the colour, striking shards of shock at the darker edges even as the contact was lost.

He felt his heart quicken in response as some far-off memory tried to reform and appear.

'Secrets define us, my lord, like small sharp pebbles caught in a shoe. You have yours and I have mine. To be rid of them is to tread a pathway differently.'

'Do I know you, Mr Rutherford?' He hated the way his voice sounded, foreign and tight.

'Know me as the artist or know me as the man?' There was no kindness in such a question. 'I do not imagine either would be possible for I rarely visit London, my lord.'

But Rutherford's hand shook as he clutched the charcoal and real anger crossed his brow.

'Of course.' James settled back into quietness, but something had changed between them and he could not quite work out what it was.

His eyes were no longer relaxed, she thought, no longer languid or threaded in humour. He'd remembered something, she was sure of it, the first finger on his left hand rapping out a rhythm against the wooden armrest on the chair.

She wanted to leave, to escape, to be far away from those probing pale eyes that saw everything, and nothing.

If she cried it would be over. If tears escaped from her eyes and ran unheeded beneath her glasses down to the skin at her cheek she would be exposed. So instead she gathered her courage and tried again whilst she still could.

'Do you think on the whole you are a good man, Lord Winterton?'

'As opposed to an evil one, Mr Rutherford?'

That small humour heartened her. 'Nothing quite so damning, I imagine. More of an overall summation of your character, if you like.'

'Then, yes.'

She relaxed, pleased for his answer. 'And do you believe in fate?'

'The concept of fate based on the belief that there is a fixed natural order to the universe that can never be changed, no matter how hard you try?'

When she nodded he went on.

'Oedipus struggled to escape his fate and couldn't.'

'Do you think that was because he was forewarned?' She asked the question lightly, but a lot rested on his answer.

'You are asking me, Mr Rutherford, if I believe man's character is his fate.'

'Perhaps I am.'

'A fatal flaw. Like Hamlet. Unchangeable. Constant. Set in stone?'

'The idea that no matter how much one endeavours one cannot change one's destiny?' She looked towards the books all lined up at one end of the room. 'You have shelves and shelves of Shakespeare and wasn't he the master of proving that fate, not will, pre-determines the order and course of events.'

'Anything you do is pointless and will not be made different, no matter how much you wish it?' He shook his head and the light caught the gold threaded through darker shades. 'No. I myself don't believe in that sort of fate.'

His fingers were alive now, as he spoke, not the quiet things that they had been before. Eloquence and intelligence had a certain line that whispered beneath the skin. Wiping out the charcoal, she began anew with her drawing, the energy within quickened, different marks appearing.

'In all of my reading in the subject, Mr Rutherford, characters aware of their fate inevitably try to escape it?' He finished that sentence in the cadence of a question and she could not help but to find an answer.

'Because *She* is a motif in folklore that draws people in and keeps them under her spell.'

'You see her as a woman? Fate, I mean?'

'I do.'

'Capricious? Often unfair?' His voice held laughter.

'Confident. Unfailing,' she returned, with the same sort of humour. 'A power applied by the truth of certainty.'

'A feminine muse who does not take kindly to her hand being forced?'

Florentia heard the regard in the words just as strongly as she felt the pull of his intellect, though his words cut close to the bone. Her hand had been forced by his on the road all those years before and it had brought her here to this moment, in disguise and hiding, the trust she had held in people shattered and torn.

'If you could begin your life again, Lord Winterton, would there be things you would do differently or change even a little bit?'

He shifted at that and uncrossed his legs, sitting

straighter, the fingers on one hand playing with the ring he wore on the other.

'Who would not admit to that, Mr Rutherford? Who would not relish the opportunity to have a second attempt in getting it right? There have been things…' He stopped and she saw a flat sadness in his eyes, the empty desolation of honesty. 'The Realms of the Lost Chances…?'

He said it like the title of a book or a song. He said it without any attempt to hide the sorrow in his voice. He also said it like a man who knew these things would never come to pass for him and something inside Florentia turned and changed.

Amazement. Wonder. The chance to speak with all her heart and soul and wit and to be answered back in the very same way. No limit in the opinions, no careful edging around truth. It astonished her this conversation, this discourse full of diverging thoughts, which echoed promise and honesty.

She wanted to know more about him, his place of birth and the people who had formed him, but did not quite know how to ask.

'What would you change if you could?' His question came through the growing silence.

'My brother's death.' She was astonished she had said that right out loud. She had never spoken to another beside her parents and sister about Bryson at all.

'How old was he when he died?'

'Sixteen.'

'And you? How old were you when this happened?'

She clenched her lips and teeth together so that she would not say. *Sixteen years, two months and nine-*

teen days. The exactness of it cut into her heart like a sharp honed blade.

'Were there other siblings?'

'There were, Lord Winterton.'

'And your parents?'

'My father is unwell. Mama nurses him. A martyr, if you will. A woman of duty.'

The words of Maria Warrenden rung out in memory. She had said almost the exact same thing of her parents at the Allans' ball when he had asked after them. A coincidence? He thought not.

Could Rutherford be some adopted son of the Hale-Burtons, a foster child or a bastard one? Every question he formed about the man demanded tenfold other questions and then more on top of those ones.

The sun was climbing now and the beams from the window fell across them both. Frederick Rutherford's cheeks were as bare as a baby's bottom, no stubble or fuzz upon them.

Perhaps he was even younger than he had said? Perhaps he was barely out of the schoolroom, but trying to make some coin for a family who were hurting?

The price tag on the painting was ridiculously high. High enough to keep the young man's parents in food, heat and lodging for at least a year if they were frugal?

The answers were beginning to line up in a way that worried James and he dearly wanted to see Roy Warrenden and his wife again to ask them some questions.

'I shan't begin the painting of your portrait today, my lord.' Rutherford said this just as James thought he might not speak again. 'I need to look at the lines of the work and know that they are the ones I want to continue with before I apply colour.'

'Can I see what you have done so far?'

Rutherford shook his head and brought out a cloth to drape around the canvas.

'It is bad luck to look at a work before it is finished.'

'Like a bride,' James said when he saw him frown. 'The groom should not see his bride before they are married,' he added, wondering why he should have used such an example when there were so many other better ones available. 'The last freedom. The final independence.'

Frederick Rutherford blushed, as red as a beetroot, from the throat to the hairline, a brilliant firelight red. 'You don't believe in marriage?'

'Well, I never married so presumably not.' He found himself saying this almost out of anger. Once he had believed he would marry. Once he had felt whole enough to become a half of someone else.

'The Warrendens are happy.' This statement surprised him.

'And you know them well?'

'Well enough to see that of them, at least,' Rutherford answered, bending to the bag he carried, the one of canvas and leather, buckled in silver. 'I cannot come tomorrow. The next morning suits me, though.'

'Then I shall see you on Thursday morning. Do I wear the same clothes that I am in now?'

'It does not matter about what you wear. I will change it anyway.'

'I see.'

'The room will look different, too. You will be somewhere else, I think, in another place entirely.'

James could not help but be amused. 'When would you like to be paid?'

'Not yet,' he returned quickly. 'If you pay me it will ruin everything. You will own what I make and I am not sure if...'

'You want to give it to me yet?' He finished the sentence and put out his hand. But it was not taken. Rutherford merely tipped his head once and then turned away from the windows and the light, the canvas clutched carefully under one arm and the oversized satchel under the other.

'Goodbye, my lord.'

Then he was gone, the door shut behind him, the lingering smell of linseed and lavender the only things left behind.

Rafe Carmichael turned up an hour later and he didn't look happy.

'London squeezes the life out of me, Winter. It's the air here, I think, and the lack of green. All I can say is thank God for the gardens Arabella planted at our house.'

'I'm hoping Atherton Abbey may bring me the same sort of refuge, Rafe. I signed the contracts yesterday.'

'Bella said you would do that, but I didn't believe her because you have never stayed anywhere for more than a few months in all the years I have known you.'

'I think it's largely to do with my unstable childhood.'

'I had heard your mother was...difficult?'

'So difficult she killed herself. It was a statement, I think, for her loathing of my father.'

'An effective one then. How old were you?'

'Fourteen. William was seldom sober afterwards but he was sometimes kind. For that I owe him at least an overdue reprieve of the soul.'

'The man who was mentioned the other night when you were attacked. Perkins? I have been doing some looking and it seems he is the son of a small northern lord. He drinks at the Red Fox Inn in St Katharine Dock usually on a Friday afternoon.'

'How much did that information cost you?'

'I will call it square after sharing a bottle of your finest brandy and giving some advice.' He waited as the glasses were found and the tipple poured. 'Find a wife like I did. Find a woman who surprises you and who does not allow your soul the chance to fail. Bella said to tell you that she went to a soothsayer in Covent Garden yesterday and offered up your name and a drawing she had of you. The old gypsy, who can read the fate of even those who are absent, said you need to look into the places you least expect to find love and that the one you will marry has already come into your life, but you have not seen her yet.'

James laughed because he could not help it. 'You believe in this rubbish?'

'I found Arabella in a brothel. If a fortune teller had tried to tell me such a truth, I might have laughed, too. Harking back to the prophesy, Winter, who has surprised you and challenged you lately?'

'Frederick Rutherford.' James's answer came without thought and he swore beneath his breath.

His regard for the reclusive artist resurfaced. If he breathed in deeply he could still smell lavender and hear the strange cadence of his husky voice. Nothing felt safe any more. He felt as if Rutherford could see into the very shadows of his soul.

'Will you visit Perkins?' Rafe changed the subject of the conversation as sharply as his wife did and he was glad of it.

'I will.'

'Take a knife, then. It's a quieter bearer of death than a pistol and from all that I've heard of him the man is dangerous.'

'You're instructing me on battle, Rafe?'

'More like warning you, for I know you are far better at the art of violence than me. I do, however, want you settled at Atherton with the wife who you will be surprised by after you find her in a place you least expect to.'

James smiled and swallowed a good-sized sip of the smooth brandy.

Her sister met her as she came up the steps and followed her into her room, though she did not speak until the door to her chamber was locked and there would be no chance of any curious ears listening in.

'I thought you were never coming home.'

Florentia took off her hat and dragged the heavy wig from her head, spreading her own hair into the air in relief as she sat. 'A portrait is not an instant thing, Maria. It is made up of layers and every one of them is as important as the next. There is no hurrying of it. Today was the base layer, the beginning.' She flung the wig down on to the bed beside her.

'Was it difficult?'

'It kept changing, that was the trouble. Lord Winterton is one thing and then he is another. Like quicksilver.' Standing, she took off her boots and wriggled her toes before stretching out her feet. The height of the inlaid leather was uncomfortable and heavy and the back of her legs ached in a shared empathy with her insoles.

'You mean mercury?' Maria's voice was high. 'Isn't that a poison?'

Florentia laughed at her sister's horror. 'But it sits next to gold on the periodic chart. What does Roy think of him, Maria? Of Winterton?'

'He sees him as a friend. He says that he is to be trusted if he gives his word otherwise we should never have agreed to this charade of yours. Not for all the tea in China nor for all the money in his overflowing accounts.'

'Did he tell you anything of Winterton's history? It could be helpful. In my work…' she added lamely, because lying to her sister was not something she did well.

'He said that the Viscount had a difficult childhood. From what wasn't said I think Winterton has been lonely for a very long time. He was also a soldier in the first Peninsular Campaign under Moore. A part of intelligence, Roy thinks.'

'Do you know a Mr Rafael Carmichael?'

'The steel baron? He is married to a woman who was a courtesan.'

'Arabella Carmichael. I met them yesterday at St James's Square.'

Maria began to frown. 'You didn't tell me that. My God, Florentia. They sound like fast people and people who might guess…'

'My secret?'

'There is more to it than that, isn't there? You would not keep this up if it were only for the production of a portrait. There is something you're not telling me.'

'Do you believe in Fate, Maria?'

'The sort of Fate that makes you sad for ever, you mean? The sort that takes you away from life because you have been dealt such a rum hand?'

Maria walked to the window. 'Your world is tiny, Florentia, and it has been for years, but everything is a risk, don't you see, every step you take, every place you go, every person you meet. It can either turn out well or it can turn out badly.' She shook her head. 'I asked Roy the same question about Fate once and he thought that perhaps it is really your own will bending everything that happens into what you think you deserve?'

The power of her sister's reply was unexpected. 'You were talking of me?'

Maria nodded.

'Well, now I think I deserve better.'

'Good.' Her sister's smile was disarming. 'And if it takes dangerous people to drag you out of obscurity who am I to complain about it, for you look happier and more vibrant by the minute. But remember, I will always be here for you when you do want to talk about what you are really up to and perhaps I can even be of help.'

'You already have been.'

'Then I am glad for it.'

Florentia met James Waverley unexpectedly as she walked from the chapel near Grosvenor Square later that afternoon. He was alone and dressed in clothes that were nothing at all like those of a well-born lord.

'Mr Rutherford? You are a religious man?' His glance took in the church behind her.

'I enjoy observing the paintings, sir, and the stained-glass windows.'

'A belief, then, in the finer aspects of the church?'

She laughed at that and forgot to disguise the sound. Caught unawares, she found her charade harder to effect, thrown out in timing for the careful preparation of forming the persona of another. The expression in his eyes also signalled danger.

Out in the open in the street he seemed taller and bigger and much more menacing than he had inside his town house in St James's. Out here the man he had become in the Americas, the powerful and compelling overlord, was so much more visible. The adornment necessary to exist in society detracted from his menace. Here the plainness of dress and the lack of any frippery left him intimidating and threatening and more beautiful than she had ever seen him.

That thought made her blush and she knew he had seen such a shyness for he looked away as if to give her time to recover. The colour of his eyes today was almost see through, the pale green translucent.

'You are a puzzle, Mr Rutherford,' he said finally. 'A man who might be everything or nothing?'

This was said as a question, the intonation lifting as he looked straight at her, the broken truths between them filled with hate and blame and betrayal.

She thought he might see it, all that was hidden underneath as he held her glance, the barrier of her spectacles counting for little.

'You are familiar to me, Mr Rutherford. Have we met before?'

* * *

Hell. This afternoon under a darker sky Rutherford seemed changed somehow, the lines of the lad's face softer, the colour of his eyes magnified.

Beautiful.

That word stung him with a shock.

For so long in his life he had stayed out of reach of others, giving little, expecting less. But here he felt a connection. He wanted to protect the boy, keep him safe from harm or hurt or sadness. He needed to understand the distance he wore like a cloak, that prickly layer of reserve so known because he had it, too, a fierce aloneness that drove everything he did.

'Do you have many friends here in London, Mr Rutherford? Do you go out much?'

'I don't, sir. By choice, that is. I am…busy.'

'With the paintings?'

'They take a while to finish properly, my lord. Often a long while.'

'Do you have a favourite?'

James could see that Rutherford did. It was written across his face in sudden shock, though he stayed silent.

'Where did you learn? To draw, I mean. Who was your tutor?'

'Books, sir. In my father's library. I was an ardent copyist before I tried anything at all on my own.'

'And your father is…?'

'Oh, you would not know of him, my lord. He is a simple country gentleman and seldom visits the town.'

'Because he is ill?'

'Pardon?' Fright now could be plainly seen.

'You told me he was a sickly man who has taken to his bed.'

At this the other breathed out, the sound shaking with a vulnerability that tugged at Winter's heartstrings. He felt every one of his twenty-nine years even as the artist began to speak again.

'I am ordinary, my lord, just as my father is and if it were not for the paintings the London *ton* would have tired of me years ago.'

'But that is exactly the point, Mr Rutherford. You were nowhere to be seen even a year ago. Nobody has heard of you in Kent and any lineage you may lay claim to here is indeed a mystery.'

The boy lifted his face to the sky and licked dry lips, the sensuality of the movement making James reel, a hot shaft of desire snaking through him. It was the smell of lavender, he decided later, and the slender pale shaft of his throat. It was the supplication of his hands, too, bent and small, paint on the edge of the thumbnail that held the scar across it.

He could discern a tang of incense from the church on his clothes and today a button on his shirt was undone, the cloth of some undergarment beneath fine.

There was danger here. The thought came with a violent swiftness, the same nausea he had felt in his recuperation after the skirmish in the northern inn, the same dislocation, too. If he had followed his desires he might have reached out there in the busy public street and brought the youth in against him, to try to understand just who and what he was. A pull of lust so fierce it almost undid him.

Instead he moved back and tipped his hat, pleased

for the growing distance between them and the poorness of the light.

'Goodbye, Mr Rutherford.' He did not wait for an answer as he left.

Chapter Six

After such a disconcerting encounter James had spent the evening at the docks in the darkness with the smell of the sea close and the knowledge that a thousand yards of Haitian mahogany was stacked in the hull of the *White Swan* clipper moored a hundred yards offshore. It was waiting for the tide to turn and the river to swell and the morning light to break across the dull silence of the Thames.

Those he had come to meet would arrive soon, he was sure of it, for the man he had waylaid last night near the Red Fox had been most emphatic his boss would meet him, doused as he was in badly cut liquor, the stench of it on his breath. The gold coins had probably helped as had the promise of more. James had always found that generosity was a far greater persuasive factor than any force in cajoling men of a dubious morality to do as he wanted them to.

Fifteen minutes later they arrived and he pocketed his silver whisky flask and stood away from the wall. If he thought this meeting too dangerous, he could simply escape by jumping into the river. He was a strong swimmer and the current here would take him across to the opposite bank.

The tall sandy-haired man he presumed to be Perkins spoke first.

'I had word that you wished to talk to me.'

Without hesitation James gave back an answer. 'My father was William Waverley and I've reason to believe he was drinking at the inn you own on the night of his death?'

'I beg to differ. The constabulary maintained he was not in my inn at all. The Viscount's death by all accounts was from misadventure further up the river.'

'His brandy flask and hat were found in a room at your establishment.'

'Says whom?'

'The man whom I bought them from a short while ago. He would be willing to go to the law with his information, but I hoped it would not have to come to that. I thought you might see the sense in establishing your own innocence in the matter before it went further, so to speak.'

'You are here to threaten me, then?'

'No, indeed I am not. All I am after is the truth of my father's demise.'

'Many say the old Viscount killed himself. A suicide?'

'I don't believe that to be true.'

'Sometimes what is hoped for and what is are not the same thing.'

'My father converted to Catholicism the year after my mother died. A penance, he thought.'

'A religion in which killing oneself is a dreaded mortal sin?'

James nodded. 'The preservation of life for the salvation of soul. He was not an angel, but he had a marked belief in the sacredness of the Fifth Commandment.'

For a moment there was a silence between them, the sound of the river close.

'It takes a brave man to come asking his questions here in the slums of the river and amongst men who would stick a knife in your back in an instant on a single wrong word.'

'I was a soldier, sir, and I promise at least some of you would die should you try to take me.'

The man opposite smiled, but he also relaxed, his fingers slipping from their place above his belt. He'd held a knife there no doubt and there was also the outline of a firearm under the right side of his coat. Left handed. So many clues to be gained by a careful observation.

'Did you know your father had a side business of transporting illegal brandy from the Continent? A way to try and makes ends meet, he told me once.'

James nodded. It was something he had only recently discovered.

'Two gentlemen came to visit him in his room, a room he often rented to be sure, and he left with them. Too quickly, I always thought, for the bottle of the best brandy in the house still sat on his bedside table barely touched. An unusual happening with the Viscount to waste any liquor of some worth…or of none.'

'You bought the contraband from him?'

'For a sum that was often more than I wanted to pay. But, yes, because he was honest in his promises and he always delivered. I recognised one of the men who came to see your father on the last night he was alive.'

'Who?'

'Mr Benjamin Heron.'

'You would swear on this?'

'To you I would.'

'Why would you give this name to me?'

'I liked your father. The drink blurred his lines, but under it all he was a good man and I think you are probably the same. The information I give you is in all confidence and I leave you to do with it as you will, but I shan't be involved further and there is nothing else I can tell you.'

Then he was gone, disappeared into the gloom of a night that held the promise of rain. James knew he would not see him again.

Heron. The name turned on his tongue. What had the connection been between his father and the man? Was Heron augmenting his own fortune by his involvement with an illicit trade in contraband brandy? The man's wealth was legendary, but he had never heard a whisper of anything untoward.

He would need to confront Heron in a way that did not send him into hiding. He'd need to become a confidant. His heart sank. The only way he could see of doing that was to make some sort of effort with his daughters.

The blonde giggliness of Julia Heron came to mind. A woman who would worry and fuss. The prophesy of the old gypsy Bella had given his name to also rankled.

The one you will marry has already come into your life. The *ton* and its rules had a way of tripping a man up and sending even those hell-bent on avoiding marriage straight into its arms and he did not wish to be the next Winterton driven to drink too much because of an unsuitable wife.

Chapter Seven

James watched from the upstairs window the next morning as his carriage drew up in front of the town house and Frederick Rutherford alighted. He had almost cancelled the appointment after their meeting yesterday and his own unease of it, but he hadn't because a delay would only increase his anxiety.

The fellow came down the steps carefully, his hand clutching the side of the carriage door as though he might fall. The slightness of his figure caught the first morning sun, a thin light today as if spring was still wrestling with the oncoming summer and had not quite let go its chill.

Rutherford looked uncertain as he turned to collect his canvas and leather satchel, the former still draped with thick fabric, and Winter wondered why the footman did not help him with it. Perhaps he had asked already and been refused. There was something about the young artist that was prickly and isolated, a reclusive spirit caught in a commission he so obviously did not want.

Why had he suggested it in the first place when the

labour of being in another's company was so clearly trying?

The boots he wore took James's attention because he noticed the soles were thickened in a way favoured by the London fops. Was Rutherford vain enough to want the extra height? His walk was mincing this morning though he lengthened his stride to avoid any cracks on the pavement or on the steps leading up to the house.

For luck? For superstition? To meet with a Fate he'd rallied against two days ago? An inescapable future?

As the lad passed the small tubs of miniature bay trees on each side of the front doorway he reached out and picked a handful of leaves, bringing the greenery to his nose and inhaling deeply, standing there completely still in the moment. His footman, a man of considerable gruffness and age, smiled at the action as he waited, the sheer enjoyment of the young man placing a spell over all who watched.

James stiffened. What must it be like to be so lost in all of the senses? A creative mind needed such inspiration, he supposed. He himself had passed those trees many times since coming to England and he had never thought once to lean down and smell the aroma. There was a certain honesty in such an act. When Rutherford opened his hands to let the leaves go he was careful to scatter them out of the harm of being trodden on.

A few moments later his man knocked on his chamber door. He had not moved from the window because all of a sudden he felt immeasurably tired, by Rutherford's mystery and innocence, by Perkin's revelations and by the Heron girls who seemed to be using each waking hour to try to find ways to inveigle him into their company. The shock of their father being named as one who might have killed his own parent was also a part of his fatigue, but although Benjamin Heron was a man of wealth he did not quite strike James as a murderer for he was too weak and nervous of life.

Then there was his reaction to the artist outside the church yesterday. That above all else was what kept him here unmoving and unsure, a feeling so unfamiliar he could not quite decipher what his next step should be.

'Mr Rutherford is come. He is in the library, my lord.'

'Offer him a drink, then, and I shall be down in a moment.'

He turned to the mirror as the servant left and observed himself. The bruise under his eye had lightened considerably and he could barely make out the wound on his lip. The shadow of uncertainty in his visage however was worrying for the lad made him nervous somehow. Rutherford's intellect had been surprising, his wit sharp and his opinions eloquently put.

He smelt good, too.

That thought had James frowning because it was such a personal observation, a notice one might give to a lover or a wife.

'Hell,' he swore out loud as the truth of such scrutiny settled. He hadn't been truly interested in a woman in years and here he was fighting off an attraction to a damned slip of a boy.

He should simply tell his man to send the artist home and pay the whole exorbitant sum of the portrait as a forfeiture. The cost would be nothing against the worry of his attraction.

And yet…?

He wanted to see how he might be perceived. He wanted to understand who Rutherford thought him to be, the real man and not the hidden one. He wanted to watch those slim fingers run along the shaft of the charcoal as he brought the stick up against his eyes and found the proportions, the small well-shaped nails, the heavy scar across his thumb.

Swearing again, he helped himself to a drink, hoping it would calm him down.

A further rap on the door had him turning.

'The young man downstairs asked me to give you a book, my lord. He said he would appreciate it returned after you have read it.'

James looked down. The volume of *Waverley* was in his hands. He had heard of this work, of course, but he had not yet purchased it. His interest was caught.

Five moments later he walked into his library to find the large canvas was not set upon the easel. Mr Rutherford himself was gazing out of the window, his timepiece in hand. Checking his client's tardiness, James thought, and tried not to smile.

'Thank you for the book, Mr Rutherford.' He met his eyes only briefly and the dark head opposite tipped in a tense acknowledgement.

Turning the cover over, James looked at the first page. 'Did you enjoy it?'

'I did, my lord. It is a tale of tolerance, I think, and of the belief that all people are basically decent.'

'It is set in Scotland, if I remember rightly, around the Jacobite Rebellion? Does the author portray the massacre with a sense of fairness?'

'All art is imagination, my lord. To stretch the mind

to describe the events leading up to such a point of breakage is illuminating.'

Rutherford's particular scent could be smelt from here, a quiet evocative note on the edge of furniture polish and the fresh bunch of white roses on the mantel. The bay laurels were there, too, a pungent heaviness almost like cinnamon. An undernote of sensuality.

Layers. Of truth and lies. He could feel it in the air around him and knew a quick moment of panic before he had it under control.

His eyes took in the canvas still wrapped in its shroud and he walked over to the same chair he had been in on both previous days and sat down.

'I think I might prefer you standing today, my lord, by the window with the light behind you, only this time I will begin in paint rather than charcoal. A freer style will serve my message better.'

'Your message?' he could not help but ask.

'The exposure of emotion is what I do best, Lord Winterton.' He coughed after saying this, a weak forced sound.

'I'm not sure if I should be pleased to hear that, Mr Rutherford.' Winter was tired of being placed on edge and tired of feeling off balance.

'Because you don't usually show your feelings?'

'To the world? No.'

'If you do not like the portrait, no one else ever needs to see it.'

'Apart from you and me?'

The frown on Rutherford's face was more than disquieting. 'Every subject gives away a little of themselves in the process of a portrait, my lord, it is a known fact. A literal likeness or a flattering representation with nothing else to it would, in my mind, be a failure.'

'I have not followed art much, Mr Rutherford. For years I was a soldier.'

'Is that where you got the scar on your neck?'

He felt his hand lift his collar before he could stop it, the raised flesh under his fingers near the corded veins of his throat. He knew the myths that had risen around him, the half-baked truths and lies that would seek to explain what people could see of such a mark.

'No.' He left it there and moved to stand at the window.

'Should I face you straight on?'

'I was thinking to do this more in profile against the light.'

Turning, he made sure it was his good side towards Rutherford. A small vanity. A useless conceit.

'Like this?'

'Not quite.' He could hear something in the words that was sorrowful and gritted his teeth. Pity was the last thing he needed this morning and as the youth came towards him he tensed.

'If you place your fingers on the back of this chair, Lord Winterton...' When Rutherford's hand lifted from his and their eyes met, a white heat of contact travelled down through his body.

He felt like he was in a dream with thickened air and no way out, a netherworld, the taste of memory sharp upon his tongue.

And the artist simply stood there, too, gazing at him, his own reflection shimmering in the thick-glassed dirty spectacles.

Two smears across the right-hand side, of paint per-

haps. Red like blood. The accident. The carriage ride.
The girl Florentia Hale-Burton bound beneath him in
the aftermath of betrayal.

He had heard her screams and felt her pull at him,
trying to stay close, to help, to staunch the wound that
was driving life from his body.

The smell of gunsmoke, roses, hay, sweat and vomit.
The sound mute and distant, the moon small and faint
in a dark, dark sky. Her tears mixing with his blood, a
gold cross on the end of the fragile chain that she wore
around her neck.

God, please give me strength, he found himself im-
ploring. Was he going mad? Why the hell should Florentia Hale-Burton be coming so forcibly to mind here
in his London salon with the daylight outside?

Pulling away, he walked from the window, afraid
to turn as the brittle silence bound them both. It was
happening again just as it had yesterday, a mix of want
and horror and shock.

Florentia knew he had felt something, too, when she
had touched him, an echo perhaps of what had been or
of what was to come.

She was playing with fire and violence and fear and
fury. She could feel the vibrations in the air above the
thick pretence of manners, barely concealed, naked,
raw and ragged.

Winterton was all the colours of the rainbow. He
was the darks and the lights and the quiet and the vivid.
He was the rush of blood and the hush of shadow, the
pure strength of a man whose history was drawn on
his flesh with brutal and eternal strokes.

The paintbrush was in her hand before she knew

it, running across the canvas free and wild. She drew him from radiance and energy, from the bleak and from the empty. She found lines she had never placed in any painting before, soul lines, memory lines.

She drew him in red and gold and shades of brown. Scarlet was there, too, and a dark raw green. She did not stop even as she felt him watching her, she, who was always so private with her art and so very discreet.

She poured her heart into the painting and felt the shadows there lighten, felt the shifting of blame and vengeance and the welcoming luminosity of forgiveness. It was cathartic and redeeming, a liberation and a pardon, a way of moving forward and onwards. The repeal of guilt. Finally.

And after another two hours she laid her brush down and collected her satchel, leaving the painting where she had balanced it on the ledge against the window, the refracted light of the sun streaming in across the colour, burnishing it with a beauty that broke her heart.

It was over. The portrait was his. With only the briefest of goodbyes she tipped her head and left.

The painting was nothing at all as he had imagined Rutherford might draw him. It was not his outward appearance he had caught but the inner significance, his glance turned towards the sky and watching something that was out of view, stillness pervading strength.

He'd drawn him as a soldier, a uniform of scarlet and black adorning him, the mark on his neck vivid and unhidden, a human vulnerability against the anonymous and harsh force of the military.

For a moment he simply stared. For a moment the

war came back into him with a force that left him gasping, the battles, the pain, the loneliness. The lies.

On his finger there was an enormous ruby, a field of blood dripping from the intricate golden ring. Outside hanging from a branch sat a gilded cage with a sombre bird inside, its head lifted in agony. He felt that song in his heart, the melody pulling at all he tried to conceal. The hurt. The shame. The utter fury that he had lived with for so very, very long.

It was a masterpiece. Even he with only a limited understanding of art could tell that it was. It was the demons inside him translated into paint and howling to a world that would never understand.

Would Rutherford be back? Was it finished? He'd formed no plans to return tomorrow and had left no bill of purchase or payment.

He had not signed the painting either, not made it his.

'God, please help me.' The words fell into the emptiness of the room as he sat and tried to find a reason for everything that had happened.

Twenty minutes later he left the canvas exactly where it was and collected his hat and coat.

Outside he found the driver of his conveyance in a tither, the carriage still sitting in front of the town house.

'You did not take Mr Rutherford home?' He looked about to see if he could see the man, but he was nowhere in sight at all and he'd promised Warrenden he'd send Rutherford back to Grosvenor Square safely after each sitting.

'The Heron carriage collected him, my lord. Mr

Rutherford got into it on the arm of a young lady though he did not look too happy about it at all.'

'Did you hear where they were bound?'

'To the Heron town house, I think, sir.'

'Take me there now.'

Inside the moving carriage James laid his head back against the cushion and closed his eyes. Wild conjectures ran in circles around his head, but he dismissed every one of them and resolved to see what the truth was when he asked Rutherford to explain. The youth did not look like someone who would be good at lying.

His own connection with Heron also swirled in his head unchecked. Why the hell had the carriage been outside his house in the first place and why would Frederick Rutherford get inside on a whim?

Florentia was dread-stricken to find herself inside the Heron conveyance.

She had tried her very best to escape, but Miss Julia was both stronger and taller than she was and short of making a scene that would attract more attention to herself she was forced to sit down on the seat opposite and make the best of things.

'Thank you so much for agreeing to come, Mr Rutherford.' The young woman smiled though the lady's maid next to her did not look happy at all. 'Papa has been trying to find you for days and days in order to persuade you to draw our portraits, but you are most elusive. He will be so very pleased with today's visit.'

'I am leaving London tomorrow. There will be no time for more commissions—'

The girl shook her head and broke across her words. 'Papa is most persuasive and the money he will offer will be substantial.' There was now a note of desperation in her voice so Flora said nothing. 'Besides, my sisters are not without charm.' She tittered. 'At least we have been told such by our many and most ardent admirers. Winterton must have also made a lovely subject, Mr Rutherford?'

When Flora failed to reply she went on heedless. 'Did he tell you of the Abbey he is purchasing in Herefordshire?'

Florentia grated her teeth together and wondered how quickly she could gain her release on arrival. Her heart was beating fast and the thought crossed her mind as to whether she was to be subjected to enforced rides for ever because of the will of another.

'He is the man all the ladies would like to marry, though of course there is talk of his dangerous past, but that just makes him more…appealing, do you not think?' The note of gossip was most pronounced in Miss Heron's speech.

'Dangerous past?' Flora meant not to say anything, but the temptation was too great.

'He was a spy with General Moore in Europe. An occupation he continued on with in the Americas apparently. His father committed suicide last year. There is a fatal flaw in the Waverley heritage, for his grandfather perished from excessive drinking. Many are wondering exactly what his inherited weakness will be. Is that not…thrilling, Mr Rutherford, and romantic?'

'Perhaps the ladies of the *ton* should be aiming for other lords who are less…damaged, Miss Heron?'

Laughter was the result of this advice. 'You do not know women at all, Mr Rutherford, but then your youth is probably a defence on that score. Mr Ward has promised Papa that any work you do for him would climb in value very quickly so I suppose that is why Lord Winterton employed you in the first place. He has the golden touch, it is said, and with his wealth and looks what lady would seek another if such a one should be available to her?'

A short silence ensued after this. Miss Heron seemed momentarily uncertain as to whether she had said too much and the maid near her was craning her head in her haste to be finally at home, her talkative mistress and her unwise antics so obviously frowned upon.

Florentia wondered what would happen when they reached the Heron town house. She had seen the thin and tall Mr Heron at a number of soirées years ago and he hadn't looked like a man at ease with himself. There was also the worry that the disguise she wore might not measure up to the blatant and telling stares of the fashionable Heron women.

Please do not let me feel breathless, she thought. Please God just let me get through this and then be able to go home. The painting of the portrait had exhausted her. It was always like that when she finished a work and was parted from it. Just another piece of herself left behind and lost. She wondered what Winterton had thought of it.

The carriage drew up to a town house a few moments later and a number of servants came forward. Within a short time they were inside a substantial and beautiful room, the other members of the family gathered around a table, the plates upon it all filled with varying meats, breads and fruit.

'This is Mr Frederick Rutherford, Papa. I ran into

him on the street near the Winterton town house and asked if he might come back here with me in order for you to speak with him.'

At this everyone began to talk and, raising his hand, Mr Heron quelled the excitement.

'As you can see, Mr Rutherford, my daughters are most struck by the fact that you might fashion their likeness. I had had a conversation with your agent, but he was not very forthcoming and to find you here in our presence and so unexpectedly is indeed very heartening. Fate, I think, Ana…' he smiled at his wife '…and Julia's quick thinking.' His daughter looked more than pleased with the compliment. 'What is meant to be will always find a way. Is that your painting satchel, Mr Rutherford?'

'Yes, sir.'

He clicked his fingers and a servant came from nowhere.

'Please keep this piece of luggage safe at the front door, Sanders. Mr Rutherford will collect it when he goes.'

A drink was offered then and the chance to select something to eat from the overburdened table. With her mouth full of fear Flora asked for a cup of tea and was glad when it came to wet her dry lips.

The doorbell rang half an hour later and to the surprise and shock of everyone Lord Winterton himself stood beside the servant who had showed him in.

If Florentia's presence had created a furore here the Viscount's coming was a hundred times more astonishing and the young Herons rose as one from the table to greet him, eyelashes batting and hair and skirts smoothed down. Like a flock of birds preening.

'We were not expecting you, my lord.' Julia seemed the first recovered as she said this. 'Though indeed it is a most pleasant surprise.'

'I am here to escort Mr Rutherford back to Grosvenor Square, Mr Heron.'

All eyes turned back to Florentia and she blushed most horribly and stood, so relieved to be able to leave the company of people whom she could make no sense of.

'Mr Rutherford is here to go over the terms and conditions of a portrait I have commissioned him to do, Lord Winterton.'

'Such matters of business will have to be conducted at another time. The young lad has been in my employ and I have taken it on myself to make sure he arrives home on the hour he stated he would.'

His eyes came across hers for the first time since gaining the room, the shards of green cold and furious. He looked nothing at all like the man she had just drawn, every plane in his face raised into a sharp relief, the lines around his eyes far more noticeable in anger than they had ever been in repose. He looked menacing and intemperate and dark.

A chameleon? The words of the Miss Heron who had brought her here came to mind. A spy in both Europe and the Americas.

She rose, moving across beside him with gratitude. There was an undercurrent here she could not understand, a jeopardy that simmered just below the surface. She saw that Heron's hands were fisted at his sides, a vein on his forehead pulsating blue amongst the redness of his visage.

They did not like each other, these men. Winterton for all his expertise at masking his emotion was clearly furious and for the first time ever in the company of anyone she wondered if he were armed. He felt different, dangerous. He felt like a stranger whom she had never met before, a man who might do away with the other without a second's thought.

'We will see ourselves out.'

When she nodded the Viscount turned, the last vestige of social amiability lost in his retreat.

Then she was following him, on his heels and close. After she took her satchel from the surprised butler, they went through the front door and when they had gained the road she took the first real breath she'd been able to in the last good while.

He glanced at her quickly but he did not speak, not until the door to his conveyance closed behind them and the horses were moving out into the heavy traffic.

'If you wish to place yourself in the hands of a nest of vipers, Mr Rutherford, perhaps next time you will not do so on my watch.' Every knuckle on his hand was stretched into whiteness.

'I declined the commission right from the start, Lord Winterton, for I prefer to pick out my clients rather than allowing it to be the other way around.'

'The worth of one of your paintings negates the importance of your agreement for Heron, I should imagine. The man has not gained his fortune by way of soft words. You would be advised to stay well away from him.'

'And you are advising me?'

'I am, Mr Rutherford. Most strongly.'

'Why?'

'I think Heron had something to do with the death of my father.'

What the hell had made him simply blurt that out? Rutherford's surprise was about as great as his own for he seldom let another know the truth of his feelings.

'How?'

When he looked over he saw the lad stare at him across the top of his glasses as though he had forgotten to hide. The blue of quiet seas, he thought, and flushed anew. What the hell was happening to him that he should think this about a man? Moving apart to leave a wider space between them, he swore under his breath. He felt brittle and tired.

'My father imported contraband to pay for an escalating gambling habit and my guess is that his rivals decided he was making too much money.' There it was again, this strange trust he felt with Rutherford. Without it he would have stayed silent.

'Miss Heron told me your father's death was the result of suicide. She said you held many secrets and that was one of them.'

'People can say anything that they want, but it does not make it true.'

Rutherford laughed. 'I agree with you there entirely, Lord Winterton. The things that are said of me…' He stopped then and turned away, but not before James had seen consternation on his face.

What was said of the artist? He had never heard of anything apart from stories of his brilliance and his reclusiveness. Hardly derogatory or inflammatory. Another question on top of everything. A further puzzlement.

Surprisingly the lad kept on talking.

'I always thought that one should ignore what was said by the *ton*, the gossip and the unkindness. But now I am not so sure. Perhaps to rally and fight against lies is a better way of living.'

'As opposed to what?'

'Hiding. Disappearing. Forever being misplaced in life.'

'As you have been?'

'Yes.'

That word reverberated around the carriage, the truth of it and the loss.

'Can I help you?'

James thought there were tears welling in the young man's eyes at his offer, but then he turned away to look out of the window and he was no longer sure.

'You already have, Lord Winterton.'

That cryptic comment made him frown. 'The portrait, you mean?'

Rutherford shook his head, the dark hair catching the light. 'By rescuing me from the Herons.'

'They didn't hurt you…?' A sense of shock ran up his spine.

'No. But Heron is afraid of you, Lord Winterton. It was why he let me go and did not make a scene.'

'Do you often see things in people that others don't?'

'All the time, my lord. Ever since I was little.'

'Leave London then, Mr Rutherford. Go home to Kent and be safe.'

James wanted Rutherford gone, away from temptation and delivered from evil.

'Sometimes safety doesn't hold the allure it used to, my lord. There is a certain spice in the elements of risk.'

'Say those who have never lost to jeopardy and peril.'

'And you have?'

'I have killed men in the battlefields, Mr Rutherford, many times, and no man comes from the theatre of war untarnished. I think you drew that in the lines of my face in your painting?'

'Because I believe that the confrontation of such a truth might make it easier to absorb and accept.'

He laughed. 'You think it could help? Truly? You think men do not know what lies within them already? The agony of pain and the loss of compassion? If it were so easy...' He made himself stop because he did not trust what he might say next.

'*"No one saves us but ourselves. No one can and no one may."*' The artist's voice was soft.

'Who said that?'

'Buddha.'

'You are well read, Mr Rutherford?'

'I have had lots of time to become so, Lord Winterton.'

The same shock that he had felt before returned with the words and he was astonished to see that the carriage had stopped as they had been speaking and his man was standing outside, waiting for the command to open the door.

Maria Warrenden was there, too, flying down the steps and towards them, her glance going to Frederick Rutherford as the door opened.

'You are very late...' James could see Roy's wife

was stopping herself from saying more, a smile plastered across her face that hardly appeared genuine.

Rutherford had ducked his head down and was looking at no one.

'Thank you, Lord Winterton, for bringing Mr Rutherford back personally. I could not think what had happened to make him so very late and imagined the worst and my husband is not at home at the moment...'

Lady Warrenden wanted him gone. That fact was scrawled plainly on her visage and in her stance.

'You are welcome, but now I shall bid you good day.'

She nodded at that, the frown across her forehead easing as he tipped his hat and left.

Maria was most agitated, but as usual with the servants within earshot she was also being careful.

'Roy would like to see you now in the library.'

'I thought you said he was not at home.'

'Now, Mr Rutherford,' was the only reply, the anger in her tone noticeable and worrying. The fiasco with the Herons had left Florentia agitated and on guard and she felt she might not weather another onslaught of her sister's concerns.

She wished Winterton had not left. She wished he was walking alongside her, protecting her.

Roy stood as they came into his library and he asked Maria to close the door.

'Your sister and I have been concerned about the days you are spending in the company of Lord Winterton and we both think it is well past time to call a halt to this deception and return home to Kent. My business here will be concluded in a few days.'

'And to be so very late today is more than concerning, Flora. Where on earth have you been all that time?' Her sister's voice was shrill.

'I finished the portrait and Miss Julia Heron happened to be going by as I left and insisted I accompany her home to talk about a further commission. Winterton finally rescued me from the Heron town house when he realised that was where I had gone.'

Maria rolled her eyes and looked furious. 'There is talk that your work is rising most quickly in favour and in worth and this is the result, don't you see? It is dangerous, this greed, and soon someone will dig around to try and find out things of you, personal things…'

Roy took over where his wife had left off. 'If your ruse is discovered, there will be a scandal of an even greater proportion than the last one and James Waverley has been trained as a spy.'

'Which is why hours in his company are such a poor idea, Flora.' Her sister's hand fastened on hers.

She knew they were right. She knew with the portrait finished and some of her questions answered they should now cut their losses and move away from town. But still…

'I want one more short session with the Viscount. I need to sign my work…'

'Very well. And after that?' Roy was standing by the window, watching over the street.

'After that I promise that I will accompany you back to Kent.'

Even as she gave them such a troth she felt the loss of it. The freedom. The power. The ability to go where she wanted to and whenever she wanted alone. A woman was tied to convention and propriety in a way

a man was not and the knowledge of such a liberation
had been life changing.

London allowed an anonymity that was impossible
in the country and she knew bone deep that she could
not simply turn her back on such emancipation. She
still had Bryson's clothes and it should not be difficult
to travel to London on her own accord.

The small hope of this made her smile.

Chapter Eight

Rafael Carmichael called on him later that evening, James's butler showing him through to the library.

'You look like hell, Winter. How is the portrait going?' His friend asked this after James had poured them each a drink.

'It is completed.'

'Do you like it?'

'Like might not be quite the right word. Frederick Rutherford is a talented artist, though he has left me with no bill.'

'I am sure you will receive the reckoning.'

'How? How are you sure?' James was tired of being thrown off centre.

'The lad needs the money, it is whispered.'

There was a tone in Rafael's voice suggesting he knew more. 'What else is whispered?'

'You tell me, Winter. It is more than out of character for you to be open to sitting for a portrait and so very protective of the artist doing it. I've also been listening to Heron's rant about you at White's this evening. Seems as though he was not happy when you went to rescue the fellow from his clutches today.'

'I'd promised Roy Warrenden I would keep him safe while in my company and Heron had carted Rutherford off to his house unbidden.'

'He's an adult, Winter, and it was only Portland Square he had been relocated to. Hardly hazardous. I doubt Heron would have harmed the lad in the presence of his family.'

'Heron might have had a part in harming my father.'

'You met with Perkins?' Rafael took a decent sip of the drink before him. 'What are you going to do about it?'

'Watch him. Try to understand just who he is or was.'

'And how is Rutherford involved in this? Why was the artist there at the town house?'

'The Heron daughters want their own portrait and they want it badly. I think it is only that innocent.'

'Will he do it?'

James shook his head. 'Rutherford isn't enamoured by London. I think he wishes to return to Kent. God knows why he wanted to fashion my likeness in the first place.'

'How closely is he related to the Warrenden family?'

'There is a link. Why do you ask?'

'Because Roy Warrenden and his wife seem overly concerned about a lad who by all accounts has gained his majority.'

'There is something you are not telling me, Rafe?'

'I had a search carried out after we met Rutherford at your place last week and it seems Mr Frederick Rutherford has never existed in Kent at all. All my sources tell me that there is a sister, Lady Florentia Hale-Burton, who paints, but…'

It was like being stung by a bee or burnt by a flame. At first James could not quite understand the implications of such a small shocking truth and then he did. The pain flicked in without warning, almost bringing him to his knees with the sheer and bloody strength of its force.

For he knew. He knew it all.

It was her, here, in London, standing there before him trying to make some sense of exactly who he was. The portrait with his scar and blood and the bird in a cage whose song was full of raging sorrow.

It was what he had done to her, all those years before, that random chance of Fate bringing Lady Florentia Hale-Burton with her sky-blue eyes and innocence into the orbit of his life.

He'd tried to hold on to her, then, through the pain and the fear, tried to keep her fingers in his own, the warmth of them and the gentleness amidst all that was agonising. The man who had shot him was shouting and he'd heard her cry out as she was pulled away, her guttural loss reverberating into the silence.

Ruined. Both of them. By chance and poor fortune and bloody dreadful luck.

'Are you ill, Winter? What the hell is wrong with you?' Rafael's voice pulled him out of the blackness, but still he had trouble processing what was to come next.

No one else had known the whole of what had happened save for Florentia Burton-Hale and he couldn't allow the truth of it to filter into a society that would not be forgiving. He had not protected her then, but perhaps he could now, here at this time. Perhaps he could try to remedy some of the hurt.

A deeper thought also ran through his mind in

threads of relief for the attraction he had felt for the lad was now explainable.

He wanted to see her. He wanted to say that he was sorry. He wanted to understand just what it was she needed from him. Money, perhaps? The fact that Warrenden or her father might want to wrap their hands about his throat and squeeze him to death in rightful retribution was also there, lingering in his conscience. A meeting at dawn, perhaps, pistols drawn or blades sharpened, in some final resolution of blame?

Rafael was speaking again and he made himself listen. 'I can help you with Heron if that's what is troubling you?' It wasn't the problem, but James decided to let him think so because it was easier that way.

'How?'

'He wants to invest in the things that I choose to place my money in here.'

'Your Midas touch? He plans to benefit from it?'

'Perhaps. But you can profit from it, too, for we will have him close, whenever we want him, and in an enemy that is always a good thing.'

'You are staying in England then, Rafe?'

'Well, with you around things are never dull.'

'And Arabella?'

'Is happy as long as I am.'

'You were lucky with her.'

'And don't I know it, Winter.'

Lucky enough to meet at the right time and the right place and in a way that would not alienate them from each other for ever.

Florentia Hale-Burton must have hated him even as she smiled, hiding behind her lad's disguise and lifting her brush to show him the truth of himself.

She had asked him if he was a good man. He remembered that. She had asked of Fate, too, and if he could do things over again would he have done anything differently?

And all the while she was garnering enough information about him. *A freer style will serve my message better.* Wasn't that what she had told him? *It is not a showpiece I shall make for you. It will be only who you are.*

Who am I?

God. He held his head in his hands and turned towards the window so that Rafael might not see the dreadful truth in his eyes. Florentia Hale-Burton had communicated her reality in so many ways, in paint, in words and in gesture and he had seen none of it.

Secrets define us, my lord, she had told him.

'I will return later, Winter. It seems that you have a lot on your mind.' James felt his friend's hand on his shoulder and was pleased for his going. He did not feel up to any questions or confessions. He felt numb and bewildered and paralysed.

And sad.

For him and for her. For life and for honour and for the lonely places they both had inhabited since last they had met.

Fate was a siren borne on the wings of force and duplicity. He could hear the deity laughing at him all the way from hell.

She arrived in the morning at the hour of eleven and James had been sitting in his library since well before nine.

To decide what to say, he thought, and shook his

head. That was not quite true for he had already made
up his mind not to confront her with the truth directly.

He needed to understand more about her first, what
her life had been like and what she now believed in. He
had placed his portrait on the mantel so that it caught
the morning light thrown across the room. It looked
good there and solid. Like a talisman or a signpost.
To the future. To what might come from the rubble
of their past.

No one saves us but ourselves. He wasn't certain if
Buddha had quite the right of it.

He saw her gaze catch the placement as soon as
she came into the room, her boy's clothes this morning so patently a disguise he couldn't imagine how he
had not known of the charade before. The black wig
she wore was dull against the sunlight, the moustache
oddly poignant over alabaster-smooth skin.

When she coughed he merely smiled and waited till
she had stopped, reaching for a purse on his desk and
pushing it over towards her.

'I hope this is the correct amount, Mr Rutherford.'
He frowned when she did not reach out and pocket it
and tried another avenue of thought. 'In your opinion
is that the right position for the painting, there in the
light?'

For the first time she smiled as she nodded and the
dimples in her cheeks were like a punch in the flawed
wisdom of his strategies. He had no defence against
such beauty and he knew it.

'I wondered before you left if you might explain the
work to me. I have not had much exposure to the art
world before this.'

But instead of answering him directly she asked a

question of her own. 'What do you see, Lord Winterton? In the picture?'

'A man in need of salvation. A man who has lost his faith. A damaged man.'

She stood perfectly still, the sun catching her eyelashes through the glass as she blinked.

'Is that what I should see?'

She shrugged and coughed again, but he could tell shock lingered beneath the practised nonchalance. 'There are a hundred ways to read each of my paintings, my lord. Sometimes there is no true answer save for that of the soul.'

'And the bird?' He asked that quietly because he knew that it was she there, Lady Florentia Hale-Burton in a gilded cage of shame.

Anger flitted across her face and the quiet blush of it rose upon pale full cheeks.

'The bird is both fancy, sorrow and fate thrown into a palette of fury. Anyone can see her anger.'

'Because she is caught?'

'Chance can come creeping in ways wholly unexpected, my lord, and in a completely random manner.'

He should have told her then of all that he knew, should have simply confessed his mistake and his sorrow for it, but if he did? Would she leave? Would she walk out never to be seen again? Keep her with you, some voice shouted from deep within. Keep her safe.

'Could I show you something, here in London, something beautiful, Mr Rutherford? Would you come with me tomorrow to look? It would not take long at all.'

'Something beautiful?'

'A garden. The scented garden of a friend.'

Her brow furrowed as she watched him. 'How would you know I am interested in those particular sort of plants?'

'I saw you pick the bay tree leaves outside yesterday when first you came. I saw how you stood and smelt them. The garden is one of the best of its kind and it is not far.'

'I could not stay long.'

'We shall be quick then. If I collected you at eleven I could have you back by mid-afternoon. Would that suit?'

'There won't be a crowd?'

'I don't imagine so. If you wish for Lord and Lady Warrenden to come with us I would be agreeable.'

'No.' This was said quickly, without a scrap of thought. 'It is easier alone.'

She didn't want her sister there, that much was certain. James wondered what Maria Warrenden might think of her dressing as a boy. One thing he did know was that Roy and she had no whiff of his name and his part in the abduction six years ago or otherwise they'd have been on his doorstep like avenging angels. He was suddenly glad for at least that.

She stood then, her eyes fixed on his face, almost as if she was drawing him again in her mind.

He remembered the bag she had slung at him as he had tried to pull her into the carriage on Mount Street and the weighty tomes within it. The small scar above his eye was still visible there. He wondered if she had noticed the mark, but then the whole situation between them was fraught with layers.

He wished he were a better man. He wished all the demons on his shoulders would stop howling and allow him time to think. Other scars drawn into his skin in patterns smarted under the linen of his shirt and he took in a sharp breath of sadness.

Lord Winterton was different today, she thought, more unreadable. The coins that sat in the burgundy-velvet purse on his table also represented an ending that she did not quite want. The chance of visiting the scented garden with him had been an appealing one and yet she knew she shouldn't have accepted such an offer.

Every moment in his company was more dangerous than the last and there had been times when she had looked at him across the past few days when he had seemed to be waiting for something, expecting something, his jaw muscles grinding together in a way that was changed.

His hair was loose, too. She had not seen it thus before.

He suited it out, the formality of him lessened somehow and the roughness of a man who had been both a soldier and a spy more on show.

She couldn't ever remember seeing a more beautiful man anywhere. Even the images in her art books of heroes and statesmen had not held the sheer grace of line and strength.

No. Her head shook at such thoughts. She would absolve and forgive and forget. She would move on after this in her life in the knowledge that she had left behind blame and censure.

But there could be nothing else. Their past had seen to the impossibility of that and had not her father spent a great majority of the last years in bed because of Lord Winterton's ill-formed actions?

She suddenly felt in more of a tangled web than she had been a week ago before she had first met with the Viscount face-to-face. Before this she had concentrated on the disrepute, humiliation and scandal he had sent her into with his foolish and ill-considered kidnapping. She had not understood his goodness and his strength and the way that he spoke with his heart as well as his head. She had not watched him in the sunlight or spoken with him as an equal. She had not seen the secrets flit across his face even as a stronger force of will had banished them away. She had underestimated his truth.

Reaching down to her satchel, she extracted a brush and paint. Carefully she crouched before the canvas and signed her initials in the bottom left-hand corner, finishing with a flourish.

F.R.

Florentia Rowena Hale-Burton. At least such a signature held something of who she was. With another swirl she attached the year. *1816*. It had been the spring of 1810 when they had first met.

'Is it difficult to let your paintings go, Mr Rutherford?' He asked this softly.

'No.' She did not wish for him to know each time she left a piece of her work behind it broke her heart to do so.

With that she reached for the purse and felt its weight. A substantial sum. So many clients squabbled over the price of a work, but he had not. Being wealthy went some way in explaining his promptness, but often it was the richest clients who were the poorest payers.

She frowned as he extracted two glasses from a cabinet and brought forward a bottle of brandy.

'The world's finest,' he clarified and poured generous drinks. 'It seems only right that we should have a toast to the successful conclusion of your first private commission.'

Raising his glass towards her, he thought for a moment. 'To unexpected truths, Mr Rutherford, and to the future.' There was a tone in his words that she did not understand, but she drank anyway and the taste of the drink was astonishing.

'It's cognac. A Coutanseaux from 1767.'

'Old, then?'

He laughed. 'Not as old as some, but smoother than most.'

'I did not drink much before I came to London.' She offered this after a moment of silence as she savoured the taste. If this was to be the last time she was with him alone she wanted at least to enjoy it. 'Sometimes now I barely recognise myself,' she added as he looked at her.

'Is that so, Mr Rutherford? London allows a freedom, I suppose, which is different from that of rural Kent?'

'Very different, my lord.'

'And your art is admired by everyone I meet. There must be a certain victory in such praise though my next question must be one that asks is such fame to your liking?'

She shook her head before she could stop it. 'Once I had the more ordinary hope of living in a house in the country and enjoying a family.'

Once I thought to have children and a husband who

would cherish me and love me for ever. Once every-thing had seemed possible and probable and exciting. Until I met you.

Was it me who stopped you from realising all of those dreams? he wondered, and turned away, the co-gnac now only a bitter draft in his mouth and the truth of her hopes lying squarely at his feet.

He was so sick of fighting, so very tired of trying to find the best in each and every situation, the inter-pretation of which would not break his spirit.

With only a few words from Florentia Hale-Burton the Winterton title could be again dimmed and sul-lied and he did not think he had the strength to make it different.

The smell of lavender wafted close and he raised his head and reached for it, trying to find courage and tenure.

'Would you make a painting of the house I have just purchased, Mr Rutherford? I would leave the tim-ing largely to your discretion, but I am willing to pay three times more than I did for the portrait for such an endeavour.'

'*"A foole and his money be soon at debate",*' came her quick rejoinder and he had to smile.

'Your general knowledge is surprisingly wide, Mr Rutherford, and very eclectic.'

'You do not think such a truism might be of use to every man who has the need of thrift, Lord Winterton?'

'A man like you?'

At this Florentia Hale-Burton had the grace to blush and he was glad of it.

'Why would you offer me so much for a commission, my lord, when plainly the tariff should be less?'

'Perhaps because I am one who sees the true value in creativity.'

'Or...?' That word was filled with cynicism.

For the first time in a long while Winter laughed out loud.

'Or... I like you, Mr Rutherford.'

She blushed at that, vividly and satisfyingly. Her charade had kept him on edge for days and it was good to get something of his own back.

'How long were you there for in the Americas?'

'Three years. I'd been ill and it was a relief to get on a ship to somewhere else and feel the wind on my face and new possibilities in the air.'

He'd laid in that bed at Tommy's for nearly eighteen months after the fiasco at the inn, trying to regain his strength and get his body to move in the way it once had. He'd had to learn to speak again for his voice had been lost in the gunshot, ripped away in blood and flesh. It had never again been the same.

Taking a long swallow of the cognac, he liked the way it fortified resolve.

Was he telling her that it had been years until he had got back on his feet after her father had shot him?

Florentia thought that he confessed this in all he did not say and she moved closer, a feeling unlike any other encompassing her.

'They infer you are a man with secrets, Lord Winterton? Julia Heron said you were a spy.'

'A long time ago I was. With General Moore in Spain.'

'Lady Warrenden has heard you carried your particular trade to the Americas.'

'Then I was a poor intelligence officer if so much is known about me.'

'I do not believe you would be mediocre at anything you set your mind to.'

'Do you not?'

He leaned across her now, the green of his eyes bruised with caution and his mouth so near she could feel the whisper of his breath.

'Your painting was probably closer to the truth of my character than anyone has come in years, Mr Rutherford. As the artist of such a discerning work I am surprised you still allow me the chance of your company.'

A warning that was not quite as hidden as the others he had given her.

'Why should I not, Lord Winterton?' She had had enough of meanings under meanings in words, but it seemed he had, too, for he moved away, distance replacing the intimate.

'I shall pick you up at eleven tomorrow morning, Mr Rutherford.' He sounded irritated, the bruise under his eye making him look tired. She could see the last vestige of redness in the white.

'They are your friends? The people with the garden?'

'Yes. I've known them for many years and they have as little patience for the whims of society as I have. Which is a relief.'

Placing her half-empty glass on the table, she turned to go, glad to be departing for she felt uncertain somehow today, of him and of herself.

'I think you have forgotten something, Mr Rutherford.'

For a second her eyes fell to his lips, pulled by a
force that was as strange as it was strong.

'Your money.'

The sense of those words brought her back and she
bit down on regret.

'Good day, Lord Winterton.'

'Until tomorrow, Mr Rutherford.'

Maria had been furious at her refusal to cancel the
invitation to the scented gardens, but on arrival at the
house just on the outskirts of London Florentia was
very glad that she had not done so.

The Viscount had been quiet today, his words few
and far between. Even his greeting had been sedate, a
fact that she forgot about completely as they alighted
from the coach to be met with a myriad scents waft-
ing all around them.

'The land as you see it was planted a few years ago.
The plot was well irrigated and south facing and had
been a garden even before they took it over.'

Winterton's explanation was quietly given and Florentia's hand fell to the wooden rail that was on one
side of the pathway, the patina of it smooth and solid.
There was thyme and basil and comfrey. Hyacinths
and primrose filled the borders along with lavender
and as Flora passed her boots touched the greenery
and the scents lifted.

'It's beautiful.'

Bending, she reached into a thick planting of lamb's
ear, all woolly and soft, before running her fingers over
the pale blue Glory of the Snow. Feathergrass, witch-

hazel, borage, evening primrose and pansies completed the tableau, each specimen tumbling across the other in a sensory delight of smell, touch and taste, the sound of wind chimes and a water feature further afield rounding out the senses.

'It's Arabella's masterpiece,' Lord Winterton explained and Florentia knew exactly whose garden they were now in.

'The Carmichaels live here?' She could not help the trepidation that coated her query or hide the worry when Winter nodded. Last time Mrs Carmichael had kissed him fully on the lips and her husband had barely glanced her way. Would they want her here? Would they wish that Lord Winterton had brought someone else who was far more interesting and colourful? As bright as they themselves were? As intriguing?

As the front door opened, however, the woman who stepped out looked nothing like the one she had met in London. Today Arabella Carmichael was buttoned up in a soft blue high-necked gown, a large apron with pockets tied across her modest dress and her hair in a simple chignon at her nape. The red of it was muted and tidy.

'Winter.' Even her voice seemed different. Today she kissed him once on either cheek. 'You have brought Mr Rutherford to see us? How wonderful. Rafe is inside in the library if you want to go through and I could show your artist the secret garden if he has the inclination for it.'

Winterton looked around at her, eyebrows raised.

'Thank you. I would enjoy that.'

When he turned Flora followed the woman down a path to one side of the house and entered a hidden garden with an entirely different atmosphere. Shaded by trees and planted in green foliage this place was cool, dark and peaceful. A small water feature that ran between the specimens gave an added sense of mystery, as if it were a glade in some far-off forgotten forest or a place devoid of people and their noises.

'You do this yourself?' Her eyes flicked to Arabella Carmichael's hands, gloveless today.

'Indeed, I do.' Her palms turned upwards for an inspection. 'A gardener cannot boast the fine hands of a lady,' she said and taking Florentia's fingers in her own proceeded to run her thumb over the skin. 'Or of an artist.

'But it is the place that I come to feel who I am, Mr Rutherford. A garden of truth, you might say. Perhaps one day I could ask you to draw it in the way that you see it?'

'A sanctuary.' The words slipped out before Florentia could stop them.

'I told Rafe that you would understand and you do. Winter has often used my gardens for his own refuge though I doubt he would admit to the fact.'

'You have known him for long.'

She laughed, the sound joyous and honest. 'My parents worked for the old Viscount on his family estate. His mother died when he was fourteen and mine died when I was ten so we had that in common, you understand. The grief of it and the futility. I always say it is the sad emotions that bind people together with a certainty. When I lost my way and went to London it was Winter who helped me find myself again. He introduced me to Rafael.' She stopped for a moment and then carried on. 'We came to London yesterday afternoon and I saw the portrait you did.'

'I hope I caught something that you recognised?'

'I think you know the answer to that one, Mr Rutherford. But my reply to you would be to ask what you left behind of yourself in the picture?'

'Pain,' she said before she knew she had and the other nodded.

'You were the bird trapped in the cage. The one who held no voice? Do you always do that, Mr Rutherford? Do pieces shear off you in every portrait?'

'Only in the ones that matter.'

'And this one did?'

'Yes.'

'Then I am glad for it. Winter has hung the painting in his library above the mantel for it is the room he most often uses.'

So it would not be hidden then. It would be seen.

They had left the grotto now and made their way around to the front of the house. Other small flowering plants grew by the steps and Arabella Carmichael took scissors from her pocket and clipped off some of the buds.

'Did you know flowers have a language all of their own, Mr Rutherford? Lily of the valley stands for purity and pansies are for thoughtfulness.' Both the white and the blue blooms were thrust into Florentia's hands before she knew it, their scent full and heady. 'They suit you. Entirely. A gift from my garden, but also from my heart.'

Then they were inside the darkness of the house, a room at the back opening into yet another vista and it was here that Lord Winterton and Mr Carmichael sat, a number of small carved tiles on a table before them.

'Are you familiar with the rune stones? Rafe collects them.' Lord Winterton asked this of her as he saw her, a certain challenge in his voice, and Mr Carmichael laughed at her silence.

'I do not use them for magical or divinatory purposes despite Winter's teasing, Mr Rutherford. An artist like you could surely understand that their intrinsic beauty, feel and age is what attracts me and if there is a shadow of the darkness to one side then it is all the better.'

Bryson had collected bones. Of birds and fish. Of larger animals, too, caught in death unexpectedly. In swamps and rivers. In the caves at Albany, the sandstone loose and heavy. They had been collecting the day that he had died... But Flora shook that away and looked instead at the rune stones, her heart beating too fast and the taste of iron on her tongue.

The strange angular inscriptions on the tiles were perplexing. Flora knew that they were usually cast in a certain direction and that if a question was asked the answer could be found in the way they fell as a pattern.

Am I ever going to be happy again?

For just a second she thought she might have said the query out loud and the fright of such a horror kept her still.

Collections held a safety zone, a way to organise, arrange and present the world just as you wanted it to be. A place where fears were managed and calmed.

Each bone that her brother had ever found was now carefully ordered and sorted in the wooden boxes she had made and painted in her room.

Sometimes when she was younger she had seen Maria look at her as if she were indeed mad, but their white opaque stillness filled a void inside her that had opened after Bryson's passing and allowed his death some meaning.

When she caught the golden eyes of Rafael Carmichael resting upon her face, she hoped the stones did not permit him to divine her thoughts.

The normal and ordinary seemed to have passed her by and this had been magnified again by her ordeal at the inn, but as she glanced around the room she saw there were things here in this house that were also unusual.

The backs of all the chairs were notched in patterns not unlike the rune stones and a book that sat open on the table held a raised print embossed into the paper.

On the mantel above the fireplace sat five small marble busts, each depicting emotion. Besides each sat a flower, the single blooms in tall glass vases and newly picked.

Arabella's language of flowers? She looked down at the buds in her grip.

There were no paintings at all on any of the walls.

'Did you enjoy the garden?' Winterton had asked her this. His expression held the hint of something she could not quite interpret.

'Very much indeed. If I closed my eyes I might have been anywhere.'

'Or nowhere,' Rafael Carmichael said as he stood, his hands against the chair. 'Smells are evocative, are they not? Winter has an aversion to peppermint and nothing will cure him of it no matter how hard Arabella has tried.'

Peppermint.

Every time she smelt it she thought of blood and breathlessness. Imagine what it must be like for him with years of long sickness to remember and the futility of his mistake.

'So we never plant it.' Arabella added this and the tone lightened. For a second though Flora had seen in the glance of James Waverley a truth that made her take in breath.

Shame. Guilt. All the things she had hoped for in her years of ruin, though now she did not wish to see them at all.

Perhaps the Carmichaels knew what had happened on the North Road? Perhaps he had told them? What must that be like to have good friends standing by you, through all your trials and difficulties, people you could be honest with and trust?

The *ton* with all its rules and propriety seemed shallow and foolish compared to these people. She'd never felt a part of society, but was always adrift and out of step. Here, with Lord Winterton and the Carmichaels, it was like having life breathed into deadness, an energy she had lost hold of returned in all its fervour.

Maria had moved on and she had been left behind, her sister's marriage taking away some of the closeness that they used to enjoy. Bryson had been her true confidant, but she had never wanted to speak of him with her family as his death had broken all of their hearts, the hole left by his passing unending and black.

But here amongst the flowers and laughter with Winterton and his friends she felt at home, comfortable, able to be herself.

Well not quite herself, she smiled, given the disguise

that she wore and the name that she sheltered behind. But no longer hiding her honest thoughts, no longer unable to speak in the way she wanted to, no longer ruled by expectations.

She had not thought it possible to live well outside of such strictures until today where the differences allowed one to flourish and thrive, like the blooms all around them and the flowers in her hands.

She liked it when Lord Winterton came to stand beside her, showing her a book.

'These are prints of some of the oldest known maps.' His finger traced the outline of the Americas. 'They thought you would sail off the edge of the world and into the land of monsters.'

Scaly green serpents hung at each edge of the paper, the ships depicted weathering storms tiny by comparison.

'When I sailed to America I remembered these illustrations as I stood and watched over the ocean.' He laughed and, with the sunlight blending the colours in his hair and glinting against the pale clear green of his eyes, Florentia knew she had never seen a man more vibrant. The thought struck her as a blow and she held her breath as she tried to look way.

But she could not.

This truly might be the last day that she ever saw him, the last time she heard his voice or knew his smile. She drank him in even as her throat thickened with sadness and it was Lord Winterton who looked away first, his glance flickering to Rafael Carmichael and his wife watching them from the other side of the room.

'Monsters of the deep hold a certain wordless eloquence, I always thought.' There was a quiet anger in his voice that was surprising. 'An adventure that I wanted.'

'And which he got, Mr Rutherford.' Arabella had joined them. 'Did you know you are in the company of a man who single-handedly saved a whole regiment of British Hussars from the clutches of the French and lived to tell the tale?'

'Barely.' This time there was no mistaking the fury.

'He was decorated for it, too, though I never saw you wear your medals, Winter. You should. If it were me I would wear them on my chest in pride and glory daily.'

'Old friends have the tiresome habit of telling one how to act and what to do, Mr Rutherford,' He gestured her to follow him through the wide doors. They came into another smaller garden filled with crocus and hellebores.

'You don't like to remember your past?' Florentia asked this even as she bent to smell one of the Lenten roses, needing to know something of him, something of who he had been. Something to hold on to after he was gone again.

'War is glorious only to those who have never lived through the middle of one.'

'But you survived?'

'But not well and the painting you made for me showed you knew that.'

Such a raw truth kept her silent. The things people did not say were as easily heard as those they did and she was good at listening to the spaces in between. It was where she had lived for years, after all, that awkward half-hidden part of life, an invisible quiet world of little consequence and no real substance.

The paintings had brought her back from the greyness and filled her world with colour again, repairing frayed edges with purpose and delight.

But here in front of her was a man who was also good at hearing the unspoken and who had ghosts of his own. Such a kinship made her falter and hesitate, a danger here that was almost touchable.

'The room inside and the gardens without are fashioned in a way to compensate sight?'

Clear green eyes blazed. 'Rafe's father died last year. He was blind. This was where he lived for his last months.'

'You were close to him, too?'

'I was. He was like a father to me.' He took in breath and carried on. 'Most people miss all the things you don't, Mr Rutherford. Did you know that?'

'Art is made in the carefulness of notice, my lord.'

'And in the regard of the concealed?'

She looked up at that, expecting accusation. Instead all she saw was a sorrow and when the Carmichaels came out to join them again Florentia was glad for it.

James felt the rope at his ankles and his wrists and the blood running cold down his back. It was into a pit of sorts that he had been thrown, the freeze of the dirt in the Cantabrian winter crusted with ice and snow and it was raining. He could feel the steady drip of it on his face when he looked up, trying to catch even a bit of the thin moonlight.

He'd been beaten every day since the French had taken him, with a beaded rope and with a musket. Something had been carved into his back in glass and that smarted more than all the other wounds that abounded across his body. His fingers ran across raised scoured skin, trying to read by touch.

Espion.

Spy. There was no clemency in such a word.

He would die here, unheralded and unknown. Just another soldier whose bones would grace the soil of Spain. And when the French Hussars came again he tipped his head and screamed into the night, his throat aching with the sound as he tried to stop all the pain that they inflicted...

He came awake suddenly into silence and to the softness of a mattress, the sweat dripping from him on to clean linen and the moon limning the world in silver.

He was in his bedchamber in St James's. Outside came the noises of a waking city. Only a dream. Again. He had had the same nightmare for years.

Pushing back the counterpane, he sat and held his head in his hands to steady the fury and the beat of blood. The Early Cheer Arabella had sent him home with were in a vase next to his bed. He clung to the smell of them like a man who was drowning, clung to their pureness and their beauty. The first flowers after the snow.

Florentia Hale-Burton was just like the blooms. Unexpected. Impossibly fragile. Today as they sat in the garden room at the Carmichaels' he had seen things that were particular only to her. The way she used her hands when she spoke, the dimples in her cheeks, the small freckles across her nose and the grace with which she moved.

He'd seen her take in the details, too, of the room, of Arabella and Rafael, of the flowers and the nicks in the wood on all of the railings.

An artist's eye, seeing the things that other people missed, understanding secrets and accepting them. When she had looked at the rune stones he had thought she might speak of her past then and there, the truth bursting out unbidden.

But she had not. She had simply held the flowers so tightly that the knuckles on each of her fingers were white with the pressure.

As they'd made to leave Arabella had pulled him to one side.

'Look after her, Winter. She is a treasure.'

'Her?' He was wary of Arabella's accuracy.

'When I was younger I, too, used disguises. Bring her back whenever you want and make certain that she is safe from what it is she is so very afraid of.'

Him. She was afraid of him.

He was glad Arabella had not asked Florentia's name or insisted on knowing her story and was relieved to finally depart before more of the truth surfaced. The girl who at the Carmichaels had chatted and laughed was on the ride home much more silent.

'I've hung your portrait in my library, Mr Rutherford. I like looking at it. Perhaps you might bring the Warrendens to see it. I know they enjoy your work and I would be pleased to show them.'

She nodded, but made no effort to pin him down to a time at all. Rather she looked away again and spoke on a different topic.

'The Carmichaels have the best of it, I think, living out of the centre of town. Kent is the same.'

'You will go back, then?'

'I will, my lord, for I have found out all that I needed to know here.'

'And the commissions?'

'I'll draw from what I have around me and be happy with it.' Her glance dropped away.

'I have noticed that your cough is much recovered, Mr Rutherford.'

'It is asthma, Lord Winterton, and it comes and goes.'

'A difficult affliction.'

'And one far less prevalent away from the pollution of town.'

'My cousin Tommy suffered from the same, but he lives in the Americas now with his wife, Acacia, and he says that the weather there suits him far better than it ever did in England.'

The slight start told him she had caught the reference. But she was almost as good at hiding things as he was. For a moment he wondered what would happen should he simply reach out and take her hand and confess everything before they reached the Warrenden town house, but this was neither the time nor the place.

He wanted to see Florentia Hale-Burton's eyes properly and the colour of her hair. He wanted to see the dimples, too, in her cheeks and run his finger across the freckles on the bridge of her nose.

'I doubt that I shall see you again, Lord Winterton.' The words came through his reveries. 'But I'd like to thank you for your generous payment for the portrait and also for taking me to see the Carmichaels today. They were lovely people.'

Lovely? Was that the sort of word a man would use? Flora wondered and looked out of the window.

'You will not return to London?' His query came quietly.

'It is a difficult place to fit in.'

'Yet all I've heard of you is salutary.'

She smiled at that and turned towards him. 'An insincere regard given that they barely know me.'

'My offer of you painting Atherton Abbey still stands.'

'I've taken enough of your money with the portrait, Lord Winterton. Any more would be a travesty.'

'It is not because of your agent's insistence in the accelerating value of an investment that I would like more of your work, but because of the truth I see within it.'

'Thank you.' Such a compliment was distracting because it was given so unexpectedly.

'I am heading west tomorrow to see to the last of the contracts on the Abbey and shall be away for a while.'

'Julia Heron said it was a beautiful house and expensive.'

'To me it will only be home,' he returned and she understood other things about Lord Winterton, things she had not considered at all before.

He had been without roots for years, but underneath the persona he presented to the world lay a vulnerability that was surprising. At least she had had Albany Manor and a family, her life closeted but safe. His had been transitory, hard and uncertain.

She wished she might have placed her fingers over the hand that rested on the seat beside her, the one with the scars across the knuckles, webbed in whiteness, but her sister's warning came to mind.

'He is a dangerous man, Florentia, and will be hard to dupe because he is like a flame and you are the

moth. If you do not wish for discovery you would be wise to never meet him again.'

Maria had given her this advice as she had left this morning on the trip to the scented gardens and she had laughed off such concerns. But Winterton was harder to read today, although far more open, and when he had told her about his cousin Tommy she had felt a shock that she knew he must have seen.

Was he playing a double game? Did he know who she was? The horror of that thought made her sit forward, her heart beginning to thump and her mouth dry.

Another minute to Grosvenor Square and safety. The anger in her warred with sorrow and that in turn was followed by a pure and quiet grief. This was the end of everything between them and all she wanted to do was to go home.

Please God, do not let him smile or murmur words that were conciliatory and impartial and final. She did not wish to stay his friend. She did not want platitudes or recriminations or even kindness.

These grey little feelings were nothing at all compared to the burning raw-red inferno that was consuming her now, her breath shaky and her throat tight with tears. She wanted things he would never be able to offer her and as she could not have those then she wanted nothing at all.

Her father would simply expire should they come face-to-face. He sometimes talked to her as he recalled what had happened at the inn and his memory was surprisingly sharp and uncompromisingly bitter.

The number of people who'd seen the Viscount and who would be able to identify him as the perpetrator of a terrible crime was also worrying. Her maid Milly was no longer in her employ, but Florentia had heard that she'd come to London to work in one of the houses here. The Urquharts, too, were a couple who might recognise him should they see them together and their tale would not be flattering. Her father's driver and the two footmen who had accompanied Papa north could also offer information should they be asked.

The truth was like a stone flung into a still pond, the ripples widening as time passed until no tranquillity was left. If Winterton was thrown into such a scandal, she did not know what might happen to him. Would the law be involved? Would he be thrown into jail and left to rot there or sent to the colonies as an indentured felon?

It was all dangerous suddenly, this secret between them, for she had no certainty that he would be safe.

When the carriage stopped she was pleased as his man opened the door to help her down. She did not tarry, but made her way inside with the utmost speed. Looking back, she was glad he had not followed and even more glad as the conveyance readied itself for departure and the horses stepped on.

It was over and finished. She would never need to see him again. Roy greeted her as he came from his library and looked down the corridor behind her.

'Is Winter here?'

'No. He had an appointment and needed to be gone. The painting is signed and paid for so there is no contract left that binds us.'

'I am glad to hear it for these matters are never without their messiness. Once I thought I knew Winter well, but now…' He shrugged. 'He is harder and more aloof.

There is something in his character that wasn't there when I knew him at school.'

She was about to answer when Maria walked in and asked them both to join her in the front parlour.

'The Duke of Northbury has sent an invitation asking for our company and that of Mr Frederick Rutherford to a ball he is having in a week. Inside there is a handwritten note to the effect that he would be most disappointed should we be unable to go. Your name is specifically mentioned, Flora. Well, Frederick's is, I mean.'

Roy looked horrified. 'The Duke was a particular friend of my father's. I can't see how we might decline this.'

Maria handed him the gilt-edged paper, the red-wax seal broken and beribboned in blue. 'I knew something bad would come of all this. I knew we should have left London sooner and now to be stuck with another charade. It is all just too, too much and you cannot possibly attend in those old clothes of Bryson's.'

'I think clothes are the least of our worries, Maria. The very least.'

Her brother-in-law's eyes ran across her face, the brown full of concern. 'What of you, Flora? Do you wish to do this or would you rather…'?

She did not let him finish. 'I have got this far, Roy, and no one could be more discerning than Lord Winterton.' Even as she said this, however, she felt vaguely sick. 'I am sure I can be convincing for one last outing if you feel it necessary to stay.'

'We will call my tailor in to measure you for a set of clothes befitting the occasion. We will also make it known that we will be leaving the day after the Northbury ball which will effectively stop any more invitations coming, no matter how important the sender.'

Maria tucked her hand through Florentia's arm. 'We will be there this time which will allow some sort of a barrier between you and the other guests and we won't need to tarry long. An appearance is all that is required. Still, it would be better if we tried not to engage others in conversation for there is only so much luck in the world after all.'

She stopped and the unspoken lay between them. *And ours could very easily be running out.*

Chapter Nine

It was a whirlwind week of fittings and bustling activity. The Warrenden tailor had come and measured her up for the clothes and, on a generous retainer from her brother-in-law's coffers, had been the very soul of discretion and confidence. If he guessed her figure was not one pertaining to a youth he made no mention of it whatsoever, fashioning the clothes around her form and fitting them with barely a word uttered.

Standing in front of the mirror an hour before they were all to leave, Flora looked at her reflection and was shocked.

This was what Bryson would have looked like had he lived. She could see the lines of him in her face and the blue of his eyes gazing back at her. The wig and the moustache blurred the resemblance a little, but at that second all she could feel was the unexpected closeness of her twin.

'I wish you were here,' she whispered. 'I wish you could help me.'

She smiled because all her antics and movements were completed with him in mind. The way he walked, and spoke and was. Without Bryson she knew she should never have chanced such a deception.

Her fingers went to a ring he'd worn that now sat on her hand. The gold was solid and real somehow, a circle that had not broken.

Would Viscount Winterton be there tonight? Would he come if he knew she was invited or was he still away seeing to the specifics of the property he was acquiring? She had not seen him since she had exited the carriage outside the Warrenden town house. But she had dreamed about him. She had dreamed they were before a beautiful country house in the sunlight and that he had pulled off her wig and kissed her, hard and true.

Ridiculous, she thought, and shook away the image. He was probably doing his very best to never see her again.

She had drawn him every single day, late at night when the others were asleep and when there was no chance of interruption. She had drawn him in colour as well as in all the shades of grey.

She hoped he would be there. She did. She wanted to meet him again and feel his eyes on her own. She wanted to ask of the portrait and of his new home.

My God, what was she thinking? James Waverley, Viscount Winterton, would hold no interest in who she was. Every woman in society was angling to catch his eye after all and with his investments in the lucrative timber trade he was exactly the sort of man the society mothers would want for their daughters.

The night suddenly seemed less of an adventure and much more of an ordeal to get through and when Maria came in with her new blue gown, her hair a cascade of ringlets, Florentia felt suddenly sick.

'I know that look, Flora, but you have to come. Roy would be devastated if you did not and we have already sent back our intention of attending.' She suddenly smiled. 'I never realised how much you looked like Bryson. It's nice, because I miss him.'

'Me, too.'

'If Father were here…'

'I doubt he will ever be well enough to return to society.'

'Maybe if your abductor had been proven dead he might have, but to never hear a word again and your reputation ruined as it was, I think he simply lost his will for life really. If Roy was to act like that I'd probably simply hit him over the head for I certainly wouldn't be pandering to his moods as Mama is want to suffer Papa's.'

The room was crowded when they arrived, the Duke of Northbury's town house one of the largest and grandest Florentia had ever seen. From one end of the first salon right along to the other there were lengths of blue shot silk hung with corded red tassels which in turn were threaded in jewels. In front of each hanging stood huge urns filled with flowers, the aged terracotta embellished with drawings of ancient Grecian gods. Arabella Carmichael would have enjoyed such bounty, Florentia thought, for many of the blooms were out of season and must have been brought in from warmer climes. She wondered about the cost of it all.

It was like a wonderful tapestry of colour and form and texture, a beautiful living painting that faded and reformed under the light of chandeliers and the shadows of quiet darker corners. With the music playing and the chatter constant Flora closed her eyes so that she could memorise it, for the grace and movement was a tableau she might never see again. But to paint it with strokes of energy and boldness...

'I thought you had returned to Kent, Mr Rutherford?'

Her eyes snapped open. Winterton stood before her, dressed this evening in black save for the snowy cravat at his neck, folded high across the scar.

She chastised herself for feeling so uncertain, her newly found bravery reduced by his presence. 'This is the last social occasion I have promised to attend, my lord, before I go home.'

'Then it is a fine choice. The Duke's soirées are always...interesting. The man has a genuine notion of the theatrical and a budget to indulge his very eclectic taste.'

As she glanced up at him she saw the bruise on his cheek had almost gone. The pale green of his eyes against his tan always surprised her.

'You are here with the Warrendens?'

'I am, my lord.'

A servant dressed in the exotic clothes of an Indian maharaja came and offered them wine, the golden tray he held inscribed in Egyptian hieroglyphics.

'One cannot be over-concerned about mixing up dynasties when the serving tools of the Raj are so very hard to come by.' Winterton stated this dryly when he saw her observation. His expression was distant, a man with a thousand masks and not one of them the truth.

The danger in him was shocking and for a second Flora forgot how to breathe, but stood there watching him, the thickness in her throat wrenching and unfathomable. When a striking and sensual woman stepped in from one side to take the Viscount by the arm she moved back.

'I have finally found you, Winter, and so many of my friends are asking for your company.'

There was a quick flare of anger in his eyes, but this disappeared as instantly as it had come. Tipping his head, he gave her his farewells and accompanied the newcomer away without any resistance whatsoever.

Maria joined her a moment later. 'The Heron girls have just asked me if my sister was still unsure about stepping into society. I told them she has no care for the deceptions prevalent here.'

'A brave rejoinder, perhaps, given our circumstances?'

Maria managed a smile. 'Winterton is always surrounded by females and looking at him I can understand why. He does seem to favour the Heron girls, but then they are awfully attractive.'

A bevy of the most beautiful women in society had indeed gathered about the Viscount and he by no means looked disconcerted. The hand of the woman who had spirited him away lay possessively upon his arm.

'James Waverley is soon to be thirty. Hopefully he will settle on someone to take as a bride if only to put all of these desperate females out of their misery.'

Florentia laughed, but she could hear the falseness in it as surely as her sister probably could. As she glanced across the room his eyes met her own and she stood transfixed at what she thought she could see. A fine regard and respect.

She took in a breath, the wig tight about her head and the stock at her throat constricting.

The other woman had turned to see what had caught Winterton's attention, anger crossing her brow, but, seeing only the thin form of Frederick Rutherford, merely smiled and turned away.

No competition there, Flora thought the gesture implied, the soft rounded womanhood relaxing into an amused benevolence.

When Roy came to claim Maria in a dance it allowed Florentia the chance to move into an alcove with long windows overlooking the garden.

She was glad for the moment of aloneness though she felt a presence behind her and knew that it was the Viscount. Without turning, she waited for him to come and stand beside her, the lights in the gardens reflected on both of their faces.

'Could I show you a painting, Mr Rutherford? I am sure you would find it of interest.'

'A painting?'

'It is in the Duke's library and he has allowed me the use of the room.'

'I am not sure…'

'It would just take a moment.'

She glanced around, trying to see her sister, but there were only strangers standing about them and, short of a rudeness, she could not dredge up any true excuse as to why she should refuse. He would expect her to be interested and so as he gestured to her to follow him she did so, down a short unlit corridor and into a chamber at the very end.

The painting stood on the far wall, the lights around it giving its darkness a particular space.

'It's a Van Dyke.'

She moved forward with amazement. 'I cannot believe that this portrait should be here, close enough for me to touch.'

'The Duke's great-grandfather gave a particular service to Charles the First, it seems, and the painting was his reward. It has been in his family's hands for years.'

Florentia moved closer to see the brush strokes and the small details of the work. 'The elegance and authority are traits in all of his works. He painted the King and his wife many times.'

'You are well informed, Mr Rutherford.'

Winter had moved up next to her now and close, the smell of sandalwood and freshly washed male easily discerned. The darkness around them and the silence was complete. Much further away she could hear the sound of music.

When he lifted his hand to run a finger across the line of her cheek she was shocked by such an intimacy.

'Your knowledge of the arts is beguiling.'

She swallowed, the horror of her situation unfolding. Was he attracted to her as a boy? Pray God, he would not take this further.

'You asked me once if I believed in Fate, Mr Rutherford. Perhaps this is ours.' His interest had fallen to her lips, a gentle tracing of the shape under the pad of his thumb.

She could not understand just what might happen next.

'Perhaps it is our fate to meet in the most unexpected of places and under the most dubious of circumstances.'

'Dubious?' Her voice was strained.

'Me and you…here. Like this. Alone. Do you not think it fortuitous?'

There was a new tone now in his words. One of humour if she might name it and careful question. A game of cat and mouse was the bread and butter, no doubt, of any spy, and he was rumoured to be a good one.

She could feel the breath of his words against her cheek as he spoke and his hand had fallen lower across her shoulder and down the line of her arm.

If he truly did not know her, then this game was dangerous, but if he did…?

'Do you ever play the rune stones, my lord?' She asked this because she knew the answer even before he shook his head.

'Then perhaps you should. For protection.'

'Against what?'

'Enemies come in all shapes and sizes and society holds a narrow view of what is right and what is wrong.'

He laughed at that and when he ceased he leaned across and whispered in her ear.

'Is this wrong? Are you my enemy, Lady Florentia Hale-Burton?'

Her world simply stopped, the whirl of colour turning grey and all balance lost under the pounding beat of her heart.

Dread rendered her speechless.

'If you expose me, Florentia, I will not deny the charges. Everything that has happened to you was my fault. I accept that.'

'Do you?'

'You tried to save me when we fell from the carriage even after all I had put you through. Why?' His words came soft and when she did not answer he carried on. 'I thought perhaps…' Again he stopped.

'You thought what?'

'That you might not have hated me as much as I believed. That there was a chance you could forgive me for what I had done to you and your family. What I am still doing to you, with your disguises and your secrecy.'

'Pity isn't a flattering word, Lord Winterton.'

'You think it such?'

'I have been an outcast for years. How could I think anything different?'

'Marry me, then. I can protect you from them all.'

She could not believe he could possibly have said this. 'Guilt is not a solid basis for a union, either. Even a ruined woman hopes for more than that.'

'Marry me and we will leave London and society. We will make a new life at Atherton Abbey.'

'And my family? You think Papa will give his blessing? You think he will not crow your name in distaste from every rooftop he could find when he sees your face? When he knows it was you who kidnapped me?'

'I think he will see sense and do what is the best for his daughter's reputation.'

'The best? The best.' She repeated those two words, sneering at him in a way that she knew was not attractive but she no longer cared. It was one thing to be married in love and quite another to be married in shame or duty. The best of a bad situation.

'No. I cannot marry you, my lord.' She could barely get the words out.

He wished he had said it differently. He wished he could take his words back and start again, this time not immured in guilt but in respect.

Florentia had removed her glasses and was wiping them against the silk in her waistcoat and for the first time he truly saw her eyes for more than a fleeting second.

He remembered them like a punch to the stomach. Their blue honesty. The grey at the edges. The flashing shards of anger mixed with sadness. He wanted to reach out then and take her hand to hold it warm against his own, two people beached up by history on to some sort of foreign shore that neither could fathom. Shipwrecked by uncertainty.

She was beautiful. He had always known that.

She had turned now and was out of the door before he could stop her, making her way into the busy melee of the main room. As he caught her up an old friend, Frank Reading, slapped him on the back.

'Been looking for you, Winter. I have some need for timber and I hear you are just the man to provide it.' His eyes went across to Florentia, who had replaced her spectacles and regained her composure.

'You're the artist, aren't you? I have been hoping to make your acquaintance for society is abuzz at your talent with a brush.'

'Mr Frederick Rutherford, this is Lord Frank Reading.'

'Pleased to make your acquaintance, sir.'

James heard the timbre of her voice lower and gain that certain cadence of masculinity. He had not realised how convincing she sounded as a boy until she had spoken to him in a different voice altogether.

'I don't suppose I could persuade you to make a painting for me, Mr Rutherford?'

'I am afraid not, my lord. I am leaving London for a

long while. Family commitments and the need for privacy,' she went on and left the words hanging.

'I hear you have done a portrait for Winter. I for one cannot wait to see it. From the whispered gossip it is magnificent.'

Florentia shrugged and James understood what her art truly cost her in just that small gesture. It was as if she did not wish to acknowledge or discuss the paintings she had left behind, a sort of bereft anger displayed on her countenance that was gone as soon as he recognised it.

Others had joined them, too, squeezing in around them, asking questions of him and of her, dissipating any closeness. He wished he might have simply lent forward and led her away, to take her into the garden in the moonlight and…kiss her.

That ludicrous thought made him swear beneath his breath in a single heartfelt curse. She had dismissed his marriage proposal summarily less than five minutes ago. She would hardly be interested in less.

The words had astonished him even as he had said them.

Marry me. He had never once in all his life uttered that to any woman before and there had been many vying for such an offer both in America and here. He could not believe how he had meant it either, how he had hoped that she might say yes.

Had Lady Florentia Hale-Burton upended his sense in some way as to render him into this man that he barely recognised? He had not seen her for almost six years, and still did not truly, for the disguise she wore was a good one.

Maria Warrenden had come out to claim her now

and they were walking back to the main ballroom, the light catching them both as it streamed through the large glass doors.

Florentia was so much thinner than her sister, more fragile, brittle almost. Was this his doing? He could see the platforms built into her shoes and he frowned at the shape of her legs through thin silk, glad that her jacket was of a long length and covered much of what he did not wish others to see.

He swore again. He had no right to such opinions, no mandate to even think such things. When he saw that Reading watched him thoughtfully he turned away and arranged his face into the more normal expression of indifference.

Nothing seemed quite right any more. It was as if his life had slipped a cog since meeting Florentia and he could not get it back on track. He wanted to follow her inside and talk to her again just to hear her voice and listen to her odd opinions.

God, she must be laughing at him now with his ill-considered marriage proposal and his patent desperation. Swallowing his brandy in three large gulps, he felt all the better for it.

Julia Heron was watching her intently from the small distance where she stood with a few of the other girls whom Florentia recognised from her first foray into society.

Just as she was about to walk away the Heron girl broke from the others and came directly up to her.

'You have the look of the Hale-Burton brother, Mr Rutherford. Bryson was his name. I thought to tell you before another does. I puzzled on the resemblance the other day when you came to our town house, but could not quite put my finger upon it. Tonight it is right here before me.'

Flora saw the frown deepen on Maria's brow. 'Ancestry often has that certain trick of stamping likenesses on those who come next, Miss Heron. My sister and I have often been mistaken for each other as well.'

'Your sister? I sometimes wonder how she is faring, Lady Warrenden?'

'She fares very well, thank you, although she is busy with her life at Albany.' Maria was quick in her reply.

'I had heard she was dabbling in painting?'

'She is indeed. Mr Rutherford here has been her tutor.' Her sister's answer held a note of panic that Florentia hoped Miss Heron did not detect and, setting her mouth in the grim line she had perfected over the weeks of playing the artist, she nodded.

'And how is it you are related to the Hale-Burtons, Mr Rutherford, to hold such a resemblance?'

'Loosely, Miss Heron. Our fathers were second cousins.'

'Just a trick of nature then?' Julia Heron opened her fan as she spoke and glanced out from behind it, a girl who knew her worth in the market place of the *ton*. 'Lord Winterton looks well tonight, does he not? I saw you speaking with him earlier and you both seemed most intense?'

'Art has its deep conversations and its age-old fascinations.' Flora tried to moderate her tone into one of indifference.

'Papa is still hopeful he may entice you into our home to draw us all.'

Maria interrupted. 'Mr Rutherford is returning to

the country the day after tomorrow. He will have no time at all to be able to consider taking on more work in London.'

The arrival of Roy allowed a natural end to the conversation and Julia Heron begged her leave and left them.

'I thought you might like a dance, Maria.' Roy looked to have had quite a bit to drink, his face flushed.

'If it stops you from taking another brandy for a few moments I think it is probably a good idea. But what of Flora?'

'Oh, I am sure I can lean against this wall without getting into any trouble.'

'Are you certain?' Her sister looked torn.

'Go and dance, Maria. I shall be more than fine.'

As they went she watched them, Roy's hand within his wife's, a sense of trust there and respect.

Marry me, then.

The three words reverberated through her body and she swallowed away the emptiness she had heard in them. How long had Winter known her secret? When had he guessed she was not as she seemed?

The Viscount was over on the other side of the room, talking with a group of men. She could see him easily for he stood a good few inches above everyone else. He did not look at all like a man who had just had a marriage proposal turned down as he threw back his head and laughed. Under the chandelier his hair appeared lighter and it contrasted markedly against the black in his clothes. Julia Heron was cosied up beside him and he appeared to be paying her a good deal of attention.

Another side of his character was present tonight. Here in the *ton* he looked at home and relaxed, a man who would welcome the discourse of others, a viscount whose lineage was easily discerned in every line of his body and in the indifference on his face. A man who was lauded and admired by others. A man far above her station in life in all the ways that counted.

She would have liked to have drawn him like this. Even as she stood there she could feel her fingers move across his form, picking out the strengths and that which made him unique. She would have fashioned him in charcoal, the thickness of it garnering attention, bold strokes of confidence and ease, the sombre clothes against his lighter hair, muscle pressing against superfine.

She wished she might have been standing there in a gown that was beautiful and feminine, her hair paler than his own and falling in long cascading curls. The cloth she had shoved into each cheek to try and change the lines of her jaw felt dry and foreign and she accepted a glass of wine from a passing waiter to try to alleviate that.

Marry me, then.

Had he even truly asked it? Without a scrap of knowledge as to who each other were and with a history between them that could only foretell disaster? What was he thinking? Why would he imagine it could be possible? Perhaps he felt sorry for her, their enforced proximity in St James's Square having the effect of allowing him a glimpse into her life since the incident at the inn? Guilt could be a factor. Or plain old pity. A man like him could not possibly have asked her in love.

She failed to see the drunk fellow weaving across the floor because he was behind her. She did not observe him clutch at the hangings of one curtain and drag it down so that it fell heavily in her direction, the banner from the pelmet above sheering away from splintered wood.

She did hear the screams, though, echoing through the room, and she did feel the moment something sliced through the fleshy part of her right calf.

A body landed on top of her before rolling away, the smell of alcohol strong, one burly arm rising to graze her cheek and leave it stinging. She felt the heavy tightness of the shock and the sharp agony of pain. A young woman to her left began to cry and the sound of the orchestra playing a waltz quietened with an awkward lilt until it had all but stopped, only the last strings of a wayward violin vibrating into the silence.

Her leg was bleeding all over the parquet floor of the Duke of Northbury's ballroom. Indifferently she wondered how much damage had actually been done to her and then all she felt was coldness.

Florentia Hale-Burton was on all fours trying to get up, her leg pushed beneath her in a strange fashion. He could tell she was hurt even before the curdling cries of those around her took away the sense of it. Through the gaps of all the colourful silk gowns between them James saw that the tie of the ugly black wig had come unfastened and the hair now fell in a macabre way down her face, the lifeless strands covering her like a shroud.

It was as though time simply stopped, the room full of horrified onlookers and the whispers growing even as he strode across to crouch beside the pale Lady Florentia Hale-Burton.

Her eyes met his own, the spectacles fallen and the

blueness in the light of chandeliers astonishing. Repositioning her hairpiece, he found her glasses and perched them once again across her nose, praying like hell that no one had noticed something was amiss.

'I am fine.' She did not cry or try to explain. No, instead she simply sat there, attempting to draw a steady breath, a slight still figure in the centre of chaos doing her best to be brave.

More and more people were coming to join the throng, their expressions shocked at the blood that was pooling beneath her on the floor.

'It is the artist, Mr Rutherford. My God, he has been injured and badly, too.'

Maria Warrenden pushed through the crowd, shouldering those who were close to let her through. Roy came behind, his face a mixture of worry and horror, but James had untied her neckcloth and was winding it about Florentia's knee just above the wound. When he knotted it tightly the bleeding on the fleshy part of her calf seemed to slow and he let out his breath. For this second she was safe, though he could feel the wolves gathering.

'*Rutherford is very thin, is he not?*'
'*And remarkably young and girlish.*'
'*What is his story, exactly?*'

Interest spread around them and as Roy's wife's gaze caught his own he simply bent down to lift Florentia into his arms, her lightness as surprising as the fact that she did not fight him but rather buried her face into his chest and stayed still. Winter hoped those in the room would see Florentia only as a young and sensitive youth who had been brought to tears by a shocking and unexpected accident. The blood helped her case, he supposed, though his anger mounted at the thought.

'Bring him through to our carriage, Winter. I have called for my driver to bring it to the front.' Roy Warrenden beckoned him and James was glad for the direction.

'Hold on,' he whispered to the shaking figure he held. 'It will only be another moment until we are out of here, I promise.'

But she did not answer as he walked along one side of the ballroom, people scattering before him, looks of horror and speculation on each face he passed.

Flora knew that Viscount Winterton did not wish for an explanation. Yet. He had looked at her in something akin to warning, the clear green eyes taking in everything.

She knew he was angry, but the mask that had dropped over his features allowed no certainty of anything else, no shared ground at all save for the recent congress of an artist and subject.

Later there would be questions, she knew that, but for now the shock of everything made her cold and shaky and she felt the first tears pooling behind her eyes.

Winter's clothing held the same smell as his jacket had all those years before. Citrus, amber and sandalwood, smoky-dark and rich. She watched him because she did not wish to shut her eyes, the stillness that was gathering in all the corners of her body frightening and complete.

When he laid her down on the seat of the conveyance she tried to scramble up into a sitting position, but he held her there, raising her injured leg and securing a blanket beneath it.

'I hurt my thigh once and this is what the army doctor did,' he gave as an explanation. 'You will, however, need to sit very still.'

Maria looked sick with worry and Flora was glad Roy was there to hold her sister's hand because at that moment she had no energy for anything or anybody else. Closing her eyes, she prayed she would not be ill all over the expensive clothes of James Waverley. Again.

Blood was still seeping through Florentia's trousers and her face was so pale Winter thought she might just faint dead away.

Maria Warrenden watched him, he could see the questions in her eyes and he hoped that her husband would have the driver ready to move off soon.

He had sent one of his men to summon a physician and take him to the Warrenden town house in Grosvenor Square. James prayed that the man might be quick in his task and that the injury sustained was not a substantial one.

She was cold, he could tell that, but short of pulling her into his own warmth all he could do was to allow her the heat of his jacket which he tucked around her. Her fingers curled across the edges of light wool and the shivering seemed to be tapering off a little.

With care he unstoppered his brandy flask. 'Take a good mouthful and you will notice a difference.'

But she simply looked away, ignoring the offer completely and rocking back and forth on the seat. He took a swig himself.

'Does the injury pain you?'

There was a quick nod.

'Then that is a good thing. Without that a wound is always thought to be far more serious. It was the same with me after I was injured out of Lugos.'

When he saw her tilt her head as though she was interested in his answer he carried on. Roy was still fussing around with instructions with the driver and Maria Warrenden was now standing beside the carriage with her husband.

'It was snowing and the pass was high. I thought when I did not feel the pain that I was simply freezing, but afterwards they said I was as close to death as they had ever seen anyone be before and survive it.'

Blue eyes came across his own, worry stamped within them. 'I am cold, too.'

'Don't worry. You always feel that after any accident.'

'I hit my head…and it's hard…to breathe.' Her teeth were chattering now and air that she took was compromised.

He remembered this from last time, the blueness around her lips and the way she spoke as if every word were difficult. Maria had climbed in now and was crying. Ignoring the noise, he simply placed his fingers against Florentia's throat and talked quietly.

'Breathe with me. Just quiet breaths. Don't try to take too much.' Her heart was racing so fast he could barely hear the silence between.

'Good. You are doing well.' He made his voice calm as she began to do as he asked.

Her fingers came up against his, searching for warmth, her slender artist's hands covered with a crust of blood from the accident. The whole side of one sleeve was drenched in red.

Florentia wished her sister might stop crying. She wished she were home in the grove of trees at Albany. She wished she might have curled up and slept in Viscount Winterton's arms and stayed there for ever.

So many differing wishes.

Bryson was in the mix, too, for this was how he had died, his leg bleeding out from the wound upon it after she had dared him to jump the fence. The tears she had held back so far spilled over. Winter wiped them away without saying anything.

And then there was a flurry of activity as Roy rejoined them, the horses called on and the carriage jolted into motion.

But the Viscount had disappeared. He was gone and Maria was there beside her, face crinkled with horror.

'I knew this was a foolish idea, Florentia. I knew that we should be caught finally and that more scandal could follow.'

Roy, sitting opposite, laid a hand upon her shoulder.

'Only an omnipotent deity could have had such a vision, my love, and if the upshot is that we all retire back to Kent, well, we were going anyway.'

'Everybody was looking at you strangely, Flora, and if they guess what we have been doing you will never be allowed to come back into society. You will always be an outcast and you will never sell another painting.'

'I don't think your bedside manner is h-helping me, Maria.' Her sister sat closer to her at that and took her hand in her grasp.

'There are things that are so very unfair in life and its time you had some luck.'

'Luck?' Flora winced as she moved her foot for her toes caught against leather and the shooting pains made her shake. Blood had begun to seep out again and was staining the seat. 'Where is the doctor? Will he come soon?'

'Winter has sent for a physician. He will be at the house when we arrive in a few moments' time, I am sure of it,' Roy said, his tone full of question.

'And the Viscount?'

Maria frowned. 'He left. Why do you ask about him?'

'He…helped me. Did you thank him?'

'I did. He seemed…more familiar than usual.'

Florentia lay back against the seat, the pain in her leg making her feel dizzy.

Chapter Ten

James called into the town house on Grosvenor Square the next morning because he had dreamed all night that Florentia Hale-Burton's health had worsened and he wanted to see for himself that it had not. The physician had assured him the lad was recovering, but he had seen the amount of blood she had lost and she was so very slight, after all.

Roy took him through to a bright room at the back of the house where Florentia was lying on a sofa, her leg raised on two pillows. Warrenden seemed tense and uncertain, giving James the impression that his presence here was as welcome as the plague.

Today Florentia's colour was better and he could see she had been reading. The lad's clothes she wore were less formal than those he had thus far seen her in and she wore no neckcloth or jacket. On his entry she scrambled up to a sitting position and the wince of pain across her brow at such a movement had him swearing.

'Winter has come to enquire about your health, Frederick.' The tone Roy used was strained, no doubt wary of further participation in such a charade. Still, James thought, he could use it to his advantage.

'I wonder if I might have a word with Mr Rutherford in private, Roy?'

Short of rudeness there was little the other could do but agree, for there was no reason whatsoever to refuse the request of a lord wanting a small and private chat with a younger man with whom he had done business. James was pleased Maria Warrenden was not about as he doubted she would have withdrawn without a fuss.

'I shall be in the room next door, Frederick, should you want me.'

Not far. Within earshot. A simple shout will have me back.

When the door shut behind him there was a deafening silence which Florentia sought to instantly fill.

'I am much recovered this morning, thank you, Lord Winterton.'

'James,' he drawled, trying to keep out the anger. 'I am certain we have long since passed the point of such formality, Florentia. Even Winter would do.' Unsure as to whether Warrenden was listening on the other side of the door, he kept his voice down and was glad when she nodded.

'I do not think your charade has been discovered. The gossip this morning is on the severity of the wound and of the amount of blood lost. I have heard no mention at all of more worrying things.'

'That was because you replaced my glasses and wig quickly and I thank you for that.'

He could see in her eyes as he looked away the shadow of his foolish proposal and he wished like hell that he had not made it.

'I must also thank you for sending your physician to attend to me. He was a c-competent d-doctor.'

Her niceties were disassembling under the burden of manners, the voice of the lad lost into a higher and sweeter inflection.

But he did not let this distract him as he came to the point. 'If the disguise you have donned as a boy is anything to do with my abduction of you all those years ago…?'

She stopped him. 'It is not.'

He frowned because her expression was showing the exact opposite. 'I do not believe you. I think you agreed to do my portrait because you wanted to understand exactly what sort of a man I was.'

She stayed silent.

'And when you found out that I was more than sorry for my part in your…numerous difficulties since and wanted to rectify them, you ran.'

'Rectify them?' Now she had found her voice.

'With marriage, and my offer still stands. It is the only honourable path that I can see to follow. A linkage of the Hale-Burton name to my own to ward off further controversy and awkwardness.'

'Controversy and awkwardness?' Her anger worried him as she scrambled up her face six inches from his own, blue eyes blazing. 'Your first marriage proposal was dreadful, Lord Winterton, but this one is even worse.'

'Is it?'

The control that he had held for ever suddenly snapped as he dragged her against him, his lips coming down across her own. He could not remember ever being so angry or so aroused, but as he slanted his mouth over hers he understood the danger that she presented.

He had kissed so many women, but this one was unlike any of them. It was like kissing quicksilver, one moment one thing and the next something entirely different. It was like meeting his destiny.

'Hell.' He broke away without explanation and moved back, breathing so heavily he could hardly find air. 'Hell,' he repeated again, the world turning on its axis.

'Fix up your moustache.' It was all he could think to say, the thin disguise unpeeling to one side of her mouth.

Florentia Hale-Burton made him into a man he no longer recognised, a dolt with the manners of an oaf. Beneath the door he saw the shadow of Roy Warrenden marching up and down.

'I realise that you can never forgive me for my appalling mistake all those years ago, so if it is money instead that you have a need of...'

'No.' She limped to the door and opened it, allowing him no recourse but to leave. Roy was outside, the look on his face dark.

'Thank you for coming to enquire about my health, Lord Winterton, but as you can see I am fine.'

For the first time ever Winter understood her prowess as an actor, no tremble in her words, no expression that would give away even a little of what had happened between them.

'Then I am glad for it, Mr Rutherford, and I promise that I shall not trouble you further.'

With a tip of his head he walked out of the house,

relieved to see his driver in place and the square empty of other traffic.

It was over. He had offered a fair and reasonable compensation to alleviate his own guilt, but she had not accepted it. Swallowing, he wiped the fabric of one sleeve across his mouth, trying to remove the sweetness of her lips from memory.

Florentia sat down heavily, her leg aching and heart thumping.

She hated him, hated Lord Winterton for his supercilious and patronising arrogance. To offer money and marriage in exactly the same breath and then to kiss her as if she actually meant something to him, his mouth hot against her own exploding into a feeling that was both dizzying and inexplicable.

She'd kissed him back, too, she knew she had. She'd given herself away before she had even had the chance to think. She could not even bear to imagine what might have happened had they truly been alone.

Swallowing, she looked up at Roy, her whole body shaking.

'I think you should not see Winter again, Florentia, and we will say nothing of this visit to Maria for it would only make her worry.'

'Thank you.'

'The Viscount is a man who always got his way. Even at school. The charm of the devil, we used to say, but there were darker parts in Winter, even then. He saw through your disguise?'

She nodded.

'At his house when you were drawing his portrait?'

'No, it was only afterwards.'

'Praise the Lord for that, at least. He's a womaniser. The very best that there is, by all accounts. His conquests are legendary.'

'Well, I am not one of them, Roy.'

'I am glad to hear it, Florentia. I do not think you could survive such an onslaught for his taste is eclectic and not at all salubrious. Maria was at pains to tell me that every unmarried woman in the *ton* is holding out for a chance to bear his name, like lambs to the slaughter.'

The irony of such an observation had her standing. 'Well, if you will excuse me I think I shall go and rest upstairs.'

'And tomorrow we will retire back to Kent?'

'Yes.'

She wished desperately and with all of her heart to be home.

James knew that the society wolves were circling and he needed to stop them. Already this evening at a soirée in Chelsea three days after the Northbury ball everybody he met had regaled him with the news of the artist's accident.

'Mr Frederick Rutherford is the talk of the town, Winter, and questions are beginning to be asked.'

Frank Reading was quick to tell him this as he came upon him in the card room about halfway through the night.

'Questions?' James tried to make his tone as nonchalant as he could.

'Questions such as how Rutherford is related to the Hale-Burtons given his likeness to the family. There is also another strain of mystery which expounds the theory that nobody in the *ton* seems to have met him before this.'

James understood well how gossip worked; the first stirrings, the quiet queries that then led to further unanswered puzzles and deeper mysteries. Part of him wanted to simply move away and leave Florentia Hale-Burton to cope on her own, but another and greater part found it hard to simply abandon her. Her problems had been caused by him, after all, and despite her personal anger at him he needed to make reparation.

'From what I have heard he is a second or third cousin to Albany's daughters and one who had only just moved up from the West Country.'

He sought to make the geography and the relationship as vague as he could manage it and was glad that the Honourable Phillip Wiggins had joined their group because the man was a notorious gossip.

James lent in to give his next words quietly. 'Rutherford has taken ship to the Americas, according to my sources, to try his chances in a new land. I think he felt after the incident in the Northbury ballroom he could no longer fit in here.'

'He did seem to take the injury rather to heart,' Wiggins said. 'Perhaps he was younger than we thought him to be, more emotional.'

'I am certain that could be true,' Winter returned, weighing the new theory with a heavy consideration, for anything to take the focus off Florentia Hale-Burton was to be encouraged.

Heron walked by and he felt the man watching him. For a moment it looked as though he might indeed stop and speak, but then he moved away. The anger in James twisted and it was all he could do to stop himself from confronting him directly.

'Warrenden is probably rueing the day the lad came into their life for all the problems he seems to have caused them. I know his agent is furious that he should have simply disappeared. Most inconsiderate of him, really. There was some talk about the younger sister, too, as I recall.' Wiggins offered this quietly as though he were trying to remember the particulars.

'The Albany girls have had their detractors for the scandal with the younger daughter was something that was never resolved.' Reading leaned in to add his piece. 'I myself always thought they seemed like nice and sensible girls. Very pretty, too.'

'Well, all that talk of scandal was a long time ago and it was a rather scrambled story.' Now James made his contribution.

'Scrambled?'

'There were no real witnesses to any of it from what I hear and Lady Florentia was back at her family home before nightfall.' James kept his tone light.

'Then why did she not return to society?'

'It's widely known that the Hale-Burton sisters never really fitted in here. My guess is the younger daughter did not wish to return and was glad for the conundrum. Kent was a sanctuary and she ran for its cover and protection.'

Wiggins nodded. 'Perhaps it could be true. Warrenden's wife is certainly direct to a fault, although he seems more than enamoured by her. Besides, Albany was always unusual and his wife was much the same. My own mother knew her at school and said she was strikingly unconventional.'

The conversation then moved on to other topics, but the first seeds were planted of a different theory and one which dismissed the sisters as uncommon rather than ruined.

It was all in the semantics, James thought, as he swallowed his brandy. A slight question, a skewered truth, the niggle of uncertainty and the hint of doubt.

Wiggins would talk as would Reading and those they talked to would talk as well. A widening pool of knowledge about Rutherford and the Hale-Burtons, about the artist's desperate flight to America and the sister's need for quiet down in Kent which, after all was said and done, was almost expected in a family as unusual as the Hale-Burtons.

This was how the world worked and how society made sense of itself. Years of intelligence in both Europe and America had at least taught him that.

He had heard that the Warrenden party had repaired to Albany the day after his ill-thought-out visit. He wished he might have heard how Florentia fared there, but with the history he had with her father he did not dare to enquire. Warrenden too, was another consideration. Roy had known something had been amiss the other morning though he was too polite to take it up further. But if his part in her abduction ever came to light...

The glow of the social occasion seemed dimmer without the clever and measured repartee of the youngest Hale-Burton. Every other woman here seemed dull, ordinary and witless. He wondered if he would ever see beauty again in the flirtatious shallowness of the *ton*, with its penchant to breed girls totally consumed with what they looked like and whom they would marry.

He wished he had met Florentia Hale-Burton properly in society six years ago, when all the world was before her and she could have chosen him on his merits.

He smiled at such fancy, for even an impoverished Earl's daughter might have had second thoughts about a man with no land or prospects and an army career that had left him in tatters.

And therein lay the crux of it all. He was richer now and the title was his, but his abduction had left her with a distaste for him and all that he had done.

Still, he could not allow his foolish mistake to erode his sense of justice. He would make sure that she was safe and back in the fold of the *ton* that was her heritage and then he would leave for Atherton Abbey to see out his days there and far away from the prattle of society.

A movement to one side of the room showed Benjamin Heron slipping out to the balcony. Perhaps tonight he could lay more ghosts to rest and, although a crowded ballroom was probably not the place to bring up his father's past, he none the less would use this opportunity to do so, feeling that there might never be another presented.

As he strode outside he saw the older man standing to one end of the small enclosure. In the lamplight Heron looked worn down, his face lined and frightened as he recognised who the newcomer was. That emotion made James wary for it was so unexpected.

'I wonder if I might have a word with you, Mr Heron?'

At that the man paled and sat on a small seat behind him, this reaction so out of character Winter wondered momentarily if he was ill.

'I knew you would come, Winterton. I knew that

one day this moment would arrive between us and I should be left asking myself why I had not been honest before it, why I had not been honourable. Alfred Perkins talked, didn't he? He told you about your father? He said I had something to do with his death?'

Lord, this conversation was going places James had no notion of, no true way of answering without blatant accusations. He decided to chance it. 'Did you?'

'William was my friend and had been for a very long time, but…' Perspiration beaded at his temples and on the top of his lip. 'But he betrayed me.'

'How?'

'He slept with my sister under the nose of her husband and got her with child.'

'When?'

'Twenty-two years ago. The boy gained his majority last year. I thought they should meet at least once and William should know the face of the son he had never wanted to acknowledge. A boy caught between dalliances…between a true identity. A young troubled man with needs of his own.'

This news was unexpected and life-altering. Winter had never had much in the way of family and here was a half-brother who was suddenly and shockingly presented.

'What was his name?'

'Trevellyen Hartington. He took my sister's husband's name though they were already distant when he was born in Wales.'

'And he did not return?'

'Not until early last year when he came to London. He wanted answers.'

'I should imagine he did.'

'He demanded to meet William and so I arranged it, but there was a quarrel and recriminations and unfortunately your father was deep into his cups. The meeting did not go well and to try not to attract the attention of others at the busy inn we walked down to the river bank for some privacy. When Trevellyen told your father he was off to the Americas William said he was glad to be rid of him and that he would never get a penny from his estate and there was a scuffle. They both fell into the river where the current was particularly strong and I did not see either of them again.'

The truth of what Heron was not saying began to sink in. 'You tried to cover up the evidence. You left my father's clothes in a pile by the water's edge and walked away.'

'His jacket, gloves and neckcloth. William had taken those off when he was shouting and I didn't want an investigation so I folded the clothes and left them there for others to find. In a neat pile because that way I thought there might not need to be an enquiry which could only hurt all those who were left behind.'

'So the constabulary would come to the conclusion of suicide?'

The older man nodded his head and there were tears in his eyes. 'I did it to protect my nephew Trevellyen and my sister and your father as well. I did that to protect everyone.'

God, thought James. There was a certain sense to what he was saying, even an honour if it could be called such. The man was outwardly sobbing now, the powerful and rich man reduced to a shadow. He prayed no one else would come through the unlocked door and see them here.

'Amelia, my sister, had two other sons and they have children as well. A lineage that would be tainted should all of this be known, a scandal to walk on down through the decades with them.'

'And what of my lineage?'

'Scandal is the Wintertons' life blood, do you not see? It is what makes your family stand out and be… different. But mine…? I have built the family finances on being…righteous, on toeing the line if you like, and I have three daughters who need husbands, one who is not even out of the schoolroom yet…'

The sniffing stopped and he looked up. 'I betrayed your father and my friend in his death and if it is my blood you demand, Lord Winterton, then I will agree to it. I will meet you at dawn in any location you desire.'

'You are talking of a duel?' James could barely believe the arc of this conversation.

'I would not draw my pistol against you.'

'You want me to kill you?'

'No. That is my burden alone.' Now he squared his shoulders and stood. 'I would use the loaded gun on myself.'

'God.' James went over to the balustrade edge, the greyness of the night creeping into his very bones.

'I decline such an offer, Heron. Your secret is safe with me and I do not demand your life for it.'

'Why?'

'William did not do the right thing for his son.' As James said this he heard the anger in each and every word. 'Or indeed for your sister. This way my father can repay at least some of his debt.'

Benjamin Heron had taken a handkerchief now from his pocket and was wiping his face briskly.

'Your father used to be like you before the drink ruined him and if there is ever anything that I can do for you in return for the keeping of this secret…'

Winter began to smile.

'Well, actually there is one thing that might balance the books, so to speak….'

He was glad to see Heron move forward and listen.

Chapter Eleven

Florentia could not believe the name on the card delivered into her hand by the butler at Albany Manor twelve days later.

'Mrs Heron, Miss Heron and Miss Caroline Heron have come down from London to call.'

Her sister clapped her hand across her mouth and whispered between her fingers, 'Why on earth would they travel all this way to see us unless…?'

The door opened, however, before Flora could reply, leaving them both to rise and meet the fashionably dressed new arrivals. Julia came across, offering her hand to both of them, a look of concern in her eyes.

'We heard the news about Mr Rutherford from Papa and came to see if we could be of any help. It is a sad fact of life when a man as sensitive and talented is harried out of society for an accident that was hardly his fault in the first place. If your own family suffers with the connection, well, that is even more unfair.'

'Indeed.' Maria seemed to have recovered her wits faster than Florentia had. 'What was it your papa had heard exactly, Miss Heron?'

'That Mr Rutherford has taken ship to the Americas in the hope of escaping the ugly gossip about his unfortunate wounds and that he did not intend to return. Ever.'

'Which is such a very long time.' Caroline Heron seemed determined to add her thoughts now. 'And it was hardly his fault, any of it.'

'Perhaps he imagined society might censure him for such sensitivity, but it is my opinion that an artist should be able to express himself in such a way and not be thought the less of for it.' Julia had taken over the conversation again, her clipped and rounded vowels horrified by such censure.

Flora, who had finally found her wits after the shock of entertaining the family in their parlour, wondered who might have spread such a rumour in the first place. 'Society can indeed be cruel...'

She left the thought hanging.

'Which is why we have come to see you.' For the first time Mrs Heron spoke. 'My husband is most insistent that our family be seen as the one to hold out an olive branch and ask if you all might like to come to a ball we are having in two weeks' time at our town house.'

'I am not sure, Mrs Heron.' Maria had the tone of worry and politeness exactly right. 'My sister has had her detractors in the past...'

Julia leapt in to clarify things. 'But we should be there to see an end to it, Lady Warrenden. You will all come as our guests of honour and no one would dare to question such an authority under our roof. Your relative, Mr Rutherford, has left England needlessly and unfairly, but as his cousin, Lady Florentia, the very least we can do is return you to the fold.'

Her eyes were worried and tear filled, leaving them in no doubt of her sincerity.

'It is of course such a shame that no one else now will see the talent of your cousin and be able to procure a portrait. But perhaps in time Mr Rutherford might return—?

Maria broke her off. 'No, Frederick is adamant he will never set foot on England's soil within his lifetime again and he is stubborn to a fault. I should never expect him back.'

'Those words were almost exactly Lord Winterton's, were they not, Caroline? He, too, was most certain Mr Rutherford would not be back. He saw the lad take sail apparently, in the dead of night on a rising tide. The Viscount said he barely took a thing with him, save his paints, of course, and one small leather case.'

Flora's heart had begun to beat quite violently at the name. Was it Winter himself who had started the gossip about Mr Frederick Rutherford? They had been hearing various versions of the same thing since they had returned to Kent and a further thread of their family's unusual outlook had been attached to that. Could Viscount Winterton possibly be trying to help them from afar?

Was this new development of invitations to the Heron ball his doing, too? Had he wangled the whole thing using his particular kind of cunning and deceit? She smiled, rather thinking he just might have.

When their visitors finally left two hours later Maria sat down next to Flora on the sofa and began to laugh.

'My goodness, Flora. Could it possibly be this easy to both be rid of Frederick Rutherford and reintroduce you to society?

'I don't know. Mrs Heron said that it was her husband who was most insistent on the help.'

'Can we trust them, do you think?'

'Do we have any choice?'

'Well, if we want this scandal associated with your name gone, I do not think so.'

Away from the prying eyes of others later that night Florentia allowed the tears fall.

Marry me, then.

Winterton's words came back, echoing as they had done in her mind every night since he had said them.

Yet he had not called in to see how it was she fared or even sent a note. Every time there was the sound of a carriage on the driveway she tensed up, but Winterton had stayed away, lost to her somehow, as if finally all the problems that seemed so attached to her name had scared him off and made him reconsider.

He knew that she had masqueraded as Frederick Rutherford, so the newest rumour of the artist relocating to the Americas was fortuitous and opportune, the protections winding around her in a way that was ingenious.

Spies operated in netherworlds and hidden places, shrewd resourcefulness a part of their code.

But if it was he who had circulated these new theories, then why had he been absent for nearly all of two weeks?

The answer came without doubt. He did not care and he would not come. Perhaps it was only guilt that led him along the path of atonement and reparation. A tit for tat, so to speak, and then his duty to her would be over. Having reintroduced her into society, he would leave her again in the same position as he had found her six years before, older perhaps and undoubtedly wiser, but still able to live a life and function.

'Every man is guilty of all the good he did not do.' The words of Voltaire echoed in her mind.

The kiss they had shared still sent a shiver down her spine every time she thought about it, thrills of want bursting unbidden. If he hadn't kissed her she might have been able to move on with more ease, to relegate what she hoped for into the impossible. But the desperate way in which they had come together suggested other things, headier yearnings and different anticipations.

Crossing to her wardrobe, Florentia hauled out the painting she had done of him all those years before and leaned it against a chair in the candlelight.

James Waverley watched her from within the canvas, his clear green eyes suggesting both pain and faith. His lips were full and sensual and the dimple in his chin was deep. She had fashioned his mouth in a way that she recognised.

Passion and lust had a certain ripeness that was unmistakable and distinct. When she ran her fingers across the thickness of paint it was almost as if she could feel the warm and living man beneath.

Winter. Even his name held a hint of mystery within.

'Come back,' she whispered to the likeness. 'Please come back and find me.'

The tears fell across her cheeks and she shook her head firmly. Life was not a fairy tale and she was not the sort of woman Lord Winterton would wear his heart on his sleeve for. Yet, she felt a bond with him that had nothing to do with guilt or shame. He had not betrayed her when he had discovered her charade. Indeed, if gossip was to be believed, all he had tried to do was help her become reinstated in the society she had been banished from.

Another chance. A further choice. Because of him.

Everything she wore was beautiful, so beautiful she felt like a stranger inside such finery as she stepped down from the conveyance and made her way into the Heron ball with her sister and Roy by her side.

The interior of the Heron town house was more opulent than she remembered, the world of the *ton* on show in a way it seldom was. English society tended to err away from showiness, but Benjamin Heron's wife was of German heritage and obviously held firm with the notion of excess and surfeit. The Heron sisters greeted them warmly as they made their way into the huge reception.

'You look lovely in that colour, Florentia. Yellow suits your hair.' Julia Heron took her hand and tucked it under her arm. 'Papa is most insistent that this should be a wonderful night for you and your family.'

'Thank you.' The turnaround of attitude in the Heron sisters was still as surprising as it was welcomed, but in a room like this Florentia knew she needed as many allies as she could muster.

Mr and Mrs Heron were equally as effusive as they bade her welcome.

'It is seldom we have the company of such lovely young women, Ana,' Heron remarked, his wife's smile showing an edge of strain as she looked at her own daughters.

Perhaps it actually could be this very easy? Perhaps with influential people like the Herons supporting her entry back into society anyone who dared to have it different would be silenced.

Roy and Maria made it a point to stand on each side of her as they walked into the main salon and as the seconds progressed into minutes and then to an hour Florentia allowed herself the luxury of relaxing. Maria must have been thinking along exactly the same lines as she leaned in to whisper her encouragement.

'Your dance card must be full by now?'

She nodded, for indeed it was. Every few moments since being here another one of Roy's acquaintances had stepped forward to inveigle a dance so when Timothy Calderwood came over she smiled at him.

'I could not believe you were here, Lady Florentia, and it is so very good to see you again.'

His voice was exactly as she had remembered it, a kind and friendly man whom she had immediately liked. Once.

'Is your wife here, too, my lord?'

A shadow fell over his eyes. 'My wife unfortunately caught a chill and passed away early last year. I am surprised you had not heard of it?'

Horror filled her. 'No, I am afraid I had not and—'

He stopped her. 'Celia was…fragile even before her sickness. She found life difficult, if you will, almost unbearable.'

Was he saying his wife had had problems? She was surprised when he reached for her hand and spoke with real feeling.

'I am sorry to have cried off all those years ago. I should never have been so cowardly, but I have paid the price for my intransigence.'

'You are forgiven, my lord.' She could think of no other words as she pulled her fingers away from his grasp and looked around. Maria was watching her.

'If you would honour me with a dance tonight, I would be very relieved.'

'Of course.' She wrote in his name beside a quadrille and was answered with a delighted smile.

'I see most of your card is filled and you are the talk of the *ton* this evening.'

'I hope not.'

He laughed and as she turned to look at him she caught sight of Lord Winterton across his shoulder observing her from further away in the room.

The Viscount was finally here? She had been looking for him ever since she arrived, but had seen no sign at all of him. Her heart fluttered and the blush that rose on her cheeks made Timothy Calderwood braver.

'I was hoping I might have the pleasure of a dance tonight for I had heard that you were coming.'

Winterton had turned now, making his way further down the room, another man beside him who was almost as tall as he was, and the disappointment that welled was painful.

'Perhaps we might even be able to resume our relationship where we left off?'

'Left off?' She could not quite get the gist of what Calderwood meant.

'I would be most grateful if you might let me call upon you at the Warrenden town house. Tomorrow, shall we say?'

Understanding dawned. 'Tomorrow would be fine.' She would instruct Roy to warn Calderwood off gently.

The first strains of a dance were beginning to be heard, an orchestra to one side of the floor tuning their instruments in readiness for the entertainment to follow, and as a young man stepped forward to claim the dance Florentia thanked him as he led her across the floor.

When Winter had first seen her a good half an hour ago he had been astonished all over again at how beautiful Florentia Hale-Burton truly was. But beyond that she looked happy, her golden hair knotted at her crown and falling in long ringlets down her back. He remembered the colour, all the wheat and gold and flaxen. He remembered her face, too, the dimples in both cheeks even when she frowned and the startling blue of her eyes. He kept his glance well away from her lips.

A myriad of young swains had stepped forward to petition her to place their names on her card and he thought that this was how she must have been once, lauded and fêted and admired, a golden girl of the *ton* before his ill-thought-out actions had ruined her reputation and any chance of a marriage. He was glad to see the Herons placing their weight into her re-introduction.

Smiling grimly, he caught her form as she was whisked past him in the company of Lord Alton Gower.

The man was a lecherous cad and Winter could not imagine what had made her agree to a dance with him in the first place. He was even more amazed that she was laughing at something he said, her dimples deep in the light of the chandeliers above. All about the dance floor other men watched her, a beauty without guile or pretence.

The pale peaked visage of Frederick Rutherford had been weary and cautious and in his persona she had seldom laughed or allowed her feelings to show.

What must it feel like to be suddenly free of all criticism, to be able to hold your head up in a society you had once belonged to and been a part of, before censure had torn you away from it?

The anger in him escalated until he wondered if it might be seen there on his face, in the burning fury and in the regret. The air he took felt restricted and when he realised his hands were tight fists at his side he made a concerted effort to relax them.

'You look…dangerous, Winter. Dangerous and beautiful.' The voice was Lady Elizabeth Hilliard, one of the most handsome women in the room. Years ago he had kept her company for quite a time until he realised that she wanted all of the things he could never give her. His love. His name and his loyalty.

'And if it is the Hale-Burton daughter you have your eye upon I might warn you that you have competition. Calderwood gives the impression of a decided interest given the loss of his wife and the history between them.'

'History?' he could not help but ask.

'They were all but betrothed once, it was rumoured. Lady Florentia's unfortunate incident put paid to that, of course. But now…she is risen from her shame and supported by some of the richest families in society. Who would dare mention her dark days in the face of such adulation? And true beauty has its own triumph after all, do you not think?'

Her laughter was harsh but not unkind and as her fingers threaded through his he allowed her to pull him towards the floor and into the first strains of a waltz.

'It is my favourite dance, Winter, and if I were to have the choice of any partner I am glad that it is you.'

'You were always a flirt, Elizabeth,' he answered.

'But I could never catch the only man who matched me,' she returned and pushed her body into his, the pure sensuality of the movement surprising him. 'We are each of us lost in some past tragedy, I think, something that stops us from living for this moment. You could have your pick of any woman here yet you do not stake a claim, and I suppose I am exactly the same.'

'Your philosophy is flawed. I have no interest in any of the ladies present and nor do they have any disposition towards me.'

'You see, Winter, that is what makes you so…appealing, this complete disregard for your allure and beauty. If you were a woman it might almost be seen as a practised vanity, but in a man…' Her laugh was merry and sweet even as the pressure of her fingers increased against his own. 'In a man such a lack of ego is overpoweringly sensual.'

Such nonsense annoyed him and he was glad when the music finished and he could lead her back to her friends. He moved away even as Elizabeth tried to detain him.

He was alone and he was drinking, a darkness in his eyes Florentia had seen before as they had travelled together. She wished he might ask her to dance or glance her way or nod his head in kinship and memory. Even friendship might do.

But he did not look towards her and as the night aged and each and every dance partner gave her the words that once she might have longed to hear, all she could feel was a growing disconnection.

She had kept one dance free just in case Winterton might cross the room and ask her, the empty space on her card taking on a greater importance than all of the others put together.

Yet still he did not come.

As she saw him move off in the direction of the balcony something in her suddenly set her own feet in motion. She intercepted him before he reached the double doors leading out into the night.

'My Lord Winterton.'

'Lady Florentia.' Careful, polite and distant. He looked as though he would have given anything at all to be able to avoid this meeting. He looked at her as though he had forgotten their kiss altogether.

'You are well?' Her words. She wanted to take them back as soon as she had uttered them.

'I am.' The silence between them howled with the awkward unsaid.

'And the portrait?'

'Is hung.'

'In the place above the mantel?'

He nodded and a muscle on one side of his jaw ground into movement.

'I am sorry.' She could not think how else to express all that had happened between them. Her hands bunched the golden silk of her skirt into tight fists. 'For this. For the lies.'

'You made a good-looking boy, but you are a beautiful woman. There is nothing at all to be sorry for.'

She had not expected such a compliment and felt a blush rise from her chest and travel in a bright heat across every part of her face.

The card was in her hand before she knew it and the pencil there poised above the one last space. 'Would you dance with me tonight?'

He looked down, his eyes dark and guarded.

'I saved it.' Another truth that she should never have confessed and just for a moment she imagined he might refuse. But he did not. A quick nod and then he was gone, back into the melee of the crowded room, away from her neediness and her desperation.

Had he agreed to the dance or not? Had he seen which number on the list it was she had kept for him and would he remember to come to claim her?

Maria was there then, her hand outstretched and a deep frown crossing her forehead.

'Winter is not a man to be played with, Flora. He is dangerous and hard.'

'You think that is what I am doing? Playing with him?'

'To ask a man like him for a dance is close to lunacy. Did you not see Lady Elizabeth Hilliard all but throwing herself at him not half an hour ago? He incites something in women here that is not…safe. Play with fire and you will be burned.'

Again.

The sound of her father's gun, the blood, the ache of flesh ripped open. The grasp of his fingers in her own. Holding on. Shaking. Every second falling into memory.

Sometimes she wondered why time had not softened

the horror of that moment, had not melded it into the history of the past where it could no longer hurt her.

'What is Lord Winterton to you, Flora? What makes you seek him out like you do?' Her sister's query was whispered and urgent.

'I painted his portrait. There is a connection.'

'Well, if you keep this interest up he most certainly will recognise you as the artist Frederick Rutherford, and if that happens no amount of cajoling on your behalf shall save your reputation.'

Flora felt the dance card in her hand, the edge of it cutting into flesh as she closed her fingers hard. He had promised her a waltz.

She swallowed and smiled, taking a glass of wine off the silver platter of a passing footman. If Lord Winterton came she would dance with him. If he took her hand she would follow.

Timothy Calderwood was there now, beside her.

'I think this is my promised dance, Lady Florentia.'

She did not even need to glance at her list to know that what he said was true.

'Calderwood looks like the cat who has the cream,' Frank Reading stated. 'But it is good to see the Albany girl so happy.'

Guilt wrapped around the heart of his anger as he made himself look away.

'Tonight every man in the room who is unattached or interested in changing their circumstances has made their feelings known. Lady Florentia has a full card and no shortage of compliments and it is a pleasing sight.'

Swearing softly under his breath, James finished his drink and laid the glass down on the polished surface of one of the tables marching down the length of the room; the delicate crystal meeting the hard marble with barely a sound.

He'd always lived with shadows. Seeing Florentia in the light of such adoration reinforced such a fact. He was damaged and scarred and the distance he held between himself and others had widened without his even knowing it. Arabella had warned him of such things and so had Rafe.

But tonight he was tired of fighting it, this inertia. Tonight as the music swelled about him and the golden dress of Florentia Hale-Burton caught in the light all he wanted to do was to be alone and outside away from the noise and the laughter.

He wondered if Reading had caught all he tried not to show as he turned away, the weary naked core of himself harder and harder to hide.

He was leaving, Florentia knew that he was and he had not come to claim his waltz for the first strains of the dance were being played. He had not even come to apologise for it either—a man who had asked her to marry him without any emotion at all and then failed to turn up for a single promised dance.

Timothy Calderwood on the other hand was hovering at her elbow and if she tarried he would see the gap. Claiming she needed a drink, she threaded her arm through her sister's and asked Maria if she would accompany her for a stroll about the room. Once away from Timothy Calderwood she unlaced her fingers and spoke quietly.

'Maria, you are the most wonderful sister in all of

the world but I am going to ask you now to do something for me that you may not quite agree with.'

'It is something to do with Lord Winterton, isn't it?' The retort was sharp.

'The Viscount has promised me this dance and I need you to walk with me over to him so that I can claim it, for I think he is leaving.'

'Roy said there is much unknown in Winter, Flora. He implied there are things that are hidden within him.'

'Please…' Flora swallowed as she asked this. 'Please will you help me?'

Maria looked stricken, her eyes wide and frightened. 'If he hurts you again…'

'Again?'

'Oh, Flora, I know you so much better than you think I do. All these meetings with Winterton. All your interest. The scar on his neck that he hides, the pull that he seems to hold over you and the drawing of the portrait…' She stopped. 'He was the lord who kidnapped you, wasn't he?'

'Yes.'

'Yet you still think this wise?'

They had reached the trajectory that brought him directly to them, another few seconds and he would be there.

'I do. There are many things you don't know about him, Maria, good things that I need you to trust me with. Please?'

'If this turns out badly…'

'It won't. But if I don't try, I will always regret it.'

Maria raised her hand and pasted a smile across her face, signalling her surprise at finding Winterton right there beside them.

'Lord Winterton, how very fortuitous for my sister was just saying that you had promised her this dance, and here you are. I shall leave you both to it and go and petition my own husband to join me on the floor.'

A warning placed around social niceties, but at least James Waverley could do nothing else but agree to accompany her into the waltz.

Florentia felt his arm beneath her elbow shepherding her through the throng of others, the warm sandalwood of his scent familiar and known.

'I realise you were just leaving, but I needed to speak with you. To explain.'

He had taken her into his arms now, the intimacy of the dance allowing them privacy, and she could not quite meet his gaze. All night she had stood up with a variety of lords and all night she had wished only for this one.

'I want to say that I absolve you from any wrongdoing, Lord Winterton. You owe me nothing more now. My own charade was ill advised and risky and I want to thank you for the story of a broken-hearted Frederick Rutherford scampering from London on a ship bound for the Americas. From all accounts the narrative seems to be your doing.'

'Says who?'

'Every one of the Heron women. Phillip Wiggins. My brother-in-law. The list goes on.'

He smiled at that, his teeth white against sun-burnished skin. 'I had forgotten and underestimated the temerity of the London *ton* in determining the source of any scandal. But be warned, Lady Florentia, a benevolent and sainted defender is far from who I am.'

Now there was no humour at all, the scars across

the knuckles of his hand across hers opaque beneath the lights. Her finger ran softly over one of the marks.

'Who hurt you here?'

He stiffened perceptibly and she turned her own thumb over when he failed to answer. 'This came from the inn when you fell to the ground beneath me. There was glass on the road and it cut deeply. Afterwards it was a memory. Often I would feel along the raised ridge of skin when I thought you were dead and pray for your soul. It helped, I think, to try and find forgiveness in something so very terrible.'

His green eyes met hers directly and they were full of pain.

He felt the shock of her words run through him like small daggers into the heart of his darkness. The scar. The one he had seen a score of times in the company of Frederick Rutherford took on an importance that was poignant.

But she did not truly know who he was.

He'd always been divided since he was little, one side of him turned to the light and the other to the shadows and fear.

His early family life was partly to blame, his own mother's indifference and bitterness part of the tableau, and his years of soldiering had deepened the dislocation.

Florentia had been damaged by him in a number of ways and yet she seemed to have survived in forgiveness, the elemental hell that he had thrown her into lessened by the mercy of a pardon.

God, he'd tried to understand people, but he had seldom managed the trick of it. Rafe and Arabella had been the closest friends he knew, but they were both as damaged as he was so perhaps they did not count.

Florentia on the other hand was blameless. An innocent thrust into notoriety by his poor actions and living out her years in the seclusion of the Kentish countryside, filling her mind with images of art in all its forms. He didn't deserve such goodness, that much was certain, and if he allowed her into his own particular ruin she could only be hurt further.

The most honourable path would be to beat a retreat and flee to leave her to the sort of life she had been born to, kind un-complex men and women who found joy in all the things he never had. Still he felt an ache surge in the very pit of his belly.

'I am leaving for Herefordshire in the morning and I am not sure when I shall be back.'

'I see.' Her words were small. He felt the breath of them against his cheek.

'London has palled in its delight for me and I yearn for more open spaces.'

She made no attempt at all in answering this.

'I have done everything I can to see that your reputation is recovered and tonight you are undoubtedly resurrected.'

'I am.' This was stated in a tone that held the promise of a fight. 'Like a phoenix.'

'A state of affairs that gives much delight to all of those around you.' Such a platitude made his mouth dry.

'I prefer you when you are at least honest, my lord. The patronising words of a man who knows he has slipped a noose whilst proclaiming its very beauty does not become you.'

'You will thank me for it one day, Florentia.'

'Will I, Lord Winterton?'

At that he stumbled, the misstep bringing her into him closer. He could feel the rise of her breasts.

Hell, would this dance never end? He could see others watching them and moved back again.

Roy and her sister were near now, a few feet away, Warrenden's wife's frown full upon her brow.

And then the music sidled into silence and the world crashed in on them again, pulling them apart, the uttered thanks, the quiet goodbyes. An inch, a foot, a yard away.

The smell of lavender followed him from the room and out into the night where he stood under the shadow of a tree and leaned against a wall.

'Please protect her. Please God let her be safe.'

It had been so long since he had prayed to any deity he could not remember the proper form of entreaty. But the wind heightened and the clouds scudded across the dull London sky and for just a moment he felt honourable.

Half an hour later the Warrenden carriage was heading back to Grosvenor Square.

Maria was unusually quiet and Flora knew there would be many difficult questions about the Viscount on arrival.

'Winter told me that he was off to the country on the morrow to visit the property he's just bought. Somewhere to the west, I believe.' Roy reached into his pocket for his flask. 'God, but I am so glad to be away from all that joviality. Calderwood looked enamoured by you, Florentia?'

'He used to be a long time ago before...' Maria stopped.

'Before my ruination.' Flora smiled gently. 'I think now he is only sad.'

'A frightened kitten, but at least a moral one.' Her sister's eyebrows raised as she looked straight at her.

They'd played this game years ago, divided people into various animal personas. And if Calderwood was now a moral cat, then Lord Winterton was a wolf. An alpha wolf, she amended, with his teeth fully bared.

She had seen the women there watching his every move, young women and old. He had that sort of aura that was undeniable and magnetic...

The leg that had been hurt at the Northbury ball was aching from standing for so very long and she wanted to be home in her room, alone to think.

Once they were back at Grosvenor Square, however, Maria came to her room and she looked anything but happy.

'You should have told me, Florentia, about Winterton. You should have said something.'

'So that you could warn me off him? So that I could not discover what sort of a man he was by myself?'

'And did you? Discover that?'

'He is remorseful for what he did. It was by mistake that he took me from Mount Street in the first place—he thought that I was his cousin's lover.'

'I don't think this is making me feel reassured, Flora.' Her sister looked shocked.

'He never hurt me, Maria. He protected me. He was kind and good and beautiful. When Papa shot him...' She stopped and lowered her voice. 'I have never ceased to hope that he would be alive and when I knew that he was… I felt whole again and so very relieved. He asked me to marry him in order that he might protect me.'

Maria sat, her pallor whitening. 'What answer did you give him?'

'He does not love me. He asked out of duty. What could I say?'

'My God, Flora. If Papa ever finds out that it was him…'

'He would probably die of shock. I have thought of that, too.'

'So where does that leave you?'

'I am not sure. Lonelier, I suppose. Less hopeful. He is leaving London and he wished me a happy life without him even as we danced.'

When Maria began to pace across the room Florentia felt a rising worry.

'When did he propose to you?'

'At the Northbury ball and also when he came to visit the Warrenden town house the day after I had been injured.'

'Twice? He has asked twice? You have never been able to see what is right in front of your nose, Flora, for you do not value yourself highly enough and it is time that you learnt to. There is something about Lord Winterton that is hardened and distant, but perhaps you are the only one in the world who might find his softness and retrieve your own happiness in the process.'

With that her sister kissed her on the cheek and retired, leaving Florentia to mull over and try to make sense of what exactly she had said.

Chapter Twelve

$\sim\!\!\sim\!\!\infty\!\!\sim\!\!\sim$

Winter rode across the lands of Atherton, the wind in his face and the promise of rain in the west across the Black Mountains.

For the first time in a long while he felt able to breathe, to take in the air that was somehow denied to him in London.

He skirted the rocky knife edge of the ridges, the narrow single track leading past peat bogs and cairns. Down in the valley he could see the Olchon River cutting into the land and further away the slopes of Hay Bluff rose above Hay-on-Wye, the barren summit clouded in mist.

He had bought Atherton Abbey because his maternal grandmother had lived her years out here at Craswell Village and this was where he had enjoyed some of the happiest moments of his childhood.

He understood this land like no other. He knew the birdcalls, the red kites, the kestrels and carrion crows and when he noticed the birds of prey riding the thermals on the edges of the hills he felt a familiar tug of memory and was comforted by such recollection.

He wished Florentia was here so that he might have shown her the majesty of the place.

Florentia. He could no longer make out what to do about her. Marry her or ignore her? She had refused his offers of marriage twice and yet he felt a pull between them that was undeniable.

He imagining how she would have drawn the outcrops and screes and the spring-line flushes. The birch and oak and alders stood in the valleys, the bushy slopes and the barren summits. Like a portrait. A portrait of an ancient knowingness, red-brown sandstone and solid bedrock.

Breathing out, he closed his eyes, taking in the particular smell of this corner of England. Here he felt whole again and healed.

Home.

An hour and a half later when he was back at Atherton Abbey he asked his man to begin hiring more of the local villagers in preparation for his move here permanently.

'And the furniture, my lord? What instructions do you have there?'

'Keep what is here and we will add to things as we see fit. The roof will need some work as will the salons in the west wing. Other than that a good clean and tidy should do it.'

They had reached the kitchens now and a small maid curtsied to them as they came into the room, a wriggling and rough sack in her hand.

'What do you have there, Mavis?' His factor's voice was stern.

'The last of the puppies, sir. No one wants the thing

as it is scrawny and sick and the old stable master told me to go and throw it into the lake.'

'Very well.' Kenning stepped back to let the girl pass, but James stood in her way.

'I will deal with the stray, Kenning. You may see to the other orders I have given you.'

It was so good to have the brushes back in her hand, Florentia thought, and to be in front of a canvas in a secluded section of Hyde Park. The Warrendens had re-established themselves again at Grosvenor Square a few days prior, Roy having urgent business to deal with in town.

She had taken up painting again, carefully and in isolated spots for she did not wish any notice from society.

Her maid sat on a wooden seat some twenty yards away. Her own seat was the grassy bank above a line of trees stretching into the distance.

Early morning in town had that certain light to it and she wanted to capture the nuances before the sun was higher and the day was dispersed. Hence she worked quickly, the pink blush on the horizon committed to paper and the deep green at her feet juxtaposed against it. Shadow and light. Cloud and grass. The hard edges of the trees seemed to float against an amorphous sky, like sentinels, and she was lost in the beauty.

'I did not expect to see you here, Lady Florentia?'

She turned to the voice and Winter was standing there, looking into the sun, a thin brown and white puppy on a leash at his side, its ears floppy and skin wrinkled. She could not help but smile as the dog pawed at her with one loose-skinned leg. The canine looked a lot less wary than the man.

'Her name is Faith. I acquired her unexpectedly.' It seemed as if he might turn away, his glance taking in the pathway behind, a man caught in a place he wished he was not.

'She is beautiful.' And she was, brown soulful eyes staring straight into her own.

'She has just eaten my best pair of boots for breakfast. If I had not brought her out to the park, I think my valet may well have murdered her.'

The humour was welcome and the clothes he wore countrified. She could imagine him on a horse with more dogs like this one running beside him and a magnificent estate in the background.

'Would your puppy sit still for a portrait, do you think? It will not take long.'

He motioned to the dog to lie down and she did.

'You have trained her to do this?'

'It's the first time she has obeyed any command since I got her a week ago. I doubt she would do so twice.'

Florentia used charcoal, the lines of a hunting dog appearing over the sweet-tempered calmness of the puppy.

'You work fast?'

'She is an easy subject.'

'Whereas I was not?'

'You have many layers, my lord, and each one is blurred by secrecy. Faith's face is open and simple.'

She did not look at him as she said this, the words coming easier with the charcoal in hand.

'I've been in Herefordshire at my new home.'

Her fingers stilled with the words and she looked straight at him then, the small scar above his eyebrow in this light much easier to see today and curling into his brow.

'The mark is from your books,' he clarified when he noticed such an observation, though when she frowned he carried on. 'The ones you hit me with on Mount Street. The ones that were in your bag.'

'I had just bought them at Lackington's. They were expensive books on art and difficult to find.'

'Perhaps I could replace them, then. If you gave me the titles, I could ask at the shop in Finsbury Square.'

Florentia swallowed and gathered her courage. 'I accept such an offer, but would you meet me there tomorrow at midday so I can show you exactly which titles are the ones I lost?'

The caution across his face was easily seen as she tore the picture of Faith from her sketching book. He reached out to take it.

'A peace offering, Lord Winterton. Between us.'

But when her fingers touched his she felt the sharp shock of that which was not so ordinary, a jolt of recognition that sizzled in every part of her body.

If he saw her reaction he swallowed any comment, his own face allowing no glimpse of emotion.

'I shall leave you to your drawing, Lady Florentia, but I will see you at Lackington's tomorrow, at twelve.'

When she nodded he left, the dog pulling at her leash as she gambolled across the long wet grass in front of him, its patterned coat darkening with the moisture.

Patricia, her lady's maid, had joined her now and looked at her with interest as she bent to collect her things. Packing her brushes into her leather bag, Florentia tried to act as natural as possible. But her heart raced and her breath became shallow and the knowledge that she would meet James Waverley tomorrow alone sung in her mind.

She dreamed that night of things she never had before. She was in his bed in an estate somewhere, a Gothic splendid house before a lake. The moonlight covered him as he came across her, his hair loose and his eyes pale, hands on places of her body that only she had touched.

'Love me, Florentia,' he had whispered, his voice broken with want.

'I do, Winter,' she had given back, and then there had been no space at all between them.

She came awake with a jolt in the pink room she always used at Grosvenor Square above the front entrance on the second floor.

She felt hot, disorientated and breathless, the time on the face of the clock on the mantel just past the hour of three.

Where was Winterton now? Did he prowl the nighttime reaches of town? Or was he with friends somewhere in a smoke-filled dim bar in a dangerous part near the river? Did he sleep alone? Did he ever think of her? Of their shared past?

Questions. So very many of them. Standing, she walked to the window to look over the square and the rooftops beyond. Her nightdress stuck to her heated skin and so she took it off, letting it drop to the floor around her ankles and enjoying the cool air that flowed across her nakedness.

She was glad the candles were out. Only the light of the moon came into her room, muted and silver, the paleness of her skin reflected in the mirror.

She was thin.

Was that a good thing or a bad one? Before the accident she had been fatter, more robust, but now no matter what she ate she remained the same weight. Thin.

She was also not a young girl any more, her twenty-three years soon to be twenty-four. Once she had imagined she would be a wife by this age and a mother. She had conjured up a house in the country with dogs and chickens and a garden of flowers that she would gather and bring inside in joyful colourful bunches.

And instead…

They had both been shattered by a mistake, their lives changed and turned on different courses, roads that they might not have taken otherwise. Him to the Americas. Her to painting.

Could they find their way back? To each other?

She smiled and saw the movement of it in the glass, blurred and indistinct.

'Please God, help me.'

To understand and to forgive.

Chapter Thirteen

He had barely slept on his first night back in London. The puppy had been fretful and afraid. He wondered for the twentieth time whether he should have brought the dog back with him as it was proving more than a handful. But when he had opened the sack and the small thin wet thing had fallen out of the folds of hessian he had had an instant recognition of himself as a child, confused, frightened and in desperate need of a proper guardianship. He'd taken the dog in his arms and placed it in his carriage on a blanket and it had sat deathly still beside him for all the hours of the journey back to London.

Once at St James's Square it had followed him up the stone steps, ungainly but with purpose, the small yelps of despair as he had deposited the dog on a rug by his bed only subsiding when he had dragged it up on to his counterpane. The shaking cold of fear pulled at other older memories and in the darkness he had allowed it under the sheets against his own body where it had settled in a long sigh until the early dawn.

When the bells of the small church a half a mile

away had rung the following morning he had been woken by the pensive dark eyes and the scratching tiny paws.

'Faith. I will call you that,' and he had laughed when the dog had tipped her head and listened as if the name meant something that she had not yet realised it did.

Permanence. For them both.

Now he was getting used to the small loyal presence and their bedtime routine. He enjoyed feeling the dog there beside him, warm and alive and responsive. Following him. Waiting for him. Constant and adoring.

The sketch from yesterday in the park was up on the wall beside the fireplace, two pins stuck into the top of the paper, Faith staring out from charcoal with all her rambunctious and impossible energy. The gift Florentia had of rendering the inside to be seen without was remarkable. She had done the same on his portrait, the one he kept in his library, the one he had shown to nobody save for Arabella and Rafe.

Such truth unsettled him, he supposed, and made him realise the extent he had withdrawn from the world.

Everything was turning upside down with an ever-increasing motion, like the points on a compass rose drawing him in. He wondered suddenly if he were like those cardinal directions and their ordinal intersects with their degrees of separation and interpretation of space. Scattered to the four winds but now drawing back, facing home and finding hope.

Was Florentia like some true north and he the filings lured in by a magnet no matter how hard he tried to escape her? For her own happiness, he said to himself, but he could barely believe it any longer.

He would meet her today at Lackington's and say what? I know I should stay well away from you, but I can't help myself? I can only hurt you again with all the things you do not know of me? The Spanish pit. His appalling childhood. His dislocation. The want to tell her all these things sat on his tongue like sharp points of the truth. Not once in years and years had he managed to sleep through a night.

'God,' he swore into the silence and Faith whimpered.

'Not you,' he said and held her as close and as tightly as he possibly could.

Standing in front of Lackington's waiting, all James could feel was dread. When the Warrenden carriage stopped before him he took in breath and watched as Florentia Hale-Burton alighted.

'I hope I am not late, my lord.'

'No. I am early.' He tried to alter his tone into one of light inconsequence, but failed.

'London and its demands makes things difficult,' she told him. 'The clothes. The hair. The shoes. The rules. There is hardly ever a stop to think about what one should do and what one should not. In the end it eats up all of your time and inclination.'

'What is it you would rather do?'

'Paint. Read. Think. Anything at all except look at myself again in a mirror.'

He laughed and was surprised by it, the sound so unfamiliar.

'Men do much better than women in the time-consuming business of appearance, Lord Winterton. For example, how long does it take you to get ready?'

'Today?' He thought about it for a few seconds and

then answered. 'A half an hour, perhaps. Less if I could have found one half of the pair of shoes Faith had run away with.'

She groaned. 'Make a guess as to the time of my *toilette*.'

He looked at the pink-sprigged day dress and the light green pelisse she wore above it. Her hair this afternoon was less fussy, the thick gold of it entwined in a smooth chignon beneath a small and jaunty hat.

'I do not dare. Too little and you will think I don't give you enough credit. Too much and you will imagine I perceive you as vain.'

'Of course, you are a diplomat with that particular knack of discretion.'

'No longer. I gave in my resignation last year before coming back to England.'

'Why?'

'Honesty has its degrees just as treachery does. Sometimes at the end I could not see much difference between them. *"I am myself indifferent honest."'*

'Hamlet?'

'Impressive.' His energy felt watered down and lost today, a weariness covering everything. 'The truth of espionage is that it makes you less trusting. After a while you only see the blackness in people and life becomes skewered.'

'So you are fighting your way back to the light?'

'Isn't that what you tried to show me in your painting?'

The blue eyes widened. 'Most people never understand such nuances.'

There was a certain sadness in him that was heavier this afternoon. He looked as if he had not slept well, dark bruising beneath his eyes.

'Have you ever drawn yourself, Florentia?' His query was surprising.

'Once. A long time ago.'

'I'd like to see it.'

Her arms around him, her nails digging runnels of blood into his skin. The flesh between them joined at the hip. She had drawn it a month after her accident when she believed him most likely dead. A violent depiction of a sexual encounter which even now made her blush.

'I doubt I will ever show you.'

'Do you always say exactly what you feel?'

'I used to once. Before…'

He took her gloved hand and held it, his fingers tight about her own and it was as if the world about disappeared into a swirl of greyness, the colour between them bold and true.

'Before I hurt you. Before I took you from one life and discharged you into another.'

'I was always out of step, Lord Winterton. You allow yourself too much blame for my fall from grace as it may have happened anyway.'

At that he let her go. 'People here admire you, Florentia, and they should. Because you are rare and honest and good.'

Surprise kept her silent, for the deep frown on his brow was at direct odds with the lovely compliment he had just given her.

Inside the bookshop was busier than she had known it and almost every patron looked their way. The Viscount did that to people, she thought, with his height and his bearing. He was a man who incited strong opinions, a man who would never be invisible or anonymous. Preferring such states herself, she hurried him through the lobby, pleased when they gained the stairs at the back of the room.

'The art history section is up here.' She tried to keep her voice neutral though every part of her was aware of the fact that once he followed her up they would probably be alone. Few others seemed to browse this section of the Temple and this was one of the reasons she'd always liked it so much.

'I've bought books here for years,' she began as they walked along the shelves towards a window at the other end of the aisle. 'They seem to have copies of things that one seldom finds anywhere else, you see, and so each time I visit London I invariably come to this place to browse. Mostly I buy, but sometimes I simply look. I can always find something that interests me even when I think I may not.'

'You talk more when you are nervous. Did you know that? You did it as Frederick Rutherford, too.'

'Oh.' The strangled sound escaped from her throat as she wrung her hands together.

'But you seldom speak about yourself. Almost everything I know of you comes from others.'

'I am not really that interesting,' she began, but he stopped her.

'Tell me about your childhood. What was it like?'

'The same as everyone's, I suppose, until my brother died in my arms.' She had not meant to say as much, but then she found she could not stop herself. 'For a long time I thought his death was my fault because I dared him to jump a fence, you see, on his horse. I made him do it even though he did not truly wish to.'

'Did he dare you to do things before his fall?'

'Often and often.'

'Then you both dared each other. It is the way of most siblings, I have heard, the way children grow and risk and learn. Surely you know that?'

And she did. Suddenly. It had been like a game to them. This fence. That gate. This ditch. That hedge. All of their lives they had egged the other on to new heights and further distances, to harder jumps and more difficult feats.

'Papa said I was the most undisciplined of his children. He said if it wasn't for me Bryson may still be alive.'

'Did you ever give consideration to the fact that had it have been your brother who lived your father might have said exactly the same to him?'

Truth. It came in shades from white to black and all the hues in between, like a spiderweb stretched across different facts and opinions and gathering them in. Piecing them together. Making sense of the little bits.

'If your brother was here now perhaps he'd be urging you to get on with living?'

We need to live a hundred per cent. Another catch phrase Bryson, Maria and she had often used. Perhaps her brother's death was not her fault. Perhaps Winter was right and her father was wrong. It could have been any of them who had come to grief at a high fence on a lonely road. She'd jumped that same hedge a few moments before and her horse's hooves had also clipped the tangled canes of wood. Relief filled her.

'Has anything so terrible ever happened to you that you have thought you might never recover from it, Lord Winterton?'

He nodded.

'Well, Bryson's death was like that for me. Before it I was someone else and after… I could not find my way back.'

'And now?'

'Now I can see a pathway.'

When she smiled at him joy lit up her eyes, a new warmth radiating in that dusty room ringed with books. Such joy held him spellbound, the lightness so foreign.

'As payment I will draw the house in the country you have bought for no fee whatsoever, my lord. Such a grand place would undoubtedly look well in a frame.'

'A discount that is generous.'

'A discount to thank you for always being kind to me.'

He could no longer simply ignore the harm he had done her. 'Especially after I did such a fine job of ruining you on the North Road?'

'Looking back, I think perhaps you did me a favour. If I had stayed in society I would probably be married to the Honourable Timothy Calderwood by now and wondering where my life had gone so badly wrong.'

'Words not entirely strong enough to compensate for my brutal kidnapping?'

She smiled. 'You tore my dress off and discarded it.'

'I did save you from the dogs.'

'After rendering me unconscious.'

He frowned. 'Yes, that was unconscionable and I even thought so at the time.'

'Why did you ask me to marry you?'

This question came right out of the blue and he decided to give her back the honesty she had given him, for he was tired of lies and pretence and caution.

'Because I wanted you, wanted you more than I have ever wanted anyone.'

Not quite the truth either, but he liked the way her eyes widened and the dimples on her cheeks were deep against the light. He did not say that she was his salvation, his last chance to find a link back to a world he had become disenchanted with. He did not tell her that every woman he looked at was only a pale reflection of everything she was. To him.

She hated the way he made her breathless and uncertain, lust burning across his face.

'My sister, Maria, says that you are like fire and that I shall be burned by you if I am not careful.'

'Careful?'

'Careful to remain distant, I expect she meant.'

'And is that what you would want?'

She did not look away at that, but stared straight into his perplexity. 'No, it is not. I am twenty-three years old, Lord Winterton, and what I want is for you to kiss me again.'

The run of confusion across his face almost made her turn, but she held to her course and did not flinch.

'I offered marriage and you refused twice? A kiss would have undoubtedly resulted from that.'

'It is not marriage I am angling for. It's the knowledge of the delight of passion that I require before I return once and for all to my life in the country. And in all the whispers that I have heard you are the master of such things.' She swallowed. 'I would, of course, require confidentiality, but then with the scandals that are known between us, I think…'

She did not finish.

'I'd be in no position to…gossip?'

'Exactly.'

That held him still. 'With no feelings at all involved?'

'Pardon?'

'A kiss might take you places you'd find addictive, Florentia. You might indeed want more. Much more.'

His fingers ran across her cheek as he said this, light and airy, barely touching. The timbre of his voice was deep, almost hypnotising, and a feeling began to build inside her that was astonishing.

His eyes were pale in the slanting light, the clear green in them turned velvet limed and fine. And then his lips came down in a hard need, his arms gathering her in, close and then closer.

She tasted exactly as she had before, of sweetness and of virtue, but it had been so long since he had felt those particular things he was careful.

They were in a public space and he understood the danger of being observed. Yet still his hand crept up into the gold of her hair and he tilted his head to come in more deeply.

There was a rush of connection, the red-hot wash of it pounding through his veins, making him reel slightly as he tasted further. His fingers cupped one breast rising ripe against the thin cover of silk and her neck arched in response. So very easy to simply take.

He pulled away. For his own safety. For a sanity that he could not understand, rationality and sense twisted into question over a complete void of control.

She was looking at him in the same way as he was probably looking at her, in shock and unrest, amazement in her blue eyes and her full lips swollen. His thumb wiped away a single tear that fell from her right eye down on to the alabaster smoothness of her cheek.

'Thank you.' Her words, whispered. 'I will always remember that.'

'God, Florentia, you slay me.'

Steadying her, he stepped well away, as far as he could move from her in the narrowness of the cubicle. He had never once in all of his years been concerned enough to put a woman's reputation above his own needs of the flesh. Women had thrown themselves at him, at this event and at that one. But they were always leavable, forgettable and interchangeable.

Until he had met Lady Florentia Hale-Burton with her cleverness and her honesty. He wanted to drag her beneath him and understand the lust he was consumed with, but he shook his head. Lust was the wrong word, but at that moment he did not wish to consider what might be the right one.

He could not do it wrong again. He could not hurt her or cause any hint of scandal. This time he must do what was exactly right for her because he had waited too long to rectify the harm he had once caused.

She felt him withdraw, saw the gleam in his eyes fade to some further-off place and the heartbeat at his throat settle.

Had the kiss been tepid to him, unenthusiastic, indifferent? After all of the women he was reputed to have been with, was her small offering laughable and pathetic?

She did not know the way of it. That was the trouble. She'd had no practice or tutorship in kissing.

The desperate need to be touched and taken consumed her, no consent in it save for a desire that made her feel beautiful beyond measure.

Her right breast still tingled with the feel of him, the out-of-bounds taboo so carefully disregarded. An ownership of the male domain. She could not imagine reaching out and touching him in the same way.

But, oh, how she wanted to.

And the most surprising thing of it all is she felt neither shame nor embarrassment in what he had discovered. She was tired of all the hiding and even here in a space so open she would have still allowed him exactly what he wanted to take.

But he had turned, his fingers trailing across the leather spines of a pile of old books on one of the tables, the edge of the scar on his neck so easily seen at the top of his neckcloth.

'Does your father come to London at all, Florentia?' His tone was measured.

'Hardly ever.'

'Your sister said he had been ill for a number of years. Was it since this?' One hand gestured to his wound, the pale green of his eyes bruised with anger.

'Yes.' She did not keep the truth from him or try to soften it. Her father had returned home from the inn and within a matter of days he had gone to bed. He'd barely left Kent since.

'And it was all a mistake. That was the hell of it. My cousin had bid me to bring his…lovebird up from London and I thought she was you.'

'You thought I looked like a woman of the night?'

The first glimmer of humour crossed his face. 'You were wearing a red dress and Tommy's lady was supposed to have been, too. I had not had much practice with identifying women like that, though of course on reflection you could not have possibly been one.'

'I am not sure whether I should be flattered or not by such a comparison.'

He smiled and began to speak again.

'When I finally woke up after the debacle at the inn the only reason I didn't up and die was because I wanted to say sorry to you. You had told me your name and who your father was.'

'Yet you did not come to Albany?'

'I was sick for a long time and largely penniless. I imagined the very sight of me again would send a young girl into hysterics and so I went to the Americas. When I returned I met your sister at a ball about a month after I got to London and then I received your agent's letter about the portrait. I knew there was some connection between Rutherford and the Hale-Burton household and I needed to find out what it was.'

'Why did you spread that rumour of Frederick Rutherford's leaving?'

'Because his disappearance made it safer for you.'

'Safer?'

'Acceptance in society is a nebulous thing. A word here and there in the right ear can do wonders and a quiet shift of understanding is often the result.'

'The right ear?'

'Mr Benjamin Heron was listening.'

'Which is why the family sponsored me at their ball. I always wondered how you might have accomplished that.'

'The Winterton family history is convoluted and dissolute. Sometimes such reckless disregard can be an advantage.'

'An answer that allows me no clue at all to your methods.'

'Heron did not kill my father. I think I told you once I thought he might have. My father did not commit suicide either.'

'An accident, then? A terrible accident with its own secrets attached?'

'You are too quick by half, Florentia. But then I always knew that.'

'Did you, my lord?'

'From the first time you came to my town house. I thought you unmatched.'

'A dangerous realisation given I was a boy.'

'I still think that.'

Such a confidence left a silence between them, stretching across surprise, and Florentia was about to talk again when she heard the sound of footsteps on the staircase. A moment later one of the men at the desk from downstairs came around the corner.

'We had hoped to still find you here, Lord Winterton. One of our best customers, Lady Ecclesfield, who heard you were here, was most insistent to have a short word. By all accounts she was a friend of your grandmother's.'

'Of course.' Winter's reply sounded forced and the frown across his forehead deepened as he saw the man waiting to accompany him down. Tipping his head in a gesture of polite social discourse, he spoke quietly.

'Thank you for your recommendations on the books

on art history, Lady Florentia. I shall be certain to keep such titles in mind.'

'My pleasure, Lord Winterton.'

When he took her hand he held it for a second longer than was appropriate. Florentia wished that he might never have let her go but a second later he was gone completely. Leaning back against a wall, she closed her eyes, taking in a good deep breath to steady herself. What had just happened? Had he felt what she had? Where did this leave them?

She did not dare go down just yet for she knew her cheeks would be flushed and her eyes glitter bright.

No man now would measure up again to this new knowledge of what was. All the suitors who had asked for dances in the past weeks faded into a grey oblivion against the crimson truth of James Waverley, Viscount Winterton. The hues around him were vibrant and rich, a violent boldness that left her gasping, the soft and sombre others cast into shadow by his light.

Closing the book before her, she repositioned her hat and tightened the loosened fastenings of her cloak. Once downstairs she looked around for Winterton, but there was no sign at all of him, the scene before her returned to a normal softness after the force and power of his parting.

Outside she smiled her thanks as a Warrenden servant helped her up into the waiting carriage and the horses moved on through the busy streets around Finsbury Square.

It was either over or just started, this game between her and Winter, and right now she had no idea at all which way the dice might fall.

* * *

Winter hailed a hackney cab and gave it his direction. He wanted to be away from Lackington's and away from Florentia because he honestly did not know what he would do next should he see her. Fall on to his knees and make a public spectacle of himself or simply take her in his arms and kiss her to find again the magic and the grace? He did not want to do either until he understood what the cost of any troth might finally be to her.

Albany was two hours south and he knew that if he made a start now he could be there before nightfall. His own conveyance would not take long to ready and he could find lodging tonight in some inn near the Manor. And yet other considerations kept rushing in.

The Earl of Albany had been largely housebound since his daughter had been kidnapped six years ago and from what James had found out he was a nervous man, inclined to odd turns of behaviour.

Roy Warrenden was often in White's in the early afternoon so Winter took the chance to find him, banging on the roof of his cab and changing the directions of his travel. He needed more information on the family and who better to give it than Maria's husband himself?

'I am very glad to see you here, Warrenden.' Winter slid into the empty seat beside him, removing the sheets of today's early edition of *The Times* as he did so.

'Are you indeed? I thought you might have come before this, Winter?'

'How so?'

'You are as astute as any man I have ever met in my life and I have been hearing the rounds of your well-placed gossip about the artist Frederick Rutherford. Florentia also confided in us that you now knew of her charade?'

Ignoring this, James formed his own query.

'How old was the brother? The one who died?'

Roy looked startled. 'I am surprised your numerous sources did not tell you Bryson was Florentia's twin. He died in her arms after mistiming a jump on his stallion. I think her heart was broken.'

'Hell.'

A twin.

There was in all his reading a special closeness between twins. How bereft Florentia must have felt at the loss of hers for every time she had spoken of her brother he had felt the sadness.

'Maria worries about her constantly, though I myself think she is far stronger than anyone imagines. To pull off the stunt of imitating Rutherford required nerves of steel and she did it well. Why are you now so intent upon protecting her?'

'I will leave it to her to tell you that. What I do want to find out is if you think the father is up to a personal visit?'

'From you?' Now Roy sat bolt upright and lowered his voice markedly. 'Lord, are you saying what I think you are…?'

When Winter did not answer he went on. 'Albany is self-centred and inclined to enjoy poor health. I think like all the other members of the family he does not enjoy society and an accident in the north allowed him the chance to opt out altogether. Which he has.'

'And the mother?'

'She is easier to understand, though she is also browbeaten by a husband who refuses to get truly well.

Maria and I do not see them often as a visit usually ends in my wife trying to cajole them back into the mainstream of life which, as you can gather, they do not take to kindly.'

'And how does Florentia fit into all this?'

'She supports them with the earnings she makes from her paintings, which will be sadly lessened now that Frederick Rutherford has disappeared to the Americas. I have tried to gift them money, but the Earl is too proud and too stubborn to accept it though Maria manages to get around some of that and slips help in now and again. Florentia has more recently had some offers of marriage presented which would alleviate all financial responsibility, but she has turned each and every one of them down.'

'Are there any more on the table that she might accept?'

'I don't know, Winter. Certainly I have young men of good heart and family calling on me daily. Whether she is interested is another matter entirely, for she is most reticent to talk of her personal affairs. Perhaps there is someone for whom she already holds a *tendre*? Should I take it from this conversation that you may be interested in throwing your own name into the ring?'

'Don't let her say yes to anyone until I have spoken with her. I need to go down to Albany tomorrow.'

'You could not speak with me now? I have taken over Albany's duty of vetting suitors, after all.'

'No. There is more to it than that.'

He could see the workings in Roy Warrenden's eyes and knew the minute his old friend had understood the truth.

'It was you? You were the one? The one who took Florentia? The bastard who changed all their lives?'

'Yes.'

'God.' He ran a hand through his hair and breathed out heavily. 'If I thought Florentia truly hated you for it, Winter, I'd want to run you through with the sharpest sword I own.'

'But you don't?'

'My wife told me the other day that her sister has not understood her destiny yet or the fact that you are going to be part of it and Maria is seldom wrong about anything. But what if Albany himself kills you? He'd hate you enough to do it, I think.'

'Then I'd be dead.'

Roy unexpectedly began to laugh. 'He's an academic, Winter. The heroics in the inn was his finest hour and I doubt such bravery will ever be repeated. Still, he keeps a loaded pistol in the drawer on the right side of his bed. If he reaches for it, I would duck.'

'Thank you.' Holding out his hand, he was glad when Roy took it.

Chapter Fourteen

Albany was a grand old manor perched on a hill and set back from the river which meandered before it, the banks resplendent with white arum lilies and tall blue flowers Winter did not know the name of. The family seat looked as if it were only just hanging on to the glorious earlier days by the fingernails, the cracks of time imprinted in the lines of the place. Like many of the old and titled names of the *ton* the Earl had obviously fallen upon hard times, and harder times still for his family, Winter imagined, with a lost entailment looming before them.

He'd stayed in the carriage until the village when he had asked for his horse to be brought around. With a light breeze and the promise of a warm day in the air he had enjoyed the exercise of riding. The worry of what this visit might bring also hung across him.

At the front door he was met by a slight older servant, his uniform too big for him. The fellow bowed as he took his hat and coat.

'May I tell the Earl who has come to call, sir?'

'I am Viscount Winterton.' Even with the threat of

what might happen Winter gave his true name. If the Earl chose to crucify him then that would be a punishment he would have to take, but he hoped he might talk the fellow into an acceptance of all that had happened.

'Very well, my lord, but the Earl is upstairs in his chamber and so it might take a little while to rouse him. If you would like to go into the library, perhaps, there is wine there and I will have the cook bring you some sustenance after your journey.'

'Thank you.'

He proceeded to follow the man a little way down the corridor. Standing in the middle of the empty room as the servant hurried off once again, Winter saw many of the things that Florentia had never told him. Her father kept a library that would have been the envy of every thinking man in Europe and the paintings on the wall were like no others he had ever seen.

He corrected himself. The portrait hanging now above his desk in St James's Square held the same freedom of lines and boldness of colour. Florentia's work. He walked over to the nearest canvas that presumably depicted her parents. They were both slight and lost looking. The wife had her hands firmly fixed in the husband's and on her breast was embroidered a picture of a boy.

Bryson? There was a startling likeness in his features to that of Frederick Rutherford. No wonder she played the part so well, he thought to himself. She was emulating a dear and lost twin. The poignancy of that thought made him swallow.

'The Earl will see you now, my lord, in his suite of rooms. I shall take you up.'

The runners were threadbare and there were several

spindles missing from the grand staircase, but a frieze had been carefully painted all the way up on the hand-rail, one of flowers and plants and entwined leaves, the same arum lilies and blue blooms in the design that he had seen by the river.

The curtains were drawn as he stepped within the bedchamber, so for just a moment he did not see the man sitting in a leather chair by a fire that was blazing even in the considerable warmth of the morning.

'Lord Winterton?' The voice was steady and pleasant. 'Thank you, Murphy. I will see to our visitor now.'

Winter waited until the butler had left before moving in further. The room had a smell of mustiness and sickness, a carbolic astringent scent laid on top as if even with all the cleaning in the world the underlying malady could not be erased.

'I do not have many visitors these days and was wondering…'

The words faded off as the man got a good look at him.

'You? Is it you? My God, I have seen your face for all of the days since we met, every night in the darkness, every moment as I eat.' He had stood up now, though his right hand was still anchored to the solidness of the chair, as if on letting go he might fall unstopped to the floor. Sweat poured down the old Earl's forehead and beaded on his top lip. 'You are not dead and buried all these years, but alive?'

Winter could not quite decipher his tone. Albany sounded shocked and shaky, his hands trembling. He had expected fury and he was being met with stupor and distress instead.

'I have come to apologise for taking your daughter,

my lord. It was a mistake which I have regretted immensely ever since.'

'A mistake?' Now the older man sat on the bed again, quite abruptly. His mouth worked up and down without sound as he swallowed.

'My cousin had asked me to bring his...paramour up from London. She was to be dressed in red and standing on the corner of Mount Street at the hour of five o'clock. She was blonde and I was warned would be feisty, but it was for her own good that he wanted her out of London so my orders were to insist until she came.'

'My God.' Anger seemed more apparent now and Winter's eyes flicked to the cabinet there with its two small drawers.

'I did not know about the scandal that ensued. I have been away in the Americas for years and came back to England only a few months ago. If I had known...' He stopped. What would he have done? Confronted the Earl so soon after he had almost been killed by him? Returned from the Americas? He was glad he had not had to make that choice.

'Have you seen my daughter? Have you seen Flora?'

'Yes.'

'And she knew you?'

'She did, Lord Albany. Though I had trouble knowing her. She was dressed as a lad. An artist, Frederick Rutherford.'

He nodded. 'Maria has told me of it.'

'I want to make things right with your family. I have come down to see if I might have your blessing in asking your daughter for her hand in marriage.'

'My blessing?'

'I want to protect Florentia. I want to make sure that she is always safe. I am wealthy now and have a large property in Herefordshire as well as extensive land in the Americas. I will see she never goes without and is always happy. I would swear it to you on my life, my lord.'

There was silence and then Winter noticed the tears that were falling down the older man's cheeks. Breathing in deeply, he tried to take charge of the situation.

'I am sorry for all the harm I have caused you and your family, Lord Albany. It was unprincipled and unacceptable and if you feel my presence here is too much for you to bear then of course I will leave.'

But Albany shook his head. 'I am not crying with sadness, Winterton. These are tears of happiness. Instead of the horror of killing someone in my mind every and each minute, now I can be free.'

'Free?'

'To live again. To feel again. Repentance has given way to absolution and sorrow to joy. I am unfettered from the guilt of taking a young life for here you are standing before me.'

Of all the things Winter had imagined of this meeting this was not one of them. 'And your daughter?'

'It is up to Florentia to decide if she wants you. She has been lonely for so many years, but she has also found a great gift in her painting.'

'Of course.'

'May I ask you something before you leave? Something personal?' He waited for a nod. 'Your throat was ripped to threads and there was so much blood at the inn. How did you survive?'

'With luck and determination. Your daughter tried

to help me as I fell and I wanted to give her my apology in person.'

'And have you?'

'Yes.'

'Then you have my blessing to try and see your way to right such a travesty, Lord Winterton.'

Florentia was sitting in the garden at the Warrenden town house watching the sparrows playing in the blossoms of an apple tree. She had been out here for a good while now, trying to decide in the quiet of nature just exactly what she should do about Winter.

She had thought to send a letter, but had decided not to. What could she say after all? *You kissed me and I was wondering if you might do so again? Please.*

She smiled, but a welling unhappiness stuck in her throat, making her feel sad and furious at exactly the same time.

Winterton had left London according to Roy. Did that mean he had left for good or would he be back? Timothy Calderwood had offered her marriage as had a dozen other men of the *ton*. They had trooped in to see Roy at every hour of the day and she had ceased to even answer her brother-in-law when he had called her to his study after each departure and asked her if she had any interest in pursuing the latest request.

She had not been able to paint or sleep or eat wondering what might happen to her now that Winter was gone. He had ruined her reputation last time, but this time it was even worse. This time it was her heart that lay in tatters at his feet.

The sound of voices inside the house took her attention. It would be Maria probably returned from her afternoon tea or Roy from his men's club where he went most afternoons to read the paper and meet friends. The normal everyday noises of a marriage and a house that reflected the happiness of Lord and Lady Warrenden. Her sister was more content than she had ever seen her and her own uncertainty was magnified because of it.

The door opened to the garden and the butler came forward with a card.

'Viscount Winterton has called upon you, Lady Florentia. Shall I ask him to come into the garden?'

Shock ran through her, but she waited perfectly still as his footsteps came closer. She did not wish to look up and find something in his face that would shatter her. She did not wish to see a return to tepid friendship or the more sombre shades of some awful truth she could not cope with.

'Thank you for seeing me. I know that you are here alone and I hope it is a good time to speak freely.' His voice was deep and husky; the voice her father had left him with.

At that she did look up and saw his eyes were full of trepidation. That alone frightened her more than anything else could have for he had always been so sure every time she had met him. She decided to get in first.

'If you are here to apologise for the kiss we shared, Lord Winterton, I do not want to hear it.'

'Pardon?' Now he looked perplexed.

'At Lackington's.'

'Why should I apologise?'

'You shouldn't and I am most certainly not sorry for it.'

'You aren't?'

'I liked it a lot.'

When he laughed she thought she might begin to cry, but he stepped forward and took her hands, drawing her up before him and then falling on to one knee.

What on earth was he doing? Could he possibly be…?

'Will you marry me, Florentia? I know I have been instrumental in many of your family's problems, but I swear to make it up to you, all of it, for every day of my life.'

'Why would you want to?' This time she heard other things beneath his words. Desperation. Anguish. Worry.

'I have always been alone, but lately I have become lonely because of you. Talking with you, dancing with you, seeing you smile, watching you paint. I can't imagine my life any more without you in it.'

She could not believe his words. Was she simply imagining this happening out of hope? 'You are asking me to be your wife, but this time because of love?' She whispered it. To say it out loud might take the truth away.

'I am if you will have me.'

'Yes.' The word came unbidden in a cry of sheer joy, disbelief making her shake. She could hear her heartbeat in her ears and feel the shallow quickness of breath. Then his mouth covered hers and she understood magic as he showed her without words his troth was indeed honest, the same swell of desire beaching across her.

'I love you, Winter. More than life itself.' She said this as he finished the kiss, his hands cradling her face.

'I don't want to wait, Florentia. I can't. We can be wed quickly by special licence if you would wish it.'

'I would.'

'I don't deserve you, God knows that, but I will never give you up. Not for anyone or anything. Yes is for ever by me, Florentia. Know that.'

'My father...?'

'I went there to Albany to ask him for his blessing. I needed this to have everything right because the last times...' He didn't finish.

'It was all so very wrong.'

She could feel the smile on his lips as she pressed against him.

'I have dreamed of this moment every night since I first saw you.'

'Good, for so have I.'

When he kissed her again it was different. This time as the warmth of his breath touched her skin she looked at him and saw things there that were now unhidden. The heat in him shocked her.

'I want you.' Her words came slowly and with feeling. She felt dampness on her skin and the running whorls of want inside like living things, dancing to a tune she had not heard before.

Everything was brought into focus. The clear green of his eyes. The streaks in his hair pale from sunshine. The stubble on his chin that showed her he had not shaved since early dawn. He smelt of the outside, of exercise and horses, of leather, sweat and hard riding.

His hands were not those of an idle lord either, the palm toughened in a way that spoke of work and toil and labour. Such a hard and lean masculinity made her smile. When his thumb ran over the fullness of her lips she marvelled at the way she responded to him.

'I never forgot you for all of those years.' His words, broken with hope. 'I remembered you every single day.'

Tears came, brimming in her eyes. 'What a waste,' she answered, but he shook his head.

'Not that, Florentia. For me it was an apprenticeship in love.' He held her hair and tipped her chin up, his tongue touching where his thumb had just been. 'I did not know what it was like to lose your heart to someone until I saw you again. Even as the lad Rutherford, I loved you.'

The intensity of his eyes drew her in, the sheer longing and veracity.

'Because without each other it was so hard to exist?' She thought of her empty days and nights, of the long and lonely years and of the painting in the back of her wardrobe that crouched in truth. Her fingers came up and touched a living breathing cheek in the same way she had caressed her canvas. He leaned into her.

'I have missed you.' Her words, fractured with conviction.

Closeness. Certainty. Desire and faith. They melded into an emotion that made her shake until his mouth came down and he allowed her to know just what she meant to him, nothing at all held back.

She answered his desperation with her own, opening wider and threading her fingers through the length of his hair.

Here she was. Her. Florentia Hale-Burton. It was staggering and astounding. The colour of scarlet and blood and fire. The hue of daring and determination and power and courage. Her. Risen in flames from the ashes. Regenerated and reborn. No longer hiding and afraid and ruined.

And then she could no longer think at all.

She was all ripeness and softness and woman, her curves sweet and full, the plump flesh of her breasts, the long line of her throat, the creamy smooth of her skin. Breaking off the kiss before it went so far he would not be able to stop going further, he brought her into his arms and kept her there.

Florentia stripped him to the bone, his naked longing exposed and vulnerable. She was so very beautiful with her innocence and her honesty, all the shades of gold across his hand in her hair and her eyes reflections of a summer sky.

An eddy of wind blew around them, lifting the fabric of her skirt and further afield he could hear the sound of horses and voices as the everyday reality of London broke again into their paradise.

With remorse he let go of her and stepped back, back to where he could only watch her, the dappled sun on her hair, the joy on her face.

'I cannot wait long, Florentia. For you.'

Then her sister was there, stopping as she saw him, her face expressing worry as well as anger.

'I hope everything is well with you, Flora?' The query hung in the air. 'I did not know visitors were expected.'

'I have come to ask your sister if she would do me the honour of becoming my wife, Lady Warrenden.'

'Your wife. Your wife?' Now there was only amazement in her visage. 'Oh, my goodness.'

Florentia took up the conversation. 'I have said yes,

Maria. We are to be wed as soon as we can. By a special licence.'

Maria Warrenden's hands were stretched across her mouth, the same dimples her sister sported deep on each cheek. 'Does Roy know?'

Florentia shook her head. 'You are the first to hear our news although Winter has asked Father and he gave us his blessing.'

Now she simply shrieked as she rushed forward, enclosing her younger sister in her grasp, the blue in Maria's gown complementing the yellow in Florentia's.

Her parents came to London the following day for a stay in the Warrenden town house and for the first time in years her father looked happy. When he asked her to the library later in the evening she knew what it was he would want to speak to her about.

'Lord Winterton came to see me, Flora. He is a good man. A moral man. He apologised sincerely for his mistake and tried to explain to me what had happened. When he asked for your hand in marriage I gave him my blessing.'

'He told me, Papa.'

'And the blinkers of my stupidity and shame through all those years simply fell away. I had not killed a man, which was a relief that was indescribable, and he had given me a second chance to get better and live again. Do you love him?'

'I do, Papa.'

'Roy said you have had many requests for your hand, but have barely glanced at any of your swains until Winterton. He implied James Waverley has been…fairly dissolute, I think is how he phrased it, but that he had turned over a new leaf and has eyes now only for you.'

'He is a friend of Roy's. From school.'

'Yes, he told me that, too. There is one worry that niggles at my mind, however. In London all those years ago there were witnesses. If any should come forward and name him…'

'I am not letting my one hope of happiness go on a chance, Papa. If that happens we will deal with it.'

'Your mother said I was to fall on my knees and thank the Lord above that you are happy, my dear, so perhaps that is what I will do. The years of our hardship are over and even with Albany entailed it shall no longer be of any significance.'

'Perhaps Bryson has been looking over us, Papa.' This time when she mentioned her brother her father smiled.

'Like our guardian angel. I like that thought.'

When he came forward to envelop her in his arms Florentia did not pull away.

The wedding had been small and quick.

It was a quiet ceremony at a chapel close to the Warrenden town house, a bunch of white roses in an opaque green vase at the altar.

Fine spring weather had swept in from the south, the sun shining through a stained-glass window.

Flora wore a gown that she and her sister had found in a shop in town, and one that with only a slight alteration had fitted her perfectly.

It was of light blue silk and matched the colour of her eyes, the bodice trimmed in cream lace and ribbon. The skirt cascaded wide from the waistline and sleeves of organza were ruched at the shoulders and fell almost transparent to her wrists. In her hair she had flowers, the ivy pulled through her curls where they were caught in a cream band of more silk. Bryson's ring hung about her neck in an ornate clasp of rose gold.

'Do I look…enough?' She turned to ask this of her sister as they stood in the small vestibule.

'You look beautiful, Flora. But more than that you look happy.'

'I love him, Maria.'

'And he loves you back. Every time he looks at you I can see it.'

'How was I so lucky?' She barely liked to ask this.

'You deserve it. You complete each other. Two halves who have been alone for a long time. Now come, I can hear the music and it is time.'

The wedding party was a very tiny one. Maria and Roy would be there, of course, and her parents and Roy's elderly mother.

Winter had only invited Rafe and Arabella. Seven people.

'So you have everything, Florentia. Something borrowed in the family garter. The old is taken care of in Bryson's ring and something new and blue in the dress. Talismans have their detractors, but for the grand occasions I have always believed in them to protect one against the Evil Eye.'

Her mother had stated this before they had left for the chapel. 'We do not want you rendered barren, my dear, so be sure to be mindful of the old rhyme.'

Barren. Flora blushed because tonight she would no longer be an innocent. Tonight she would go with Winter to his town house and she would know all the intimate delights that she had never had the measure of.

'Love lights the marriage bed, a glorious pyre.'

She saw Lord Winterton as soon as she walked through the doors. He was dressed today in a navy blue jacket and beige trousers, the white tie at his neck arranged more formally than she had ever seen him wear one. When he turned to look at her the beauty of him took her breath away and her father at her side stopped to observe her.

'Are you sure, Florentia? This is what you want?'

'It is, Papa, with all my heart.'

She would never forget the moment her father gave her over to Winter. James Waverley's fingers were warm and strong and they clasped hers in a way that let her know that they were in this together, that whatever happened in all the years to come they would both face it. With the height of his neckcloth she could see no glimpse at all of the scar. She wondered if that was deliberate.

The candles smelt of rose oil and the play of leaves from the tree near a window sent shadow against the opposite wall.

A setting that showed layers of beauty and of truth. Like her paintings. Deceptively simple. Unthinkingly complex. The colours of polished wood, the gowns and the bower of blooms a vibrant mix of shades that melded to create a perfect backdrop.

Us. We. Together.

When Winter squeezed her hand she turned to smile at him and knew the sort of happiness that was as complete as she could ever imagine.

* * *

He took her home as the day dimmed into dusk and Florentia felt an excitement that made her tingle.

She smiled as they passed the chair opposite the grandfather clock in the lobby. She had known very little of the Viscount personally when she had first come here to make his portrait and the rumours of his past had been rife. His parents were notoriously difficult, she knew that from the endless gossip of them, people who had never settled in love or in life. His own shifting lifestyle had probably come about as the result of such flagrant disconnection.

'Would you like to see how I hung your painting?' he asked, taking her from those thoughts as they veered off down the hall to the right.

The portrait had been framed in a way that showed it off to its very best advantage, the gilded and elaborate plaster moulding bringing out the tones within and giving relief to the subject and its colours.

'Is the frame French?' she asked as she walked closer.

He nodded. 'I found it at Christie's.'

'A perfect match.'

'Like us?' His eyes were darker tonight, clouded by high emotion as he reached out for her hand, lips warm on the back of her fingers. Stamping an ownership. Demanding much more than simple talk.

'I would never hurt you, Florentia.'

'I know.'

'But I want the sort of marriage my parents did not have. A true one and real. Nothing held back. A love match.'

'I want it, too.'

At that he nodded and drew the first pin from her hair. She stood there and let him make a careful deconstruction, the ivy loosening as more pins followed the first.

Her hair unravelled to her waist. She saw the colour and length of it in the shadow of his eyes even before one hand came up and knotted the fall hard in his grasp. Pinned into his want, she tipped her head back and met his gaze squarely, her mouth falling open and her lips dry.

'Let me love you, Florentia.'

'Yes.' Her breath shallowed behind the word, consent a yielded surrender.

His fingers on her cheek were soft, feeling the contours, understanding flesh. When they wandered to her ears, she smiled. Today she had on her grandmother's pearl earrings, the gold filigree in them intricate and beautiful.

'These suit you, my love, and I shall buy you whatever else you would like in the way of jewellery.'

Her skin rose at his touch and as his eyes locked into her own he took her into his arms, tight and true.

'I love you,' he whispered. 'I love you so much that it hurts.' Her breath quickened as his fingers slid against the thinness of silk, finding the bud of her nipple with his thumb and moving across it. She arched into the caress, the body's own music true and deep.

He did not halt as she came into her release, but felt the rumbling echoes of flesh when she cried out loud, the low and guttural sounds rising from the depths of a feeling that brought sweat to her brow.

And then she was limp, her head resting on his chest.

'Not here.' It occurred to him that his mastery as a lover was being tested even as he said it, lost in a feeling that was unfamiliar.

He was desperate, more desperate than he had ever been in all of his life to please her, the silk and shadows of his past melded into this one unprecedented moment when he felt the control he was famous for slipping. Slipping so far away that he carried her up the stairs and into his bedchamber like a green lad, fingers fumbling at her fastenings, a row of pearl buttons and stays and ribbons and hooks. He ripped the last layer of flimsy lawn and then his hands were on her breasts, ripe and firm and his.

Even language was deserting him. A blue garter was around her right thigh, trimmed in cream ribbon. She was the most beautiful woman he had ever seen in his entire life. Perfect. Unflawed. Glowing in the candlelight, burnished in wheat and ivory and gold.

Dipping his head, he tasted her, one pale pink nipple coming full into his mouth. Sweet and salty. Then he felt her hands thread into his own hair and bring him in closer.

'Sweetheart, I can barely think with the wanting.'

'Then don't,' she said and reached for his own nipple, flicking it as quickly.

A measured equal taking. That thought made him hard for the years of his own whispered prowess had left him always as the instigator, the leader. Here she was, an innocent finding in the tiny nuances her own sensuality and giving it back to him without any shyness whatsoever. When she leaned over and bit him as he had done her he simply lifted her up in his arms and took her to bed.

Always he was careful and thorough and clinical. Always he followed a pattern, a routine, a method. Habitual, customary and ordered.

Today passion simply ruled him, pronounced and random, the haphazard and arbitrary desperation taking his breath into large unruly gulps and his erection as hard as stone.

When she suddenly looked up and smiled, he had the impression that she knew his thoughts almost as if he had spoken them out loud.

He was beautiful. As beautiful as any man she could have drawn, with the long lines of his body and the dimple in his chin. Bur there was something else there that held her, too. A vulnerability and a tenderness, addressed only to her and translated into flesh.

He had not removed his clothes though she was naked. But he was frenzied and when his hands pushed down his trousers she understood that he would be fully garbed when he took her. He met her eyes then, his manhood poised at the edge of movement.

'I...don't want...to hurt...you...'

And he pushed in, the length and breadth of him. When she cried out he held very still, engorged now inside, the thick ache of him unfamiliar. Exposed.

Above her the ceiling was moulded plaster and the chandelier sported candles in cut crystal. She strove for the details, for the tiny things she could see that might take her mind from the pain, for the colour of the beadings, for the top of the velvet curtains around the four-poster bed, ruched into dark gold and burgundy.

And then he moved again, slower this time, a gentle rolling rhythm interspersed with quicker pushes and a feeling grew that she could not stop, like a wave gathering force, building, peaking and breaking upon some far-off shore, taking her with it, the fire and the ice, the beauty and the grace. Just her breath now and his in the room, all else forgotten as she closed her eyes and only felt. Him. His force and his power. Taking her in the way lovers had for all of time immemorial, sacrificed upon an altar of delight she had no name for.

Endlessly primal and beautiful and astounding.

She felt as if the beating heart of her lust was there in the room as a physical form, scarlet gold, orange and black. White was present, too, the colour of safety and innocence.

She had always seen life in terms of colour.

And finally the quiet crept back in, breaths shallowing, hearts calming, the movement of his fingers across her gentle and comforting. Close and content, the outside sounds of the night, the last bird calls, the roll of a carriage wending its way past, a servant moving through the corridor, the last sparks of flame in the grate.

Anchoring them to this life, returning them from the other.

'Thank you, Florentia, for your gift of innocence.' His breath warmed her shoulder. 'I think I should have been gentler.'

She answered him with a simple shake of the head. 'You were perfect.'

She felt the movement of a smile against her hair.

'I lost control. It is something that has never happened before. Usually...' He stopped and so did the movement of his fingers across her naked back. 'I have not been without women in my life, but the rumours that multiply my conquests many times over are false. I want you to know that. There's never before been anyone special. Until now, here with you.'

Raising herself up on one elbow, she looked at him, the neckcloth in disarray and the scar beneath easily seen. 'I drew you after the inn in oil on canvas in the dark and sombre colours of grief. For years the study has been hidden away, but every now and then, and more often of late, I have taken it from its hiding place and felt the lines of you.' Her first finger hovered over his jaw and his cheek before rising to his nose. 'It's as if I knew you through my drawing, like a ghost or a spirit, always there. A protection against life and the living of it. A guardian.'

'And do I measure up? Now?' The fullness of his lips were emphasised by candlelight as he asked his question.

'When Bryson died I thought in my heart that my world would be frozen and dead for ever. I thought that the beauty in life had gone with him and that there was nothing left to live for.' She saw him watching her, a small frown between his eyes.

She had to tell him, had to make him understand. 'Now I think life has grabbed me and made the blood run again and even that makes me feel guilty because in the minutes you hold me close and safe I forget Bryson. Completely. Forget all that he was and will never be again. I allow him to die.'

'It's what you paint, isn't it? His death. Again and again. I saw your work on the walls of your father's library.'

'He was my twin. Without him I was only half until you came and made me whole again. And it is a dangerous place to be in, this hope, because were you to leave as well…' She didn't finish because she couldn't.

He felt his heart lunge and shatter. Into pieces. A thousand hearts all beating just for her.

'It's for ever, Florentia. This. Us. As long as we both shall live and beyond that if I am able. There will never be another for me, I promise you that.'

'Thank God you didn't die when Papa shot you.' Her hand reached out to trace the scar and he stiffened. No one had ever touched his neck before and he had never come to any woman's bed without his shirt on. 'Can I see it? Can you undress to show me?'

Winter did not hear any pity in her voice and if he had he would have refused. All he heard was interest in the outcome of a piece of time in history that had changed them both. Besides, she'd just told him of some of her secrets and fears and he felt that there should be an equal sharing in return.

Sitting up beside her, he made his decision, but it was with trepidation that he untied his neckcloth and undid the buttons of his shirt. An armour that had been in place for so very long was difficult to remove and he knew the marks beneath the cloth on his skin to be shocking.

Please God, let her not be repulsed, he found himself beseeching to a deity he had barely prayed to for years.

'It's not a pretty sight…' He told himself to stop and be silent. No manner of words would lessen the shock of it and apologies and confessions would only make things worse.

So when he turned so that she could see the full

wreckage of his back and shoulders and neck he felt the shivers of shame turn with him.

'Esp…ion…?' He heard her pronounce the word and felt her finger trace the letters in flesh.

'Spy,' he returned, hating the hope in his voice. 'Under Moore in the First Peninsular Campaign. I was caught, you see, and held…' His voice broke as the memories he tried never to recall weighed down upon him.

'And these?'

Now he felt her gaze and touch on the long horizontal scars that covered his upper back.

'From being whipped. Like a dog,' he continued and made himself go on. The honour had left him a long time ago and the three days in the pit of hell had made him a different man altogether.

Detached. Indifferent. Callous. Cold.

'What of here?'

The softness of her fingers was now on the bands of white scars around the top of his arms.

'Ropes. They bound me and when I fought the ties tightened and stripped off the skin.'

He turned then and stopped her hands from finding more, simply by holding them together on her lap.

'I am damaged and ruined, Florentia. Much more so than you should ever think and if such wreckage is something you feel you could not stomach to look at, then…'

Her lips closed over his mouth, her small tongue finding in his silence what he had found in her. She did not hold back or half-heartedly try to reassure him that things were all right, that he was not too much damaged, that the scars were small or the shame was nothing.

Instead she simply gave him back his life in the one way she had just re-found hers.

I was only half until you came and made me whole again.

She had told him of it before, but now she was showing him, her lips on the mark at his neck careful and gentle and kind before moving on to those on his back. Not as if she might simply erase them with her attention, but as if to her they were only just a part of him, a part of them, a part of the life he had led.

'Let our past lie in the same bed, Winter, where we can allow it some honour before we forget it.'

The tears fell down his face before he could stop them, he a man who had never cried, not once in all the years of his hardships. Not when he was young and unloved and lost. Not in the pit with the French soldiers who liked nothing more than to hurt him. Not even in Tom's house after the debacle at the inn. His eyes welled with relief and release and gratefulness that he should have met a woman who could finally understand him.

Florentia with her wisdom and her difference, with her honesty, intelligence and enlightenment. How, after twenty-nine years of being alone, had he finally found a woman who was his?

Such a question staunched the sadness and brought a half-smile. He had found her by ruin and deceit, by accident and charade, by luck and by design. She had sought him out to understand just who he was and he had agreed on the portrait to get closer to the truth of who he had been. Two ends to the same question. Pole opposites whom Lady Luck had finally favoured because they belonged together.

Standing, he shrugged off the rest of his clothes and then lay down beside her. Her hair fell like a curtain of spun gold on the sheets and the long line of one leg came across him. Her eyes were the colour of skies in summer and seas on a quiet and favoured wind. They were the blue of cornflowers and sapphires and tourmalines.

'When I look into your eyes, Florentia, I can see right through you.'

'Into my heart?'

He laughed.

'And beyond.'

'Show me what you can see, Winter.'

His hand fell across her stomach and downwards and then he drew her a picture of all of the feelings in the world.

And that night he slept in her arms from midnight until dawn, all of the broken nights' sleep he had known for years lost in a calming slumber and warmth.

When the bells of London rang and there was birdsong he could not believe that it was six o'clock on the old timepiece on top of the mantel.

'Florentia?' he whispered her name.

'Yes?'

'Love me?'

'I do.'

Chapter Fifteen

It was the very last ball of the Season and as Florentia and Winter had virtually stayed away from any formal social occasion since being married they decided that they would attend the Bell-Harris soirée before leaving town to live permanently at Atherton Abbey.

Winter had bought her a gown for the evening's entertainment from a dressmaker who was newly set up in London and the current favourite of this Season. It was a deep navy interfaced with cream and gold, the sort of dress that took two maids and a great amount of time to get her into. Florentia felt like a princess.

Maria and Roy had been down in Kent in Albany for the past ten days and her parents had returned to London with them and were to come to the ball. The first time her father had been out in proper company for six years. She was pleased he had made such an effort to be in their lives again and her mother was bathing in all the marital bliss of her two daughters.

Faith had taken to her father like a duck to water and had gone down to Albany with them. She would be back this evening, too. Winter and Flora had missed their energetic and excitable puppy and were looking forward to seeing her.

Flora's life had fallen headlong into a wonderful place. Winter was everything she could have ever dreamed of in a husband and a visit to Atherton had revealed a home of beauty and substance. The Carmichaels were to visit them in Herefordshire the following week and Arabella had promised that she would show Flora how to begin her own garden.

She played with Bryson's ring that she still wore around her neck on the long golden chain.

Pride goeth before the fall.

The quote came from nowhere, but it unsettled her and made her worry. Was it even possible to stay as happy as she now was for ever? Or was there some celestial truth that balanced out luck and ill fortune so that one did not have too much and another too little?

She breathed out and looked at herself in the mirror. Money did have a particular way of softening all the edges and presenting one in a light that was…peculiar. That was the only word she could think of. She could not imagine walking anywhere in a dress such as this or indeed even relaxing in it.

One night, she whispered to herself. This night. And then we will be gone.

As soon as she arrived she felt an undercurrent that she did not recognise. Winter by her side felt it, too, for his hand tightened across hers and he stiffened.

'Your parents and your sister are not here yet. Were they expected to be late?'

'I did not think so.' Her own glance took in the many corners of the room trying to find them. 'Perhaps the journey took longer than they imagined. There has been a lot of rain lately.'

He nodded and led her over to the side of the main room to stand near a pillar that had been decorated in gold ribbon and the leaves of some plant she did not recognise.

Julia Heron came over to her side immediately.

'Papa said to tell you that he would like a word, Lord Winterton, if I was to see you before he did. He is over by the dining table in that far corner. I could wait here with your wife if you wish me to?'

Green eyes skated over her own and she saw in their depths a worry. 'I'll be gone only a moment, Flora. If you stay here?'

'Of course. I shall talk with Julia for we have much to catch up on.' She tried to keep her tone as light as possible, but a dread had wrapped itself around her heart and would not let her go. She squeezed her hands so tightly together that the crescents of her nails began to sting as they dug into the back of her fingers.

'What is it your father wishes to say to my husband, Julia?'

'I think it is a warning. There has been some gossip...' She stopped and smiled tightly. 'But I am sure it is all a misunderstanding and will be resolved forthwith.'

'A misunderstanding?'

'There has been talk that the Viscount may not have a reputation quite as spotless as others believe it to be. Nonsense, of course, and as it only requires a firm denial there will no doubt be a swift ending to any rumour.'

The kidnapping. Florentia knew without a doubt

that this was what Julia spoke of. Had the Urquharts talked? Had their marriage finally been the catalyst that allowed the couple to put together memory and come out with accusation? She looked around to see if she could see Winter and was glad to find his tall form threading its way back through the crowd and towards her.

His face was a mask of indifference and she knew instinctively that he was furious. Still, as he reached her he kissed her hand, all attention and easy smiles.

Deception and deliverance was all in the charade, he had told her once, and he was a man who understood the shifting sands of complicity.

'I hope everything is all right?' Flora tried to match her tone to his. 'For the orchestra should be striking up a waltz soon and I would love to dance.'

He looked at her at that and she knew he understood in her airy conversation that she perceived the truth of what was happening here.

Julia looked relieved. 'The Urquharts are such prattle mongers and such a far-fetched accusation could not possibly be true.'

'Gossip holds a life of its own, Miss Heron.'

'Which is exactly what I said to Percy Urquhart when I saw him the other day. Why on earth would Florentia marry a man who had ruined her? What possible motive would she have for doing that? He did insist that the scar you carry on your neck, Lord Winterton, substantiated the stories he had heard. Some fracas in an inn by all accounts. Papa assured him it was all made-up shilly-shally and that you were at that time busy with army matters.'

Flora felt her husband's hand tighten about her fingers. Together they might weather this if the Urquharts did not make a scene and accuse them directly.

A moment later she knew the futility of such a hope.

'You have a fine sense of the absurd, Winterton, by creeping into the *ton* with your newly earned money after causing such an outcry all those years ago. To kidnap a young lady and throw her into your carriage as you did was reprehensible and lawless. You deserve to be hanged for it. No offence, Lady Florentia, but if he is coercing you in any way now would be the time to admit it.'

His voice boomed out. Not a quiet assassination of character but a very public one. Flora held on to Winter's hand as if it were a lifeline in a rough and dangerous sea.

'I think you are mistaken, Urquhart. Or drunk.' Now Winter's talons were out as well, though his voice was much more quiet than that of Percy Urquhart.

'I can prove it. We were walking with Dan Collins that day and he is here standing beside me. He says it was you, too, and would sign any legal form to swear so.'

Around them other voices were adding to the allegations, a wealthy and respected family of the *ton* like the Urquharts against the dissolute and far more scandalous Wintertons. The taint of new money was undoubtedly in the equation, too, and the *ton* had cut their teeth on the dreadful antics of James Waverley's father.

He was like a wolf surrounded by a pack of yapping hounds, all out to draw blood and make menace. But if she noticed the darkening of his pale green eyes she doubted anyone else would.

Fight or flight. That realisation made her sick for she knew Winter would attack until he could do no more. For her honour. For their family. It was not his name that would keep him fighting, but hers. If he lost this battle she would lose her own protections and she knew he would never allow that.

Another voice suddenly rose across the others and when she turned she saw her father and mother with Maria and Roy pushing through the crowds.

'You are an idiot, Urquhart, and you always were.' Her father's tones were clear. Her family had come to stand beside them now, forming a ring around Winter. 'If there is anyone in all of this world who would know the whelp who tried to kidnap my daughter it would be me. I shot the man in the shoulder. I saw him die right there in front of me, his blood running across the cobblestones in a river and I have been brought to bed with regret ever since. For the taking of a life. A young life, for the man could not have been more than twenty. So do not talk to me of such foolishness, for in the death of Florentia's abductor lay a sorrow for my family that is still new and green. I remember his face as if he were here standing next to me, the dark brown eyes, the light hair, that longish face. The screams of anguish as I dispatched him to hell. No insincere and foolish assertions shall ever take that from me.'

'Perhaps I remember wrongly, Lord Albany.' Collins spoke. 'I, too, think his hair was lighter and his eyes darker. In fact, I am sure of it now.'

The crowd wavered and withdrew, the chatter building of Albany's loss, a high penance for a concerned father. The ground swell of opinion changed and altered. It was suddenly not Winterton and Albany who were at fault here, but the mean-minded and imprudent Urquharts.

Winter felt the change and knew the support of a family who had much reason to hate him. He was overwhelmed by such assistance because it had been seldom in his life that he had ever felt such succour from anyone. Save Florentia.

His wife shimmered beside him in her navy gown, her hair against the darkness of fabric like silk and honey. He had felt her fear and her terror, yet not in one tiny movement had she shown it to anyone. No, she had stood beside him and held his hand as she smiled, unmovable and solid.

With a family like this around him he could do anything.

Roy slapped him across the back as the others chatted. 'You owe the old Earl a drink,' he said quietly.

'I do.'

'Maria told me that I was to bring a knife tonight and if it came to a fight I was to use it on whoever threatened you.'

'You knew of the Urquhart allegations?'

'They have been swirling for a week or more now around the salons of London town according to Frank Reading. I found that out when we arrived yesterday afternoon from Kent.'

'God.'

'It's over. Albany saw to that quite nicely, I think.'

The Earl had come across to him now. 'That is the last of it, Winter. We will never mention any of this again.'

'Thank you.' The shake in his voice was clear, but Florentia's father ignored it as he stopped a footman with a tray of newly poured wine and asked for it to be shared around.

'Let us drink to the future,' he said as they all took a glass. 'To the years ahead. May they be full of laughter, wisdom and wine.'

Winter tipped his head and drank deeply and when he looked over Florentia was doing exactly the same.

'It's finished. The past cannot touch us again.'

'Not after your father's performance. One of the finest actors I have ever seen in a theatre or out of one.'

She laughed. 'He was often in plays before he met Mama. I think it was she who put a stop to it.'

'He was magnificent. Perhaps your own talent as a thespian comes directly from him?'

She felt his feet pull away from underneath Faith's stomach. The puppy had crawled on to the bed the moment they had arrived home and they had no heart to remove her.

'A family is a wondrous thing,' he said softly after another moment, 'for it comes in all forms. A wife who is as beautiful as she is clever. A dog who does not know the meaning of obedience. A father-in-law who looks like an owl and has become an eagle. Maria with her worry. Roy with his knife. Your mother. They were all there today for me, by me, supporting me despite the truth being exactly as they knew it wasn't. Without them...'

'That will never happen. The thing about a family is that for good or for bad you have them for ever.'

'I love you, Florentia. I love you more than life itself.'

She felt him turn and his arms came around her to pull her close. Bodies had eloquence, too, she decided as his strength closed in and she knew without words exactly what it was that he promised.

* * * * *

If you enjoyed this story, you might also like Sophia James's stirring quartet
THE PENNILESS LORDS

MARRIAGE MADE IN MONEY
MARRIAGE MADE IN SHAME
MARRIAGE MADE IN REBELLION
MARRIAGE MADE IN HOPE

And make sure you look for
Sophia James's short story
MARRIAGE MADE AT CHRISTMAS in
ONCE UPON A REGENCY CHRISTMAS
anthology!

HOMETOWN HEARTS ♥

YES! Please send me **The Hometown Hearts Collection** in Larger Print. This collection begins with 3 FREE books and 2 FREE gifts in the first shipment. Along with my 3 free books, I'll also get the next 4 books from the Hometown Hearts Collection, in LARGER PRINT, which I may either return and owe nothing, or keep for the low price of $4.99 U.S./ $5.89 CDN each plus $2.99 for shipping and handling per shipment*. If I decide to continue, about once a month for 8 months I will get 6 or 7 more books, but will only need to pay for 4. That means 2 or 3 books in every shipment will be FREE! If I decide to keep the entire collection, I'll have paid for only 32 books because 19 books are FREE! I understand that accepting the 3 free books and gifts places me under no obligation to buy anything. I can always return a shipment and cancel at any time. My free books and gifts are mine to keep no matter what I decide.

262 HCN 3432 462 HCN 3432

Name _____ (PLEASE PRINT) _____

Address _____ Apt. # _____

City _____ State/Prov. _____ Zip/Postal Code _____

Signature (if under 18, a parent or guardian must sign) _____

Mail to the **Reader Service:**

IN U.S.A.: P.O. Box 1867, Buffalo, NY. 14240-1867
IN CANADA: P.O. Box 609, Fort Erie, Ontario L2A 5X3

* Terms and prices subject to change without notice. Prices do not include applicable taxes. Sales tax applicable in NY. Canadian residents will be charged applicable taxes. This offer is limited to one order per household. All orders subject to approval. Credit or debit balances in a customer's account(s) may be offset by any other outstanding balance owed by or to the customer. Please allow 4 to 6 weeks for delivery. Offer available while quantities last. Offer not available to Quebec residents.

HHBPA17